What the critics are saying...

5 Stars "Susan Phelan's words are spellbinding. A captivating vampire chronicle that threatens to shatter the bottom of your soul with its emotional tale of humans and vampires alike searching for the one thing in life that gives it meaning. I'm a fan of the paranormal / supernatural in fiction and this is one of the best offerings right now." ~ *Cupid's Library Reviews*

"The Cure is a gripping read, filled with revenge, lust, and a desire for something more meaningful than eternal life." ~ *Fallen Angels Reviews*

"An engaging vampire tale about one man's quest to rid himself of the evil that plagues him, THE CURE, by Susan Phelan is a must read!" ~ *Romance Reviews Today*

5 Stars "Ms. Phelan writes with much emotion and feeling. She is a gifted writer." ~ *Karen Find Out About New Books*

4 Stars "The Cure is loaded with interesting plot twists. The book moves so quickly that the reader will be breathless by the time the last page is read. Valian is a sympathetic hero. Chancella blooms from an all business scientist to a spitfire heroine. Jack is pure evil and is willing to do anything to achieve his goal. I enjoyed this book. It kept me interested from the first page through the last. I look forward to reading more books by Ms. Phelan in the future." ~ *eCataRomance Reviews*

5 Stars "Ms. Phelan's words captivate not only the heart but also the soul of the reader, as the love of the two characters seems to burn the pages." ~ *Coffee Time Romance*

THE BLOOD
TAPESTRY

The Cure

Susan Phelan

CERRIDWEN PRESS

A Cerridwen Press Publication

www.cerridwenpress.com

The Cure

ISBN #1419953311
ALL RIGHTS RESERVED.
The Cure Copyright© 2005 Susan Phelan
Edited by Pamela Cohen.
Cover art by Syneca.

Electronic book Publication June 2005
Trade Paperback Publication January 2006

Cerridwen Press is an imprint of Ellora's Cave Publishing, Inc.®

The Cure

๑

For Anne Rice

സ

Trademarks Acknowledgement

The author acknowledges the trademarked status and trademark owners of the following wordmarks mentioned in this work of fiction:

Rolex: Rolex Watch U.S.A., Inc.

Armani: Giorgio Armani

Hugo Boss: HUGO BOSS A.G.

Preface

❧

Valian landed gracefully on the balcony, his dark hair only slightly windblown from the twenty-two-story leap. He reached out and with a single, effortless flip of his wrist tore off the metal deadbolt on the sliding glass door. Tossing it aside, he pushed open the full-length window and stepped into the darkened apartment.

A slow, methodical scan of the room showed definitive signs of domesticity. In the middle of the suite, a pair of fuzzy slippers were strewn across a newspaper on the floor. Not far off, a dog-eared, worn copy of *Men are from Mars, Women are from Venus* and a pair of eyeglasses, teetering dangerously close to the edge, lay atop a speaker that was doubling as an end table. Nearby an empty dinner plate, half concealed by crisscrossed cutlery, a paper napkin and a half glass of white wine, all but dominated the small wooden coffee table that stood opposite the TV.

The 12:00 a.m. telecast sent soft shades of blue and yellow flickering across the form that lay asleep on the couch, the spasms of light briefly illuminating a large, framed picture on the wall behind. The candid shot revealed a young couple clinging tightly to each other and laughing uproariously, the intensity of their embrace having apparently thrown them off balance. Valian gazed sullenly at the photograph, the room silent but for the soft droning voice of the news anchor and the occasional cry of a passing siren, its sound snaking in through an open window.

He walked over to the sleeping form, the unnatural stillness of his gait akin to the eerie floating movement of ice fog drifting across an open highway. Calmly, his eyes locked with those of the warm, purring creature that lay on the woman's stomach, the low vibration coming from its throat changing and intensifying as it raised its head. The two predators stared at each other in silent confrontation for a long moment, then abruptly, the cat jumped down and tore from the room.

Gently sitting down beside the woman, Valian languidly stretched one arm across to the back of the couch before extending a long, white hand up to her face. He delicately traced the line of her jaw and the curve of her lower lip. Stirring, she turned her head slightly to one side but did not awaken. He continued to touch her, his hand sliding down to her neck where he could feel the pulsation of her heartbeat, pounding seductively, almost teasingly, beneath his fingertips.

He could even hear it now—that slow, continuous drum beating its sensual rhythm, beckoning him closer as it seemingly grew louder. Shifting his position, he undid the belt of her robe, opening it to reveal her nakedness—the rise and fall of her smooth skin instantaneously hypnotizing him.

A soft breath escaped the woman's lips at the touch of his hand on her breast, his finger gently circling her erect nipple. Holding himself in check, he bent down and licked the tip of the rosy flesh, one hand gently kneading her hip before gliding over the silky fabric of her panties, his feathery touch brushing the top of her plump thighs. With barely restrained need, he continued to move over her breasts and throat, her heart deafening him in its increased intensity. Faster it beat now, louder and harder—crying out to him, pleading with him, and still he held back, even as the woman sluggishly touched his hair, urging him firmly toward her face and lips.

Glancing up, he saw the woman's eyes were still closed and realized she was in that half awake-half asleep dream state that humans often experience.

Valian could feel the tingling ache in his gums spread to a throbbing pain as his eyeteeth lengthened and grew, tearing the soft pink flesh in which they were embedded, the points sharpening to that of broken glass. Running his tongue along the tip of one of them, he moaned as the warm blood spurted into his mouth.

He shuddered at the sight of the bluish-purple vein in the woman's throat jerking with every heartbeat. The room was suddenly swirling around him as he bent over her, his lips pulled back in a half snarl, obsessed with the dark, aching need to drive his long, hard teeth into her soft tan flesh.

One moment his hunger was driving him to the brink of insanity, the next he was floating, the rich hot liquid spreading like fire through his withered veins, filling him, soothing him, healing him.

In his delirium he was only vaguely aware of the life form beneath him, her cries and struggling diminishing as her life left her and entered him. Swooning, he involuntarily clasped her tighter to him as her every thought, memory and sensation poured into him in overwhelming abundance.

All the while, her heart fought valiantly against his — two distinctly separate rhythms dancing around and completely oblivious to each other. On and on they pulsed until that one earth-shattering moment when the fight for supremacy, that wild syncopation ends and they fall together into perfect unison. At that moment, no mere mortal can know the feeling of two hearts beating as one. It is then that her soul, so brilliant and pure, bursts open and floods into his, so dark and pain-ridden, to illuminate the black and absorb the pain; giving him but a glimpse of that eternally sought after human emotion — love.

With that, her heart begins to weaken, falling out of time with his. Slower and slower it beats, trying feebly to keep up but with each pulse, it struggles only more.

Until, finally, there is no more.

Valian pulled away, grief clearly etched on his handsome face as he regarded his victim, her gaze fixed on the ceiling, her mouth agape. He reached over, almost tenderly, and closed her eyelids. Tilting her head to one side, he examined the two opened wounds on her throat. Then drawing one index finger along the cut-glass edge of his vampire teeth, he smeared the blood over the marks and within seconds the raw gaping lesions absorbed the fluid and completely disappeared.

Rising, he made his way across the silent area only to once again encounter the cat, its tail suddenly fluffing up to twice the normal size as it hissed maliciously at the intruder. Unfazed, Valian stepped around the spitting animal and out of the suite.

Closing the broken door behind him, he stood for a long while staring out over the glittering Manhattan skyline. Although he didn't require sleep—well, not in the way mortals did—he had the distinct sensation he was exhausted.

For nearly three hundred years he had walked this earth, drinking in the perks of his immortality as surely as he had drank in the blood of his prey. He released those weary, downtrodden and hopeless souls from their godforsaken realities and gave them what they sought most—a swift and painless end. It was a service that was as symbiotic as they come.

But in spite of it, or more likely *because* of it, he was surprised to feel the dead weight of disillusionment fall over him once again. Only now, his existence was far less bearable than before—having become nothing more than an endless parade of empty nights and unsuspecting victims with no hope of pleasure or peace in sight. The only release he could find was in the source of his agony; the blood serving to pacify his discontentment and anxiety over a life he no longer wished to live.

Indeed, how ironic was it that he, the one who had masterminded and engineered the end of so many lives, now sought his own finale.

Yet there was one prospect, one last chance for an escape from the mundane horror of it all.

A wry smile played across his full mouth, briefly softening the stern countenance as he recalled the Latin definition of the woman's name…it meant *sanctuary*.

With the quiet conviction of one of the Ancients, Valian resolved that the time had come.

Relieved, he placed his hand on the wrought iron railing and easily soared over the edge, leaving his long dark overcoat to billow majestically behind him as he fell from view.

Chapter One

ॐ

"In conclusion, I would like to thank the head of the faculty of science for his kind invitation to speak to you this afternoon. Thank you very much."

A thunderous roar of applause filled the four-hundred-seat campus auditorium as Dr. Chancella Tremaine stepped down from the podium, her diminutive stature suddenly all the more obvious. With a brief nod of acknowledgment, she grabbed her steel gray briefcase and turned to leave the stage.

Glancing at her watch, she realized she had just over an hour to get to her next engagement — a book signing across town. Then on to dinner with that visiting scholar — what was his name again? She'd been sleeping when he phoned late last night, and bits of their conversation were kind of fuzzy but she did recall his mentioning the institute in Martinique as well as his recent work with a mutual colleague. And who could forget that bedroom voice, so smooth and melodious, that at times almost hypnotized with its unique tranquility?

Groggily she drifted into a strange reverie at the recollection, irritated as a shrill sound abruptly cut in to replace the remembered silken tone. High above the murmur of the dissipating crowd, a strong, sharp-edged voice rang out.

"Dr. Tremaine! Dr. Tremaine!"

Chancella turned on her heel, scanning the mass of people for the urgent, disembodied voice. Her eyes fell quickly upon the young man — a gaunt, nervous-looking male, barely twenty, pushing aggressively through the group, his dark glasses and turned-up coat giving the distinct, almost comical, impression of someone incognito. He reached the edge of the stage, panting heavily, his shaggy light hair plastered to his forehead. Gruffly wiping the corner of his mouth with his sleeve, the unkempt teenager motioned frantically. Chancella leaned down.

"Dr. Tremaine," he whispered hoarsely, his face flushed with excitement, "I have to ask you something."

With a trembling hand he removed his shades to reveal large blue eyes, once more wiping at the accumulation of nervous perspiration on his upper lip. He glanced warily from side to side before leaning a little closer.

"They're real, aren't't they? I mean, they really do exist."

"Well," Chancella began with a gentle smile, "myth has it that—"

"NO!" he bellowed, immediately conscious of his thundering outburst. Lowering his voice to a conspiratorial tone, he started again.

"What I meant was, they're among us right now," he pressed, pointing his finger in emphasis.

Chancella resisted the urge to roll her eyes. There was one in every crowd. Preparing to back the guy down, she drew in a deep breath, but looking at the wide-eyed trembling face, she stopped cold. Deep within the childlike eyes there was an erratic twitch that revealed a genuine fear.

Or mental instability.

Or both.

Whatever the reason, this guy wasn't joking. Chancella started to speak but he cut her off, rushing on in a surge of panicked energy.

"You see, I think I've seen one. A real one. I mean, I *think* he's real," he said, gulping in a quick breath of air, his voice rising to a near-hysterical pitch. "And he's blackmailing me to do something. I don't want to, but he'll kill me if I don't. You've got to help me. Tell me what to do! I can't—"

The young man stopped abruptly at the sight of a man approaching the small crowd that had gathered.

"Terrific lecture, doctor," the university executive said, rocking slightly back on his heels, "and may I say, a fascinating subject matter. Why, I never dreamed there was so much to learn on the topic of—"

"Forgive me," Chancella gently cut in, flashing a charming smile at the balding middle-aged professor. "I'm just finishing up here."

Turning her attention back once more to the troubled young man, Chancella was startled to see he had disappeared. In his place stood a short, chunky girl watching her rather hesitantly, as did the few remaining people who stood around, some clutching copies of her book. Chancella moved her gaze quickly around the room, but only a handful of students now remained and the boy was clearly not among them. Perplexed, she turned back to the professor, who stood grinning widely, positively beaming with the glow of a schoolboy crush.

"I'm sorry. Now, you were saying?"

"Oh, yes," he started, clearly pleased that he finally had Chancella's undivided attention. "You know, I didn't realize the extent of your knowledge."

Immediately horror-stricken at the unintentional insult, he stammered, his face turning a deep shade of crimson, and quickly tried to correct the remark.

"Ah—I mean to say, that I appreciate this project must've taken a considerable amount of time and research."

"Right on both counts," Chancella replied with a kind smile. "From its conception, the book took just over two years to complete. When I first decided to write it, I began by reading everything on vampirism I could find. There are some recorded instances throughout history but they are few and far between."

Chancella paused, noting the spellbound expression on the faces of those around her. She continued on.

"The next step was my trip to Europe where cases of vampirism were first documented. There I talked and studied with some of the world's most prominent scholars and scientists in the field. You see it's only in North America that the vampire is considered to be a creature of myth or fiction. In other, older parts of the world, they are thought to be actual beings still in existence today."

"Vampires among us?" someone called out from the crowd.

"That's right," she nodded seriously.

"Really?" the professor nearly shrieked, immediately clearing his throat, the prospect having clearly alarmed him. "That can't be so."

"Well," Chancella started in gently, aware that the now intimate little gathering was pressing in closer, hanging on her every word. She would have to be careful. "I suppose it depends on one's definition of a vampire. Studies have shown that there are people who drink blood, or claim to, but their reason for doing so leads me to believe that they are *not* the genuine article."

"Mmmm—yes," the professor said slowly, scratching his chin thoughtfully as he absorbed the information, trying to make some sense of it. Detecting his skepticism, Chancella tackled it from another angle.

"Ingesting blood because one actually likes the taste, or as part of a cult or ritual, or because you *want* to be a vampire does not constitute the real thing."

"No, no, of course not," he agreed.

"So what does?" one student asked.

"You have to realize that a vampire is, first and foremost, an immortal being—an entity that cannot die. But why? How is this even possible? It is primarily due to the fact that the tissue that makes up each and every cell in a vampire's body functions on a completely different level than the human species."

"It doesn't function at all," a snickering male voice rang out. "They're dead!"

The laughter that followed swiftly died down and once again, Chancella had the floor.

"No, well, yes, that's correct in one respect," Chancella laughed, "but you see, within each vampiric cell is the ability to maintain itself for an eternity, unlike its human counterpart, which must die and be replaced by another cell."

A scarlet-haired girl spoke next, her eyes sparkling with a playful curiosity.

"But what makes a vampire in the first place? You say that it is not from a nibble on the neck."

"That's correct," Chancella seriously concurred. "Originally vampirism was thought to be a virus in which victims of a bite were infected and would themselves 'turn'. However, substantial research has shown that the human red blood cell, when completely drained and then replenished with a fresh supply, mutates into this super vampiric cell, if you will, thus perpetuating the lifelong need to repeat that process on a daily basis."

"Don't you mean nightly?" someone challenged jokingly.

"Correction, yes, nightly," Chancella conceded with a smile. "Unfortunately, that is one of the myths that is absolutely true. Sunlight does kill them."

"But why?" another asked.

"I don't know exactly but it would appear that the vampiric cell, its molecular structure altered by the blood exchange, becomes highly susceptible to Polymorphous Light Eruption."

"In English please," a voice called out.

"Basically speaking, PLE is the cell's inability to tolerate even the smallest amount of ultraviolet light in any form. It's a severe reaction, allergic in nature, that causes the skin to blister and the blood to boil to the point of, well, let's just say it is a fatal condition."

"Gross," a girl in the front spouted, screwing up her face.

"Yes," Chancella soberly agreed, "it's extremely painful and as we all know, sunlight is full of ultraviolet rays, so—"

"That's why they only come out after dark," one person proudly announced, finishing the sentence.

"Precisely."

"But I'm not entirely clear on something," said the professor, abruptly barging into the verbal volley, his cynical nature rising to the forefront. "Surely you don't mean to imply that individuals who have lost a great deal of blood will turn into one of these creatures upon receiving a blood transfusion?"

Chancella shook her head adamantly as she removed the fashionable copper and black onyx glasses that had been perched, rather precariously, on her small, slender nose.

"No, no, this is perhaps the most difficult aspect of all to fully understand. The metamorphosis from *homo sapien* to *nosferatu* is a two-tiered process. Although vampires take blood from their human victims to fulfill a very real physical need, it is not solely the corporeal aspect of feeding that they crave but also the spiritual absorption of another soul into their own. There is no doubt that the blood is a necessity—a healing, soothing elixir—but it is the merging of their spirit with their victim's spirit that first turns them and that they continue to hunger for."

"Cool," the redheaded woman said, bobbing her head in approval.

The professor, his previous demeanor of lovestruck admirer having long since fallen by the wayside, regarded Chancella with a degree of suspicion as he posed one final query.

"Really, Dr. Tremaine," he said dryly, "you don't actually *believe* that there are beings such as these walking in the world today?"

Chancella drew in a sharp breath, conscious of several pairs of eyes watching her closely. Surprisingly, she'd never been asked that question so directly. People generally tiptoed around, casually trying to assess her commitment to the subject matter that was traditionally thought of as fiction. However, she felt a sudden response welling up inside her and taking the advice of her dear ol' mother, she 'plugged her nose and jumped'.

"Absolutely!" she smiled broadly, breaking into a light chuckle at the cheers and claps that punctuated her confession.

Then, under her breath she murmured ever so softly to herself —

"I just haven't met one yet."

* * * * *

The bookstore was packed with people including several Goth-rock fans, their dyed black hair and powdered white faces drawing wary second glances from those around them. Chancella sat at a low oak table, inscribing a book for a woman in her sixties who looked particularly out of place, her nervous machine-gun babble indicative of her discomfort.

" —and these kids nowadays are really very, well, different, aren't they?"

The senior started at the sight of one especially androgynous male standing beside her. His blood red lips and black-lined eyes were overemphasized on the stark white face, which was framed by his long shaggy blue-black hair. She smiled nervously at him as her eyes traveled down the length of his leather-and-chain-clad body. When she returned her gaze to his face, he pulsed his eyebrows up and down suggestively. Clearing her throat, she quickly looked away.

"I, I don't know why my grandson likes these…people," she leaned over and almost whispered to Chancella. "I think they're all strange!"

Chancella only smiled as she handed the book to the ill-at-ease grandmother. "I hope your grandson enjoys it."

Unappeased, the elderly woman offered a weak "thank you" and quickly left, the crowd parting to let her through.

Out of the corner of her eye, Chancella caught sight of the pyramid of books that stood to one side, her picture on the back cover of one that stood upright, staring out at her.

She had insisted that her long auburn hair be pulled back for the shot. Perhaps her trademark French twist was a little severe for her delicate, narrow face but she had refused to leave her hair flowing about her shoulders like some sort of cover girl. The firm set of her mouth and the serious expression in the large hazel eyes, softened only by the slightest hint of crow's feet, also gave the false impression of sobriety but even so, she mused to herself, she wasn't bad for thirty-something.

Taking the top book from the pile, she flipped it over, studying the black gothic lettering that stood out against the somber gray background. *The Cure: Solving the Mystery of Vampirism.*

Her first book had dealt with regenerating dead cell tissue to an original functional state, laying the foundation for her second, but much to her surprise, people often asked if there was any connection between the two bestsellers. In her mind, it was quite obviously the next logical progression.

After sitting for the past several hours, Chancella arched her back slightly, resisting the temptation to stretch her arms high overhead and loosen her stiff muscles. She was sincerely delighted with the success of this hometown and final stop on her current book signing tour — even if the vast majority of those present were vampire wannabes.

As if on cue, a loud voice bearing the distinctive trace of a Transylvanian accent boomed out. The throng that surrounded Chancella turned in unison towards its source.

"Goooooood eeeeeeevening."

"Oh hi, Nick!" Chancella said warmly, not entirely surprised to see her ever-supportive lab assistant peeking mischievously through the sea of bodies. He had a habit of showing up at any and all local appearances. A blossoming biologist in his own right, Nick Lewis was one of the few in the field who had, initially, taken her studies seriously, and many a time his enthusiasm and faith in her work had kept her going. In fact, Chancella realized as she regarded the twenty-two-year-old affectionately, she might never have persisted in publishing her latest book without his encouragement. "What are you doing here?"

"Well, I thought I might take you out for a bite," he said, sounding more and more like the Count himself.

Chancella cringed at the lousy Carpathian inflection.

"Hey, dialects are definitely not your strong suit," she laughed, silently marveling at how handsome he looked in his customary leather jacket. Although far too young for her, Chancella had to admit that Nick was a bit of a hottie.

"Hey, what can I say?" he mumbled with a grin.

By now, he had wangled his way to the front and stood in a gosh-golly kind of manner, shuffling his feet as he watched her sign one book after another. When an unforeseen break in the endless line of fans came, Chancella took a moment to study her budding protégé.

As of late, the usual gleam in his blue eyes had dulled considerably and as she watched him, a strong uneasiness came over her. Something wasn't right. Silently, she noted that the regular dark circles beneath his eyes had deepened and his normally perky expression had grown dim and serious. Maybe it was just lack of sleep. A notorious insomniac, Nick often came into work with a real set of luggage on his face but these days, he was looking particularly rough. More than that, he seemed troubled. Gently, Chancella laid her hand atop his.

"What's up?"

"It's nothing," he said, quickly averting his gaze, shifting from one foot to another in an antsy display of discomfort.

"Still having trouble sleeping?" she persisted quietly.

"Aaaah!" he slapped at the air. "Goes with the territory. You know the live-on-the-edge, laugh-in-the-face-of-death world of science," he said with just a suggestion of bitterness before pulling out a crumpled pack of Marlboros. "Hey, let's go for a smoke."

Chancella looked hopefully at her publicist, who stood listening just a few feet away. Although the biologist-turned-author had no intention of breaking her ten-year abstinence from the habit, she sure could stand to stretch her legs.

"Go ahead," the older woman strongly urged, waving them off, "take advantage of this lull. Consider it the calm before the storm," she said with a wink.

Chancella and Nick made their way towards a red EXIT sign near the rear of the shop, walking past a hushed, carpeted area that housed a pair of sofas on which sat a couple of people. Quite separate from each other, they poured fervently over their respective reading material—one leafing aimlessly through a current issue of a leading tabloid magazine, the other absolutely devouring Tolstoy.

Once outside, Nick blazed up and turned to her with a funny little smirk.

"So, you're becoming quite the celebrity," he said, squinting at the smoke that curled up from the cigarette dangling from the corner of his mouth and snaked into his eyes.

"Oh, don't be silly!" Chancella said quickly, not accustomed to the spotlight and never really one to seek it.

"No, no," he pressed on, his eyes widening in earnest, "there's a lot of people who really dig your book. I mean, after all, vampires are big business these days."

"Thanks to Bram Stoker," she replied with a respectful nod to the Irish author.

"Yeah, but I can see why they're so popular," he raced on with an edgy enthusiasm. "I mean, what a life! Talk about freedom. Do what you want, when you want, to whomever you want. As far as I'm concerned, vampires are the ultimate social rebels."

Chancella burst into laughter.

"Nick, you're crazy!"

"Maybe so," he replied a little dourly, "but I'm right."

Chancella regarded him closely. All those long late nights together in the lab, she had come to know the real Nick Lewis.

He was not the lab-coated, horned-rim-glass-wearing nerd that most people saw but rather the epitome of a free spirit, confined by nothing and no one, a James Dean incarnate bent on pushing all social and moral limits to the breaking point. And although she was tremendously fond of him as a person and sincerely loved his zest for life, Chancella could never share his pent-up, angry-at-society adolescent mentality. They were both rebels, to be sure, but her rebelliousness was generally confined to the lab.

That having been said, there were times when she remembered those wild motorcycle rides along the coast with Nick speeding twice the limit, the wind ripping through their hair and the feel of his young strong body as she clasped her arms around him.

It was during those fleeting moments of those oddly spiritual flights that she felt disembodied and truly free and she wondered, just a little wistfully, if she'd ever feel that way again.

The touch of his hand on her forearm brought her back to the present and to the cautious sound of his voice.

"So, how's about it?" he asked somewhat timidly. "Can I buy you dinner?"

"Oh Nick, I can't," Chancella said gently, nearly missing the crinkle of disappointment that flashed across his brow. "I'm sorry but I've already got plans."

"Yeah, okay," he murmured, his voice taking on a strangely wooden tone.

Stopping cold, Chancella examined him once again, concerned as to what lay behind his mounting gloominess, but he merely nodded and began walking towards the door. Hesitantly, she fell in step beside him, making a mental note to herself that when this current literary tour was over, she would have to study all the facts and come to some conclusion about Nick's uncharacteristic behavior.

Suddenly struck with a thought of a completely different nature, she whirled to face him.

"Oh, Nick, listen—can you restock the pharmaceutical cabinet tonight?"

"What do we need?" he asked almost dispassionately as he let the remnants of his smoke fall to the ground where he crushed it out under the heel of his shoe.

"You'll have to check, but I know we're low on atracurium besylate," she answered, tensing at the disturbing recollection of a specimen's near overdose—the improperly measured muscle relaxant had nearly killed the lab monkey. As it was, the powerful compound had rendered the animal paralyzed for days.

"Sure," Nick said. "I might as well go in and do some preliminary testing tonight."

"Well, be careful."

"I will," he replied quietly before carrying on in a humorous mimicry of a nasal-voiced teacher. "Now remember, kids, for rodents, felines and canines, two milligrams per pound whereas people get—" his voice returned to normal, "what is it again? Ten per? Twenty?"

Chancella stared at him vacantly, her smile fading as the whine of the store's air conditioner hummed loudly in the back alley patio.

"Gee, Nick, off the top of my head, I don't know," she responded doubtfully, her words coming out haltingly. "I mean, I've only used it on small mammals but certainly, never on a—human."

Once again, Nick's odd conduct tugged at Chancella's intuition, and this time it was accompanied by the most horrific, overwhelming sensation—a raise-the-hair-on-the-back-of-your-neck kind of premonition that something terrible was about to happen.

But then Nick laughed out loud, his usual lighthearted manner accompanying the full, hearty chuckle and Chancella reluctantly dismissed her apprehensions. Reaching for the door, he motioned for her to go first, teasing her as she passed under the crook of his arm.

"Never fear, Doctor," he said in feigned seriousness, "I promise I have no intention of using this on a human."

A couple of hours of autographing and general chitchatting soon sped by, and as the mass began to wane, Chancella searched the area for some indication of the time. High on the wall, just above the revolving door to the shop, she spied an antique clock.

5:42 p.m.

Although not officially night, Chancella could see through the large storefront windows that it was already dark outside, and the house manager had begun to usher people out.

Chan-cel-la.

She froze.

There it was again—her spoken name floating, faint and ghostlike, in the air, immediately calling to mind the way the word *Heathcliffe* drifted, disembodied and mournful, across the bleak windswept moors in *Wuthering Heights*.

As was earlier, the voice that brushed her ears as soft and intimate as a whisper was still rich and melodious, the low volume of the sound giving her the unnerving impression that the speaker was standing right beside her.

Or, more accurately, was somewhere inside her.

"Dr. Tremaine?"

Snapping to, Chancella shook her head, staring at the young couple in front of her, the teenage guy decked out in a T-shirt and New York Yankees ball cap.

"I'm sorry?" Chancella smiled as she tentatively reached for the book the fan held out to her, still somewhat shaken by the strange occurrence. "Make it out to who?"

The young boy grinned, his broad smile revealing an impressive set of silver braces.

"Jush-tin," he slurred, nodding enthusiastically.

Chancella obliged, signing her name on the inside cover with flourish. Handing the boy his autographed copy, she was reminded of the young man who had approached her at the lecture that morning, his urgent, fear-filled face bringing a fresh wave of curiosity to flood over her. Although she had, at the time, questioned the youth's mental health, she now had an overriding notion that his fear was very legitimate, but what could have possibly frightened him so?

Abandoning the unresolved matter — something she absolutely detested doing — Chancella sighed and looked up, smiling at his girlfriend and the rather mischievous look on her youthful face. Just beyond, Chancella could see a boisterous horde of teenagers snickering softly as they huddled together. Clearly the girl had drawn the short straw.

"Dr. Tremaine?" she began with a nervous titter, "Is it true that vampires can't, well, you know," she giggled again, "have sex?"

Chancella stared at her blankly for a moment, working to conceal her amusement.

"How old are you?" she asked politely.

"Fifteen," the teenager snickered impishly.

Chancella couldn't help but smile as she reached out to lay a motherly hand on the girl's slender shoulder.

"Stick to someone your own age."

As the two youngsters laughed and nearly ran to join up with their posse, Chancella once again became aware of the persistent weariness that had plagued her throughout the day, that strange fogginess challenging her concentration and blurring her senses. It had been a long tour, but she took solace in the fact that within a few minutes she'd be finished, and not a moment too soon. She had even begun to hear voices, she inwardly laughed!

More seriously, she wondered how she was ever going to last through a dry business dinner with that visiting scientist.

The good doctor was really going to have to be something special to hold her attention tonight.

Chapter Two

ဆာ

The entrance to the government facility's research department was a challenge at the best of times, but this evening Nick Lewis was finding it particularly difficult.

With one arm overloaded with a tower of books and still managing to clutch his ever-present double latte, he fumbled in agitation, his free right hand moving awkwardly in an attempt to unite the key with the grooves of the stubborn lock. At the feel of the corrugated metal edge sliding into the slot, he flicked his wrist and pushed a shoulder against the heavy door, spilling into the short passageway, the metallic clang of it slamming shut behind him echoing in the small space.

Removing the coded access card which had been held, all the while, tightly clenched in his teeth, he waved it past the security scanner on the wall, waiting for the solid red light to change to green. With a monotone beep it did and he pushed through the final entryway into the darkened lab.

Well acquainted with the surroundings, Nick expertly moved through the blackness to his disheveled desk. Miraculously finding a place to lay down his books and coffee on the cluttered surface, he turned on a study lamp that stood amongst the rubble, the area directly around the workspace flooded with the fluorescent light.

"Evening, Frankie, how's it going, Johnny?" he distractedly offered to the pair of small white mice in connecting cages just beyond. As if in response, the two tiny animals blinked their beady pink eyes and, scurrying to the edge of the cage, squeaked in unison.

"Nah, not tonight, boys," Nick said over his shoulder, the worn leather jacket looking out of place in the sterile setting of the laboratory. "Daddy's got some work to do."

Taking a deep swig of the caffeine-rich drink, he caught sight of the top book on the pile he'd brought in, the sight of Chancella's name causing his insides to twist in anger. "Nick, go get this. Don't forget to do that," he grumbled, his face twisting into a bitter sneer as he moved between the supply cabinet and the counter, laying out the necessary equipment for the first phase of testing.

For four years he had lived in her shadow as her personal little servant boy, but man, if he had his way, he would show that self-serving prima donna a thing or two. One night when she least expected it, he'd —

Nick stiffened, his rage-fueled movements grinding to an abrupt halt as the creepy feeling of being watched coursed through him.

Gradually pivoting around, his eyes shot open at the sight before him as a deep, subdued voice, laced with an artificial cordiality, broke the stillness of the hushed space.

"Hello, Nick."

"Who are you?" Nick practically shrieked, peering through the dazzling white brightness to the dimness beyond.

The tall figure, partially concealed by shadow, leaned casually against the opposite counter. He didn't answer.

"How'd you get in here?" Nick persisted, shooting a quick look at the security-locked door, his voice rising dramatically.

With a decidedly unhurried motion, the stranger raised one hand, turning it palm up and curling his fingers inward, his head tilting down slightly as he appeared to study his nails. Ignoring Nick's question, the man finally spoke in an oddly drawn out and enunciated way, as if he were physically weighing each syllable in his mouth.

"Where's your boss?" the intruder asked, the last word emphasized in an acutely sarcastic manner.

Nick's shock over the mysterious individual's appearance quickly, and very obviously, changed to indignation.

"*I'm* my own boss," he snapped petulantly, his chin jutting out in defiance. "I do what I want!"

"Is that so?" the man responded silkily, his head lifting as his attention gradually moved up from his well-manicured hand to weigh heavily on the lab assistant's face. "Come now, Nick," he said almost sympathetically, moving forward, the light falling across his extraordinary face. "We both know that's a gross misrepresentation of the truth. In fact," he let his golden-eyed gaze travel across the way to the imprisoned rodents, a sly, devilish grin breaking the unusually smooth flesh, "you have no more control than your furry little friends over there."

Gasping for air, Nick gawked, stunned at the marble-like profile of the odd individual, the sight shocking him into a kind of temporary paralysis. There was something foreign, even alien about the albino-like countenance, so strikingly contrasted by the tailored silk shirt of magenta that brushed against his muscular torso and fell over the snug reptilian print pants.

Following the hypnotic intruder's view, Nick's bottom lip, now trembling pitifully, protruded into a pronounced pout. He began talking then, a soft and incoherent rambling that revealed another reason for his deep resentment towards his mentor, and it was one that went beyond his professional jealousy.

"I've slaved day and night, doing her dirty work, while she jets around giving talks and signing books, and for what? What do I get for all my trouble? What do I get for my undying loyalty? *'Maybe some other time, Nick',*" he sniped, mimicking Chancella in a pathetically childish manner. "'*I don't feel that way about you, Nick. I love you as a friend, Nick'*," he mumbled on miserably. "I'd do anything for her and she knows it! It's just not fair," he wailed. "I deserve more. She owes me!"

The stranger rolled his eyes and looked away in disgust, the corner of his thin, pale mouth pulling down into a clear-cut scowl.

"Stop sniveling!" he impulsively shouted, the volume of his echolike voice rattling a collection of beakers nearby.

It also served to snap Nick out of his pity trip.

Then just as suddenly, the eccentric figure changed his tone to one deceptively soothing and saccharine.

"But you are right," he nearly purred, his topaz eyes now shifting to a warm shade of toffee. "It's not fair, but then again, life isn't fair."

The figure went silent. For a time, a grim air darkened the plains of his ashen face and he stood perfectly immobile, staring straight ahead, unseeing. By the by, his expression slowly brightened and he resumed.

"However, I've come to help you and—" he paused for effect, the seductive smile that spread across his otherwise immobile pale face effectively distracting from the mocking tone in his voice, "to make sure you get exactly what you deserve."

"Why?" Nick demanded warily, a sense of desperation creeping into his next question. "What's in it for you?"

"That doesn't matter," the beguiling character replied, his expression melting into a menacing scowl.

"Don't you want to put that bitch in her place?" he boomed dramatically. "Isn't it about time you got some recognition for the part you played in all of this?"

The sweet, slithering call of temptation whispered in Nick's ear, and as he stared at the ominous being before him, he swore he could literally hear a voice, somewhere inside himself, enticing him to respond.

"How?" he forced out from between chattering teeth rattling together in fear and excitement.

"With the formula for cell reanimation," the pallid figure stated indifferently.

"Oh, is *that* all?" Nick cried, flapping his arms in exasperation. "What are you, crazy? *I've* never even seen it."

The tall man arched one thin, shapely eyebrow heavenward. "What of the experiments? Surely you required the serum to conduct them," he stated icily.

"Yeah, yeah," Nick said impatiently, "but Chancella makes up the batch herself and then gives it to me. I have a vague idea of the components, but I sure wouldn't want to wing it."

A heavy, dangerous atmosphere filled the isolated area as, unflinchingly, the still form wordlessly examined Nick.

Licking his lips nervously, Nick sped on in an uneasy torrent. "If I knew the elements, we'd be laughing. I mean, give me the recipe and I'll bake the cake, comprende? But you gotta believe me—it would take a freaking hacker to get into her computer!"

"Ah, yes," the stranger said, apparently unconcerned. "It is of no matter—I had anticipated as much. It's taken care of."

"But what's this all about?" Nick whined in confusion. "What do you need it for?"

"Why, to *prove* Dr. Tremaine's hypothesis, of course."

Nick gaped at the puzzling trespasser.

"Prove it? On what?"

"That too will be taken care of," the striking figure answered with a note of finality, his eyes once again locking with Nick's in a hard gaze.

"Okay," Nick could only whisper in response, appalled to discover that some mesmerizing, trance-inducing force kept him rooted in place.

The mysterious man turned to exit then, the power of his gaze lifting, therein releasing Nick from his apparent spell.

"One more thing," he said unexpectedly without turning around, "what have you in the way of tranquilizers?"

"We got a couple of things that could be classified as a sedative," Nick answered slowly. "Why?"

"How much have you on hand?" the stranger asked, ignoring Nick's question.

"Why?" Nick asked again, this time a little cheekily, his mood elevated by the peculiar man's forthcoming departure. "Feeling a little jumpy?"

The sarcastic look on his face quickly changed to remorse as the dark form glared at him over one broad shoulder. With a shaky smile, Nick backpedaled.

Fast.

"As a matter of fact, we just loaded up with enough stuff to, ah, pretty much drop King Kong."

In slow motion, the stranger turned fully around, the light dancing off something just to the left of his jaw line, seemingly nestled amongst the dirty blonde strands of his hair.

Irritated by the distraction, Nick shifted his gaze over to the stranger's face, his heart leaping into his mouth at the immediate and overwhelming sensation that he was looking at The Devil himself. And as the *thing* spoke, he only grew more certain.

"Better get more."

* * * * *

The restaurant was a quiet hideaway of sorts, its mirrored walls, lush palm trees and glittering crystal chandeliers an untraditional décor for the intimate Greek café. Soft shades of maroon and grey ran throughout the carpeting, wallpaper and chair fabric. Even the flower-surrounded candles that graced the center of each table matched the classic color scheme.

Chancella was led to a quiet little booth tucked away in a far corner that served to shield her from the din of the bustling Friday night crowd. Looking radiant in an ivory lace suit, its low-cut jacket and short skirt perfectly exhibiting her shapely figure, she placed her overcoat on a nearby hook and, straightening the close-fitting fabric of her outfit, scooted into the comfy leather seat.

Leafing through the menu, she nonchalantly glanced around, her attention briefly caught by the amorous antics of a couple at the next table. Lapsing into an intense stare, Chancella intently watched the young man smilingly steer a forkful of a decadent whipped-cream-topped dessert toward his girlfriend, depositing it into her reluctantly open mouth. Then leaning across the table, he planted a warm, tenderly probing kiss on her lips as if he were trying to steal it back. Pulling apart, they broke into a soft giggle like a couple of love-struck teenagers.

"Chancella?"

Both the softly spoken word and the hint of a cool breath brushed her ear at exactly the same moment, and she whirled quite nearly all the way around in her seat, baffled to discover no one was there. Thoughtfully she slowly turned back around, gasping at the man who now stood directly in front of her.

"I'm so sorry," the gentleman began, the velvet-like quality of his voice instantaneously soothing her tattered nerves. "I did not mean to scare you."

Sucking in her breath, Chancella stared speechless into the most amazing pair of eyes she had ever seen.

They were the muted shade of sea foam, and above and beyond their extraordinary color was the titillating co-mingled expression of amusement and desire swirling within the distinctive depths.

Awestruck, she begrudgingly forced her view away from the entrancing gaze, determined to exercise her keen knack for scrutiny and detail. Purposefully she perused the elegant person in front of her.

He was at least six feet tall and although of a lean build, he was not thin. Clearly, he was of considerable wealth, for every item that adorned his frame was of the finest make—from his shiny, dark Armani suit to the sparkling gold Rolex on his wrist. His dark hair, which barely brushed the top of his shirt collar, was luminous and served as a stark contrast to the striking marble-like pallor of his skin, the dewy flesh shining in a most unusual way. The sharp plains of his face—the long straight Grecian nose and the high, sculptured cheekbones—were out of sync with the full mouth that just now curved into a dazzling smile to reveal long, straight white teeth.

"I very much admire your work," he spoke, the unusually smooth textured tone making Chancella feel as if she were being wrapped in a warm fleece blanket. "I find your theories of —" he paused, glancing up to his right and just over her shoulder as if trying to recall some dearly departed memory, "of considerable interest."

"Th-thank you," Chancella stammered, trying to shake the fog that his speech induced. The odd blurriness that permeated her senses was further complicated by a new sensation — a sweet fluttering movement in her stomach that spread like liquid honey through her body, melting her strength, her resolve, her control.

Above it all, she could feel the penetrating depth of the man's gaze, the sheer force of his being staring down into her very soul, and she had to fight to keep herself from quivering.

An uncomfortable silence fell between them and the mysterious individual seemed to be waiting for something. Then he spoke, extending a long, pale hand out to her as he did.

"Chancella, I'm Dr. de Mortenoire."

Then seconds later he added as if to clarify, "From Martinique."

"Oh, Dr. de Mortenoire!" Chancella said with delight, the informal use of her given name immediately drawing her attention. Rising, she accepted his outstretched hand, the feel of his cool, soft skin sending an involuntary shiver through her. "It's a pleasure to meet you."

"And you," he replied serenely.

For a few awkward seconds they stood observing each other, their hands still clasped together in the aftermath of their introduction. Held captive by his oddly fixed expression, Chancella swooned as a forceful wave of lightheadedness literally threatened her equilibrium. Pulling her hand from his, she smiled uneasily as she steadied herself against the table.

"I'm sorry," he began charmingly as little sparkles of light twinkled in the spellbinding emerald eyes. "I hope I haven't kept you waiting."

"Not at all," she smiled, grateful to feel the solid shape of the cushioned seat against her trembling knees as she sat back down.

"I can't tell you how much I've been looking forward to this moment," he said quite solemnly, the radiance of his persona dimming ever so slightly.

Flushing, Chancella regarded her foreign colleague for a lengthy moment. There was a distinct oddity about the man, but it was one that she couldn't immediately pinpoint. His silken voice, softened by a near indecipherable accent that danced around several dialects and those remarkable eyes produced a near hypnotic effect and clearly, he was a cultured and educated individual. But somewhere under the surface Chancella perceived a trace of danger, almost a tremor of an arrogance-fronted menace that, much to her own astonishment, intrigued her greatly.

Returning her attention to the intoxicating stare that awaited her, she responded to his courtly compliment, her own voice sounding strangely unfamiliar.

"It's my pleasure."

The attractive doctor looked visibly relieved, as if a great burden had been taken from him, his eyes now glittering with a most brilliant shade of turquoise.

"No, believe me, Chancella," he said again, his manner most serious. "The pleasure is all mine."

A sullen-faced waiter arrived to take their orders and Chancella found her insatiable curiosity arising within her when her dinner companion declined anything from either the kitchen or the bar. As if in answer to the unspoken question, he regarded her for a long moment before offering a simple explanation.

"I don't drink and I'm afraid I'm not terribly hungry as I ate on the plane. But please, you go ahead."

Chancella nodded, her puzzlement alleviated as her fascinating colleague took up the conversation, wasting no time in delving into the reason for the proposed meeting.

"As I said, I'm most interested in the theories presented in your recent book—in particular the section dealing with the reversal of cell death."

"Yes," Chancella nodded, immediately affecting her most professional voice as she took a quick sip of the white wine that had been hastily placed in front of her. "Well, the concept of breathing life into deceased cell tissue has definitely broken new ground in the scientific community, but is not without controversy."

"I can imagine," he leaned forward slightly, his face totally expressionless. "How is it that apoptosis is not present?"

The knowledgeable question, referring to programmed cell death, was one that had often been posed to her by other scientists. As a cellular biologist, Chancella knew that, millions of times per second, cells within the human body literally commit suicide as an essential part of the normal cycle of cellular replacement. This process is also considered a safety net against disease for when mutations of any sort occur, the cell will automatically self-destruct. How this natural occurrence is absent in a vampiric cell was a bit of a mystery.

"I don't know exactly," Chancella stated matter-of-factly. "It would appear that once transformed, the new cell's permanently altered molecular structure is immune to self-destruction."

"But you can reverse this?" he asked seriously.

"Well, we have created the environment needed in lab mice—"

He held up a lean hand to interrupt her.

"Created vampirism in mice?"

"Yes, well, the cellular equivalent of it," she agreed, quickly carrying on, "and have determined that through the use of a microscopic proton pump, cellular respiration can be restored, thus activating the feedback inhibition."

"The slowing or stopping of a reaction."

"Right," she agreed.

"And you've only tested this on animals?"

"So far," Chancella shrugged as she looked directly into his eyes. "To date, I haven't had any vampires come a-knocking…"

She let the sentence trail off, momentarily distracted by the austere beauty of the man's face, his full lips curling up into a gentle smile as the smooth, alabaster flesh moved, giving way to a sexy pair of dimples.

Directly she trembled at the startling sensation that she was lifting up out of her seat, weightless and hovering as the room shimmered mystically around the two of them, changing into a surrealistic realm of swirling vapors and blurred shapes that rippled like some sort of otherworld force field.

Holding her breath, Chancella became aware that she was unable to look away from her absorbing colleague, the entrancing turquoise-gray stare holding her still. Just as an instinctive panic flared within her, she heard a gentle voice speaking to her, just like in the bookstore earlier that afternoon, the words sounding dreamy and distant, as if whispered, ever so softly in her ear.

Until now.

Blinking, she bit her lip and released from the magnetic-like pull of his gaze, looked down at her hands, tightly clasped together in her lap.

"I…I beg your pardon?" Chancella faltered, frightened by the return of the eerie faraway voice. Rubbing one temple, she closed her eyes.

"You must forgive me," she said in a barely audible tone, breaking into a nervous little laugh that she hoped would disguise her concern. "I have been a little tired lately."

Despite her many years monitoring bizarre reactions, these recurring and distressing episodes were stymieing and she was beginning to fear the worst. Maybe it was all very simple. Perhaps she was losing her mind.

Her meal arrived and, greatly relieved, Chancella reached for her fork, her mouth watering at the luscious scent that wafted up from the hot plate. She had ordered Chicken Neptune, one of her favorites, the lean breast meat covered in a creamy lobster and crabmeat sauce with a side of wild rice and a garden medley of broccoli, carrots and peppers.

Gingerly picking at the vegetables, she inwardly wondered if her strenuous tour schedule was catching up with her. After all, it had been a wild few weeks, in which she got precious little sleep and routinely missed meals. Perhaps that was the real culprit behind her apparent dementia.

For the past several minutes, the doctor had remained curiously silent, watching Chancella intently and with a singularity of purpose that made her uncomfortable.

"Tell me," she began as she buttered a hot roll, "where did you say you got your Masters?"

"I didn't say," he answered almost sharply, his eyes following the movement of her fork from her plate to her mouth and back again.

"Oh," Chancella said faintly, quite taken aback by his candor. Frowning, she felt her face grow hot, the blush not lost on the one who had caused it.

"What an exquisite shade," he said much softer, his head tilting to one side as he continued to keenly observe her.

"Pardon?" Chancella leaned forward, uncertain as to his meaning.

"The color in your cheeks," he replied, motioning slightly. *"C'est ravissant."*

He uttered the last word almost breathlessly, his eyes holding hers in a direct gaze.

"I'm sorry?" she said, lightly urging a definition for the foreign term.

"Yes, *ravissant*…it is, how do you say it? Lovely."

He finished ineptly, almost awkwardly, as though he was most unaccustomed to complimenting anyone.

Unsure of how to respond, Chancella only offered a weak smile before trying to change the topic once more.

"What did you do your thesis on?" she asked lightly, a creeping suspicion at his evasiveness beginning to needle her as she paused to delicately dab the white linen napkin at the corner of her mouth.

The perilous tone that lay beneath the words that met her sent a sudden chill down her spine.

"Have you never heard the expression *curiosity killed the cat*?"

Her eyes flew up to meet his, the odd, pulsating green depths nearly hypnotizing her until the clatter of her fork hitting her plate sharply brought her around.

"Excuse me?" she asked shakily, reaching for the dropped silver utensil.

The doctor's face, which had grown still and strangely void of emotion, then melted into charming warmth that, although mirrored in his voice, never quite penetrated his eyes.

"I'm afraid I'm terribly pressed for time and as much as I would enjoy exchanging social niceties, the unfortunate truth is it simply is not practical. However, I was so hoping to see the documentation on your latest project. I know it's terribly late but might we stop by your office afterwards?"

"Tonight?" Chancella asked, her face lighting up in clear astonishment.

"Yes. That is, if it's not too much trouble."

She opened her mouth to refuse but there was something in his manner that nearly stopped her heart. An irrational wave of desire fluttered in the pit of her stomach and as her eyes once again met his, an uncharacteristic flood of subservience came over her. Weak and distant, she heard her own voice drift out to meet him.

"Of course, Dr. de—" she began to answer but jolted herself from the foggy trance-like state, acutely ill at ease with the sense of superiority she was allowing him to tout over her. Determined to level the playing field, she took his lead. "May I call you by your first name?"

He looked at her very directly then and with an expression that could almost be construed as severe, giving her the unnerving sensation that he knew her very intention for asking. But then he made a near indiscernible bow of his head.

"As you wish," he said softly.

For a few heartbeats, he hesitated—his lips parting to utter the sound and yet no sound came forth, his eyes seeming to simultaneously beckon and reject her. But soon after he abandoned his apparent reluctance, the low pitch of his voice raising the hairs on the back of Chancella's neck as he spoke.

"It's Valian."

* * * * *

The tall, blonde man seated at the lounge across the way watched Valian and the lady-doctor leave the restaurant. Staring into his untouched glass of red wine, he allowed himself a broad smile.

This was too easy.

The malevolent grin quickly faded at the appearance of a woman at his side.

"Hey, handsome, can I buy you a drink?" the dark-haired beauty purred as she saddled up beside him, one slender bare arm slithering seductively around his shoulders as she pressed her large breasts, which strained against the tight, thin fabric of her low-cut shirt, against his arm.

The man regarded her coolly, his streaky blonde tresses falling into his eyes.

"I don't drink...booze."

The lady of the night eyed the goblet before him and threw her head back, howling in delight.

"But baby, you're in a bar. Watcha come here for?"

Without answering, he moved his gaze to the stage where a half-naked young woman swirled around the metal pole that appeared to connect the floor to the ceiling that was hidden under a thick veil of smoke, like some sort of steel shaft to heaven.

"Oh, I see," the whore hissed softly, her tongue flickering delicately along the edge of his earlobe. "You want some action."

She leaned even further against him so she could reach over with a red-nailed hand to massage his inner thigh.

"Well, maybe I can help you with that."

The man slowly turned his attention back to the prostitute. She was a pretty enough female, or had been at one time, but the heavy makeup and outlandish clothing did little for her now. Even so, his mouth started to salivate as his eyes traveled down the length of her body.

"Let's go."

Outside the street was unusually quiet, the only sound coming from the buzzing of the overhead streetlights.

"C'mon, baby," she grabbed the john's hand as they got into a cab, getting out some time later in front of a pink and blue neon sign that flashed the partially lit words Paradise Hotel. With the burnt out letters missing it read Par-di-e H-el.

"This way, c'mon now," she pulled on his arm. "Don't be shy."

Wordlessly he allowed her to lead him into the dismal lobby of the neighborhood flop house. No one was manning the front desk so they walked up a narrow flight of stairs to the second floor and down a darkened hallway before coming to a stop in front of a battered, worn door with a faded metal number on it.

"Lucky number seven," she winked at the stranger as she stepped into the shadowy room. Reaching for the light switch, she gasped at the cold hard clasp of his hand on her wrist.

"No lights."

"Whatever you say, baby," she said, peeling off her red leather jacket and tossing it carelessly on a nearby chair before slinking over to the mirror-less dresser across the room. She turned to face him.

"So, whatcha want?" she asked casually, squinting slightly at the shadowy form.

"Everything," came the low-voiced reply.

"Two hundred, up front," she stated emphatically, stifling a yawn.

When the man remained rooted in place, the hooker shifted her weight to one leg with a huff, the movement throwing her hip out to the side into a decidedly impatient pose.

"Let's go, honey. No cash, no party."

The clear rustle of money that followed brought a greedy glint to the pro's eyes. Flouncing over, she took the two bills from the man's outstretched hand, stuffing them down the front of her see-through blouse into a black lace bra. Then she reached behind her back, undoing the button of her leopard print skirt to ease it down over her hips where it fell to the floor, with only a crotchless black lace thong in its place.

She reached for him then, pressing her hand firmly against the front of his snakeskin pants, but the man took a step backwards, evading her touch.

"Take off your clothes," he ordered flatly.

"Whatever you want," she cooed.

Illuminated only by the moonlight shining in through the filthy, cracked window, she wordlessly removed the remainder of her things and stood waiting for his directive. For a long time there was nothing and she grew uneasy, sensing that he was staring at her, somewhere in the dimness of the dingy space. When he finally spoke, the sound startled her from behind — she hadn't seen him move.

"Go lay on the bed," he said, the rich, melodious tone deceptively soothing and gentle.

The hooker complied, stretching out on her back and interlocking her hands over her head. At the touch of his hands on her ankles she smiled, drawing in a sharp breath as he jerked her down to the edge of the bed, and abruptly spreading her legs, planted his head firmly between them. The ensuing wave of pleasure quickly turned to excruciating pain and, flailing frantically, she disengaged herself and scrambled back against the headboard, fumbling for the lamp on the nightstand.

Hitting the lights, she screamed in horror at the sparkling fresh bloodstain on the dull sheets where she had just been. That same blood, her blood, now dripped from the man's mouth, the rich crimson liquid flowing in rivulets down either side to his chin. Burning within his eyes was a crazed animalistic fire and a slow, sadistic smile spread across the striking, alabaster face as he stared at her.

"You said whatever I want," he growled, his long straight teeth smeared with red.

The whore opened her mouth to shout once again but in a flash he was at her side, her head caught firmly between his hands, and with a single, sudden movement he snapped her neck.

Letting her fall lifeless to the bed, the stranger used the corner of the bedspread to wipe his bloodied mouth. Standing up tall, he straightened his burgundy shirt before running a strong hand through his sun-kissed hair, absentmindedly fingering his lone earring that twinkled in the moonlight. Then without emotion, he sauntered casually past the bed and the body of the hooker and left the room, closing the door quietly behind him.

Chapter Three

ဆ

Chancella and Valian strolled down the avenue, looking to flag down a passing cab, but the night air was so warm and moist from the afternoon rain shower that still lingered on the breeze that Chancella secretly hoped none would stop. But, she realized with a secret smile, that wasn't the only reason.

The past couple of years Chancella had readily sacrificed any kind of social life for her work and it was a decision she seldom thought of and certainly never regretted for her work had always been a particular interest. However, tonight, she was startled by the budding flicker of another kind of interest, her firmly entrenched analytical nature giving way to a long repressed and somewhat irrational emotion that whispered suggestively to her at every turn. Why, she was absolutely amazed at the tiny little thrill that coursed through her as she regarded Valian out of the corner of her eye—a soft breeze tousling his dark hair to blow a couple of silky errant strands across his smooth forehead. Somewhere in the deep recesses of her memory, a picture of Barbra Streisand's gloved hand tenderly brushing back Robert Redford's hair at the end of *The Way We Were* immediately flashed in Chancella's mind and she couldn't help laughing softly to herself.

"What's so funny?" Valian asked, his low voice not surprisingly sending another chill down her spine. She was almost getting used to the erotically charged state his voice produced.

Almost.

"Nothing," she said lightly, mildly embarrassed at her departure from her normal professional manner. "It's just—"

She looked at him and for the second time since they met, Chancella could've sworn that the eccentric individual knew exactly what she was thinking. Mortified by the possibility, she hastily changed the subject.

"de Mortenoire. That's French — isn't it?"

"Yes," he said frankly.

"Then you were born in Martinique?"

"No, it's simply where I reside."

He stated the last sentence so emphatically, Chancella felt certain he wanted no further discussion of his private life, but then, almost as an afterthought, he amended the statement ever so slightly.

"For now."

There was a pronounced highbrow, somewhat haughty manner in the way he spoke, a definite assuredness that tainted every utterance as if he was not in the habit of being questioned.

Even so, Chancella waited for him to continue, walking along in a patient silence. When it became apparent that Valian would not answer her original question, she opened her mouth to ask something else but was interrupted by his cool, detached voice.

"I'm originally from Andorra," he said, the way in which he said "originally" clearly insinuating he had moved around a great deal.

Chancella stopped, frowning slightly.

"Where is that?"

"It's a small town located right on the border between France and Spain."

"Ah, that explains it," Chancella said, nodding slightly. Valian stopped then too and regarded her steadily.

"Explains what?"

"Your accent."

She had immediately picked up on the distinctively melodious roll of sentences from his mouth, as if he were singing rather than speaking—a trait common to many Romance languages. And yet, there was the obvious misplacement of emphasis in certain words, pronouncing re-MIN-der as re-min-DER, a customary intonation of the French. "Then your speech is cultivated from both?"

"I suppose so, yes. I do speak several languages, however I was raised on Catalan, which is a Latin-esque hybrid of the two."

"Really? Catalan—I'm not familiar with it."

"It's an ancient tongue and one that is mostly spoken within Andorra's borders."

"Interesting," she mused softly. "What's it like?"

He eyed her curiously as if trying to determine her sincerity.

"Say something in it," she coaxed lightly.

"Like what?"

"Oh I don't know—anything."

The rich thick roll of the cadenced phrases were nearly musical as his tongue seemingly caressed the exotic syllables, the lyrical sentences rising and falling in a baritone cascade of accentuated vowels and lilts and Chancella felt a shiver of pleasure at the sound of the mysterious dialect.

"Gosh, that's wonderful," she said genuinely. "What does it mean?"

"I said 'all the answers of the world are within your eyes'."

Chancella nodded wordlessly, surprised to once again feel a little flustered by his straightforward manner. "So your parents are from Andorra as well?"

"No," he said haltingly. "My father was…Spanish."

Another bout of silence.

"And your mother?"

"It is said that my father fell in love with my mother the very first time he saw her — a beautiful gypsy from France."

"A gypsy?" Chancella chuckled, her smile fading under Valian's serious scrutiny.

"A gypsy," he somberly repeated. "However, I believe nowadays you call them fortune tellers or tarot card readers. When my father was crowned King, he turned his back on both my mother and me. It is her name that I have taken as my own. Not his."

He glanced away suddenly and frowned, angry with himself for the unnecessary divulgence. For a second, his attention was caught by a couple of kids kissing hotly in the shadows of a dim doorway.

"King?" Chancella asked in astonishment. "Of what?"

"This is it — no?" he changed the subject tersely as he motioned to the tall structure before them, his voice returning to its formerly composed and disinterested state.

"No," she answered quickly, motioning forward as they continued on. Greatly intrigued by her colleague's lineage, she questioned him further. "So then, you are royalty?"

The words were no sooner out of her mouth than she regretted having uttered them, for Valian whirled to face her, his eyes a bizarre shade of lime, blazing with a fierce fire as his jaw clenched tightly.

"True, but it is a title that I do not wish to claim. Nor ever will!"

Stifling a gasp, Chancella backed up, staring in disbelief at the expression of anger on Valian's formerly placid face. Without a doubt she had struck a nerve and one that ran very deep. Clearing her throat, she glanced down, silenced by the forceful manner in which he had spoken. It was obvious that his royal bloodline was off limits, but her persistent curiosity was not appeased and she gingerly waded in again as they resumed their late-night jaunt.

"Did you and your mother remain in Spain?"

He shot her a hard, sideways glance, his piercing gaze still carrying the fiery remnants of his fury.

"No," he sighed as he finally looked away, his voice lessening. "We returned to Andorra, her hometown, where we remained for several years. After her death, I left." He winced slightly, glancing away again. "I haven't been back since."

"Perhaps you will return one day," she said softly, stunned by the ridiculous temptation to reach out and clasp one of his pale slender hands.

Valian stopped and looked at her fully, his eyes dancing with a transitory light, and when he spoke there was the tiniest flicker of hope in his low, even voice.

"Perhaps. If I ever have a reason to."

Shaken by Valian's magnetic charm, Chancella, relieved by the familiar sight of the steps that led to the research facility, motioned towards the angular concrete building.

"Here we are."

Entering the lab, she was mildly surprised to discover it vacant—she was certain Nick had said he would be working late.

Unlocking the tall metal cabinet that housed the majority of her research materials and files, she took out two thick volumes, a number of the worn pages within the sturdy three-ring binders black with scribbled notes and detailed diagrams.

"This is everything except the formula itself," she said to Valian, huffing as she set the cumbersome books down on the counter with a thud.

"Yes, yes," he said thoughtfully as he tore through the tattered sheets at a remarkable rate. "It would appear to work 'on paper' as they say."

He paused, inwardly searching for the flaw.

"And there are no drawbacks, no side effects to speak of?"

Chancella grimly shook her head, a clear look of disappointment darkening her bright hazel eyes.

"Unfortunately, there are some, yes. The serum still needs to be revised, a few of the kinks smoothed out. As it is, the formula works—it does regenerate the expired tissue but—"

"But what?" he harshly prodded, his dark eyebrows knitting together with intent focus.

"There are risks to the subject. The use of certain narcotics can help ease the transition and reduce the intensity of the reaction to the serum, but the patient would still suffer acutely painful consequences."

"That doesn't matter," he stated flatly, turning his back on her to further scrutinize her notes.

"I beg to differ with you, doctor," she insisted coolly. "Granted, vomiting and convulsions are not, in themselves, life threatening, but they certainly warrant proceeding with caution."

When he did not respond, she persisted.

"In some cases, subjects have died from massive internal hemorrhaging."

"So?" Valian asked as he looked over his shoulder, his face oddly void of emotion.

"So?" she repeated incredulously. "Wha—why—these are unacceptable risks!"

"Not to me!" he shouted hotly at her. "All I care about is whether cell reanimation is possible!"

Chancella was immediately silenced by his impassioned outburst and stood stunned, gawking at him for a time. The smooth waxen-like texture of his radiant skin so caught her attention that she unabashedly studied it until he hastily twisted away from her scrutinizing gaze. When she at last found her voice, it was low and cautious.

"I appreciate your enthusiasm, Doctor, but it would be remiss of me not to include *all* the findings of my work."

Valian, his back to her as he perused the overflowing pages of her notebooks once more, dismissed her with an arrogant wave of his hand.

"It's a very small price to pay for a new life," he mumbled.

Dumbfounded, Chancella could only shrug it off as she set to lessen some of the dissipating tension between them by redirecting the conversation.

"Well, there is still the matter of timing the injections."

"Oh?" Valian circled around, a renewed interest wiping the scowl from his face.

"For complete tissue restoration, the subject must be administered a series of injections. However, if adequate recovery time is not allowed between treatments, one can actually produce the opposite result to the desired end."

"What are you saying?"

"That improper dosages of the serum create a biochemical inversion of sorts, making the tissue permanently resistant to any future attempts to reanimate the cell."

At that, Valian turned an even whiter shade of pale, his eyes growing dark with shock as though he had been struck a terrible blow. Despite their heated debate only seconds earlier, Chancella felt an impulsive swell of concern at the radical change in her colleague.

"Are you all right?" she asked softly.

He didn't answer, his mesmerizing gaze fixed on some far-off point, the corners of his full mouth pulling down into a pained grimace. Delicately, Chancella reached over and cautiously touched his forearm.

"Valian?"

He had been quite clearly shaken, but the soft faltering sound of her voice caused him to turn his head slowly towards her face, regarding her with such an air of bewilderment that Chancella couldn't contain a soft laugh.

"Are you all right?" she asked again, inspecting him intently. This time she refused to waver under the burrowing weight of his penetrating gaze and for one suspended moment their eyes locked together—hers filled with a fiery defiance and his, a curious confusion. Unbeknownst to her, it had been ages since he had been called by name.

In that precise moment he took a leap of faith, a concept he had abandoned a very long time ago, and reached out to her in the gentlest, most unobtrusive way possible.

I need your help.

Chancella twitched, frowning at Valian, and for the first time noticed, once again, the way his face could take on a rather bizarre mannequin-like quality, giving the impression that he wasn't human. Or more correctly, that he wasn't *alive*.

"What did you say?" she leaned forward, her sight resolutely fixed on his mouth, determined to catch the least movement. But his full lips remained closed, parting only slightly to moisten them with the tip of his tongue and yet, again, the words sounded inside her.

Will you help me?

Seconds later came the plea.

I need you.

Before she could form a single thought, the recollection of the voice, this very voice, calling her earlier in the day overtook her. Stunned, she glared at him.

"It was you—in the bookstore this afternoon—speaking to me. That was you, wasn't it?"

This time the low, silken pitch of his voice reached her ears.

"It was."

"But how? How'd you do it?"

"Nothing more than simple telepathy, really. By utilizing thought transference, our initial connection, a meeting of the minds, preceded our physical one. It was a way of planting the seed, so to speak."

"Planting the seed? For what?"

"For your unbiased and unadulterated assistance."

"With what?" she repeated, growing leery of what was beginning to feel very much like a game of cat and mouse.

"You know," he said unsmiling. "Your writings will guide you. I am that which you seek."

The last statement, as mind-boggling as it was, came as more of an apology than a confession. Chancella could only gawk at the individual before her who, through her astounded view, no longer appeared handsome and charming but rather alien and dangerous. And still she stood rooted, caught somewhere between inquisitiveness and fright, interest and terror—the two feelings so merging that she could scarcely tell where one ended and the other began.

Unable to answer, she continued to stare at the figure before her in stupefied disbelief, held captive by the entreating expression in the aqua eyes that were so unflinchingly fixed on her face. For the last time the polite request was internally communicated.

Will you help me?

Chancella's head pounded with what felt like a million different thoughts—each working to confuse and pull her in a diverse direction and yet above it all was the preposterous notion that somehow he was speaking the truth. Bewildered, she gathered her methodical wits about her and set out to uncover his intent for making such an incredible assertion.

"What precisely are you talking about?" she stammered out sharply. "The formula?"

"Yes," he answered calmly, the mellow sound of his voice easing Chancella's anxiety only temporarily, for his next request put her right back on the treadmill. "I want you to try it on me."

"But you're a doctor!" Chancella practically cried with an exasperated huff, immediately realizing the irrelevance of the statement.

"Am I?" he posed the question to her, answering before she had a chance to. "Surely you wouldn't have agreed to meet me if I'd told you the truth."

"What?" she demanded, feeling strangely betrayed by the deception. A dark shadow fell over his face as he read her thoughts.

"Even as your heart tells you the truth, you are doubting it," Valian challenged, peering hard into her eyes. "But you must believe me. I am what I say. I have sought you out for a single purpose and it is one that will afford both of us the opportunity of a lifetime. My motive is my own but for you, I supply you with the chance to *do* what before you could only surmise, to achieve what you could only speculate, to—" he paused briefly, "to practice what you preach," he finished, nearly whispering.

"But it can't be. I mean, you can't be."

"And why not?" he asked soothingly. "Don't tell me, Chancella, that you have spent years of your life researching, experimenting and studying something that, when push comes to shove, you don't believe in?"

Chancella opened her mouth to speak but she hesitated as a desperate tug-of-war raged inside her. Flat out terrified at the prospect, she realized that she had never once entertained the possibility of coming face-to-face with a real "live" vampire. And now, when challenged with that reality, what *proof* did she have other than the ridiculous gnawing feeling that Valian was speaking the truth?

"Ah—so it is proof you desire," he said lowly, having read her thoughts. "How best can I substantiate my claim—hmmm?"

Backing up, Chancella wordlessly shook her head as the scores of possibilities played out in her mind's eye. Chances are this guy was just a nut, which, of course, presented its own problems. But if not, he was right...this was an unbelievable— no, historical—stroke of luck. Indeed, one might even call it *destiny*.

The cold, hard pressure of Valian's strong fingers abruptly closing around her wrist snapped her back to reality, and once again, she saw a hard, burning anger flaring within him.

"You must get something clear," his lips curled back and he spat out the next words from between tightly gritted teeth. "I have no intention of hurting you, but patience is not one of my strong suits. You *are* going to help me."

Then yanking her even closer, Valian held her firmly as he pressed her against the desk, his unforgettable eyes smoldering with a dangerous jade fire.

"If you insist," he said his cool, odorless breath brushing against the side of her cheek, "I will have no choice but to convince you beyond a shadow of a doubt."

With that, he parted his lips ever so slightly, just enough to allow Chancella a glimpse of two abnormally long eyeteeth that seemed to be lengthening as she watched.

Confusion quickly shifting to fear, Chancella shoved against him and backed up, getting just enough room to swing frantically and deliver a single sharp smack to Valian's cheek as she slapped him stiffly across the face. The unexpected blow, though lightweight, seemed to catch him unaware. And in the split second he loosened his grip on her, his face directly melting into a demonic-like mask of fury, it was in that window of opportunity that Chancella flew to the door.

Racing down the security-locked hallway, she frantically flashed her clearance card in front of the access pad to the stairwell and hustled down several flights of stairs before bursting out into the lobby. Speeding across the large atrium, she slid her security pass across the final locked portal — once, twice, three times before it would open and, pushing on the heavy glass doors of the entrance, she rushed out into the darkened empty street.

Stumbling forward, she bolted down the boulevard, running wildly, her arms and legs pumping hard and fast. Desperate to put as much distance between her and the lab as possible, she rounded a sharp corner and continued sprinting, taking the night air in through pained, raspy gulps.

Several blocks ahead, and just around from the bakery, she knew there was a police station. With renewed vigor, she headed forward with a steely determination, anxious for whatever assistance she could get there.

A sharp stitch knifed her left side as she ran but she pushed on, soon closing in on the small brick building. As she bounded from the curb, the heel of one pump caught on an uneven stretch of road and she tripped, tearing her nylons as she fell hard to the ground, the blood from her badly scraped knee spotting the pavement. Panting, she slowly got to her feet and limped on towards the proverbial light at the end of the tunnel. Her energy threatened to give out before she reached her desired destination but still on she pressed, stealing a hurried glance over her shoulder to confirm that, despite the virtual impossibility of it, Valian wasn't following her. Without an access card, he would still be locked within the tight confines of the maximum-security complex. If they hustled, the police could probably still catch him there.

Facing forward once again, she rounded the final corner, running straight into the arms of—Valian. A bloodcurdling scream ripped from her throat as she struggled with the reality of his presence.

"Stop it!" he growled gruffly, giving her a solid shake for emphasis, the movement rendering her ragdoll-like within the steel grip of his hands.

"How'd you...I..." she stammered in bewilderment, squirming against his angry embrace. Then, just as in the lab, she pulled her free arm back to strike him. This time, Valian caught her hand in midair and, glowering down at her, he drew so close that their lips nearly touched as he spoke in a low, menacing tone.

"Don't...do that," he hissed, his ominous gaze glittering in the harsh light of the street lamp as his cold fingers dug painfully into her skin, bruising her flesh.

Without thinking, she reacted near hysterically and leaning over, she bit the hand that restrained her, squeezing her eyes shut as she viciously dug her teeth deep into the cold, white flesh, her mouth immediately filling with the warm iron-rich taste of blood. Gradually she detected an unnerving stillness from her assailant, the realization slowing the impassioned gnashing of her teeth against his alabaster skin. Opening her eyes, she froze, her lips loosely locked around his knuckles as she felt the weight of his cold, unemotional stare burrowing into her.

"You like to bite?" he asked softly, the near imperceptible promise of sensuality lurking deep within the low intimidating timbre.

Pulling away, she shakily wiped at her bloodied mouth with her free hand, looking in disgust at the oozing cuts she had left on him, his hand still clasped around hers.

"Who are you?" Chancella pleaded as she tried to draw away, a strange sense of calmness threatening to overtake her rationale. "What do you want from m—"

Stopping suddenly, her eyes widened in a horror-tinged incredulity as she looked at Valian's injured hand again. The dark, deep gashes her teeth had made in his skin had completely closed up, leaving only a residue of all but dried blood in their wake.

Baffled, she hesitantly returned her gaze to his face and the serious, almost sad look upon it.

"I told you," he answered quietly.

"Hey! What's going on here?" a burly young officer called out as he broke away from a couple of other off-duty cops that were leaving the precinct together. Plodding over to them, he opened his jacket to reveal his shoulder holster. "Lady, are you okay?"

Turning his head to impassively stare at the advancing cop, Valian released Chancella, allowing her the opportunity to flee, and yet she hesitated, merely looking from the approaching cop to Valian and back again before she began to take tiny backward steps.

"What's going on here?" the officer asked loudly.

Chancella turned to face the policeman, stammering uncertainly for a few seconds.

"I was — we were — he — "

When she twisted back to Valian, a loud hiss of disbelief escaped her lips, the cop's soft exclamation of "What the hell?" swiftly following, for whoever, *whatever* Valian de Mortenoire was, he was gone.

* * * * *

Across the way, Valian stepped out from the dark alleyway, his soft step not making a sound on the wet cement ground. Stopping, he cocked his head to one side, his eyes glued to the entrance of the cop shop that Chancella and the rookie officer had just entered.

What was he doing? He had let the woman go. Twice. Even after he had clearly seen she had realized the truth, even when the light bulb went on in that obscure region behind her eyes, he had released her.

Surprised by his decision, he stood for a long time, staring pensively at the worn old precinct.

What was it about her that was so different? He had seen many a beautiful mortal, indeed, they were all beautiful but there was an inkling of something new here, something puzzling, that made him do the worst possible thing any vampire could do.

Hesitate.

A luscious scent hit him and he abruptly snapped his head around to the right, locating its source within seconds. Crouching down where the woman had fallen, he gingerly dabbed at the fresh stain, still wet, on the concrete before licking the rich red liquid from his fingers. A jolt of fire blazed through him carrying with it images of Chancella and every sensation that was her unique perspective on her life. *Summers at the beach, dancing at the prom, her father's gravesite, walking the dog, tobogganing in the snow.* Mixed, muddled memories of days gone by quickly overlapped, the pictures speeding faster and faster until the roller-coaster ride stopped suddenly on Valian's face when only hours earlier she had first looked up from the restaurant table at him.

He rose then, a slight smile breaking the solid lines of his face. Before this night he had sought her out, searched for her, hunted her. But now, through her blood, they were indelibly linked.

Now, no matter where Chancella Tremaine went…he would find her.

* * * * *

Unlocking the door of her high-rise condo, Chancella stepped into the quiet darkness, the soft silvery light of the moon dancing in through the windows. Letting her coat fall into a heap on the carpet, she kicked off her pumps and padded into the bedroom. With a heartfelt sigh, she fell onto the bed and, closing her eyes, began massaging her temples.

The police station had been a zoo and that lieutenant had looked at her like she was positively insane.

"A vampire?" he said, his warm brown eyes twinkling gleefully. "Maybe we should call out the garlic squad for this one — huh?"

No, Chancella had tried to explain patiently, ignoring the aging cop's bemused expression — the guy wasn't a *real* vampire — he'd only *thought* he was.

And yet as hard as she worked to persuade the elder policeman, she worked even harder to convince herself. Back there on the street, she had seen something she couldn't explain — the gashes on his knuckles disappearing, healing miraculously before her very eyes. For that, there could be no explanation. Or more correctly, there could be only *one* explanation.

Shaking her head, she got up, groaning at the ache in her tired muscles. Even though she barely had enough energy to get out of the confines of her clothes, she was certain a hot bath would do her good.

In the dim light, she stripped everything off, sharply sucking in air as she tried to peel off her nylons, the shredded sheer fabric sticking to her scratched knee where the blood had dried. Reaching for the robe that she knew was slung over the headboard, she quickly threw it on and belting it loosely about her body made her way into the bathroom.

Inspired by nature, the warm terra-cotta space contained a veritable forest of leafy green plants. Most were placed especially around the large sunken tub that, during the day, was highlighted by the rays of sunlight streaming in the large skylight overhead. The effect gave one the unmistakable impression that they were bathing outdoors. Conversely, when the sun went down, one could lounge in the soothing waters, gazing up at the twinkling stars in the dark.

Perched on the side of the tub, she plugged the drain and turned the faucets on. The relaxing space soon filled with a heavy humid steam that covered the mirrors over the sink and on the back of the door.

A crystal bottle that contained a soft purple liquid with bits of flower petals and sparkles floating within stood on one side of the tiled bath area. Reaching for it, Chancella removed the cork stopper and poured some of the mauve fluid under the running water, the gentle, tranquil scent of lavender immediately filling the air.

Removing her robe, Chancella stepped into the soothing warmth of the water and eased herself back, cringing as the water washed over her ripped flesh. A deep sigh broke free from her lips as her eyes fluttered shut, but peace would not find her for the bizarre events of the day replayed in her mind.

Frowning, she again recalled the young man at the lecture and his sincere, desperate plea for her help. Then there was Nick, with his uncharacteristic moodiness. Finally her thoughts turned to the mysterious man who called himself Valian de Mortenoire.

Valian — the name, sounding exotic and dangerous, and yet, the words strangely seductive, whispered hauntingly in her head, bringing with it a sharp pang of disillusionment.

In her mind's eye she could see him as clear as day as they strolled to the lab, his shiny dark hair blowing softly in the breeze and those magnificent green eyes, glowing and shimmering as they watched her.

Always watching her.

Despite the weird tone of the past twenty-four hours, Chancella couldn't deny that this one individual, this *being*, had in a matter of a couple of hours made her realize just how much she had missed the company of someone special in her life. Maybe all work and no play had made Jill a dull girl.

Stretching, she smoothed back her hair with wet hands, wincing at the cruel irony of the situation. Just when she'd found the one who could achieve the near impossible, figuratively and literally turning her head, he turned out to be —

What? She inwardly demanded — a crazy? A vampire?

If none of his story were true, Mr. de Mortenoire would have to be one of the best con men around. Indeed, what a charade he had held up as truth — albeit a well-conceived and convincingly related one — such an intricate yarn he had spun about his father and his disowned lineage to the throne! And those teeth! Or that trick with his skin! How'd he manage that one?

Oh, it was all too fantastic to believe, she privately groaned, and yet, there had been something so real about him.

The unmistakable sense of urgency and sincerity with which he had implored Chancella tugged at her tried-and-true intuition nonstop until she begrudgingly had to admit that although Valian may not be the Real McCoy, there could be little doubt that he *believed* he was.

Sighing deeply, she snuggled down further into the soothing waves of warm water, hoping that the wet swells of heat across her body would wash away her confusion and angst. Sometimes it seemed that everywhere she looked, there was someone in dire need, reaching out with their last breath towards her. And yet, she was forced to dismally accept that she couldn't save them all, the humanitarian within her weeping as it let drop its maternal head in defeat. In fact, she surrendered with a heavy-hearted resignation, she wasn't sure she could save *any* of them.

As chaos and concern swirled in her head, she wearily opened her eyes, directly screaming at the image of a man's face reflected in the steamy surface of the mirror over the sink.

Jumping up, she scrambled back, water sloppily washing over the side of the porcelain edge. Looking up once again, she was dumbfounded to see nothing out of the ordinary on the smoggy mist of the glass. She was so sure that she had seen the face of a blonde-haired man staring back at her but, shaken and puzzled, she slowly got out of the tub, and toweled off.

Grabbing her robe, she moved into the living room and, stretching out onto the sofa, she flicked on the remote for the radio — the area immediately filled with the soft, soothing sound of Frank Sinatra.

It's not the pale moon that excites me,

that thrills and delights me,

Oh — no —

It's just the nearness of you.

The music swirled around the room as Chancella's eyelids grew heavier and heavier until slowly, delicately, she fell into a deep slumber.

* * * * *

She was floating, high above the trees and rooftops, her body gliding and at times hovering like a feather as it drifted delicately down to the earth. Only she was moving upwards, first soft and slowly, then whoosh! in an expulsion of spontaneous energy that sent her hair and clothing flying back with the force of the movement.

Her limbs, limp and lifeless, hung loose, complacent and free and her flesh, muscles and veins, indeed every fiber of her being was coursing with a strange new vitality.

A strong pair of arms enfolded her from behind and she swooned at the warm sensation of someone nuzzling her neck. Reaching back and up over her head, she let her fingers run through the soft, smooth strands of hair of her heavenly captor, the firm caress of his hands on her breasts and thighs sending shock waves of light and love through her.

Turning around to behold him, she leaned forward to tenderly kiss the lips of the unrecognizable lover. It was a gentle exchange, the feel of his soft pliable mouth on hers like the wings of a butterfly, growing stronger with each kiss, their passion fueled by the fire that coursed through them.

Higher they flew, locked in their ardent embrace, up through the fluffy white clouds that dotted the night sky towards the sun and heat, the steady, constant warmth soon giving way to an intense feverish pain.

Squirming, Chancella fought against their agonized upward course into the increasingly excruciating blaze, and still they pushed on. Her head buried against the dark angel's shoulder as her screams merged with his—a haunting cry deafening her and echoing on the wind as it drifted out to the four corners of the world.

Chan-cel-la.

* * * * *

Chancella sat upright, blinking into the darkness, the sound of her frightened panting hissing in the stillness of the shadowy living room.

With a disoriented uncertainty, she brought a trembling hand up to her face where she wiped at the surprising tears that moistened her cheek.

Jesus, what a nightmare.

She ran a still shaking hand through her tousled hair and, moving back a bit, propped against the armrest of the sofa.

Just then, the spotlight over the fireplace flickered on to reveal the form of a man leaning nonchalantly against the mantle.

"Good morning," he offered casually, the low timbre of his voice sending an immediate shiver through her.

Chancella jumped and, swallowing hard, slowly edged up even further into a sitting position.

"What do you want?" she sputtered hoarsely, the words coming out in a sound between a whisper and a croak.

He looked sincerely surprised for a moment.

"Better watch how you talk to me. You wouldn't want me to get angry." His eyes gleamed with the last word. Then he rolled his head back and laughed, the movement revealing the tips of two gleaming white fangs that elongated as she watched, lengthening to jut down over the line of his bottom lip.

Chancella could only stare at the figure in a terror-induced speechlessness.

He had a tall, lean frame and his hair, a streaky bleached-blonde shade, fell in full, feathery waves to his shoulders. His burgundy silk shirt hung open to reveal an impressive set of abs that gave way to skintight snakeskin pants and matching tan boots. Chancella noted how his skin was iridescent in the light, almost shimmering, the strange shiny quality constant except for the slightest hint of an after-five shadow. Oddly, his eyes matched the color of the single gold earring, a crucifix, that dangled from his left ear and they flashed with a strange light as they fell over her body.

"I watched you undress," he purred. "Nice panties."

Chancella subconsciously pulled her robe tighter around her naked frame. Her mind, frantic with options, tried to locate the nearest phone but the sound of his strange voice wiped all thoughts from her head.

"Ummmm. You look delicious, Chancella," he continued, slowly licking his lips, his eyes digging into hers.

She stared at him blankly, her heart pounding in her chest. This guy was scaring the hell out of her and if the lopsided smirk on his face was any indication, he was getting off on it. Trying to buy some time, she cleared her throat but her voice still cracked as she spoke.

"How…how do you know my name?"

"I know lots of things about you," he stated matter-of-factly.

"Oh?" She could feel her mouth trembling. The man simply stared at her, a sardonic smile tugging at the corner of his mouth, the unanswered question hanging in the air.

"Well," she started again, praying that the intruder couldn't hear the tremors in her voice, "that leaves me at a bit of a disadvantage. You know my name but I don't know yours."

He observed her for a long moment before a slow, widening sneer spread across his face.

"Call me—" he paused, one long index finger tapping indecisively on his lower lip, "Jack."

Then with a pronounced twinkle glinting within the champagne-gold of his eyes, he lightly added, "I'm a *friend* of Valian's."

The way he said the word clearly implied he meant quite the opposite.

"Valian?" Chancella all but shrieked, her eyes growing wide with disbelief, urging yet another laugh from the stranger — a deep husky sound that filled the room with a strange vibration.

"Surprise, surprise," he teased, the brilliant smile on his face failing to offset the hardness in his eyes. "You do like surprises, don't you?"

Chancella could barely manage to open her mouth before the figure moved with an inhuman speed from the fireplace across the way to hover over her, the unnaturally porcelain face drawing within inches of hers, his cool, odorless breath brushing against her skin and hair when he spoke.

"Well, brace yourself, baby," he cooed in a voice that dripped with sex and danger, "I'm full of surprises."

With that, he grabbed her viciously and yanking her onto her feet, drew her to him, crushing her body against his while he pinned her arms behind her back with one hand and pulled her hair back with the other. Held captive in his strong embrace, she became painfully aware that her exposed neck was arched, ready for the taking, a ragged scream tearing loose from her throat at the cold, wet feel of his tongue moving along the length of her throat over to her ear. The sharpness of his teeth bruised her flesh as he nibbled her earlobe.

"Mmmm."

The sound of his moan rang in her ears as the terror within her literally blinded her, her heart pounding so hard that she found herself gasping for breath.

"I can hear your heart," he hissed, the strength of his lean, hard body bending hers backwards. Slowly, his little nibbles became more insistent, his soft moans giving way to guttural sounds, the ferocity of his passion filling Chancella with one unmistakable, recurring thought.

She needed no proof. This was for real.

Jack's hand moved roughly between her legs and as Chancella struggled in vain to break free, the sound of his taunt filled her ears, tears of pain and humiliation springing to her eyes.

"You like that, don't you?"

With a swift movement, he reached over and tore open her robe, exposing her bare breasts to him. He leaned down and fastening himself to one of her nipples, bit sharply into the tender flesh, causing her to cry out in pain.

"Shut up!" he snarled, his fangs gleaming horrendously in the light.

She pushed against him with all her strength—struggling, scratching and screaming and yet, above it all, she could hear the blood-chilling sound of his mocking laughter.

With a sudden motion, Chancella reached up and raked her nails across the flawless white flesh of his cheek. Jack howled fiercely, enraged, before backhanding her across the face.

The last sensation Chancella felt was the wet warmth of the blood that poured from her nose, spreading across her cheek before she fell into unconsciousness.

Chapter Four

ഌ

Across town, Rio walked briskly along the rain-slicked street, his head down and arms wrapped around his shivering form, the khaki army jacket providing little warmth. Although the afternoon sun had long since disappeared, the heavy black cover of midnight now in its place, a close humid heat rose from the city pavement, but he took no notice. He was freezing. And scared.

Turning the corner, he swore softly as he collided with a couple of passersby, his mind reeling with what to do next. He'd sought advice from everyone he could, starting with the one person he trusted most.

Simarone had been his best bud for a while now and they'd gone through some tough shit together. Hell, they'd met on the street when Rio was hustling in the park, just trying to make a couple of extra bucks. Sure, his work at that computer store was a breeze for a pro hacker like him, but it didn't pay diddley-squat.

Maybe it wasn't so surprising that when Simarone walked up to him that first night and asked if he wanted to make some real money, Rio said *hell yeah*! After all, it wouldn't be the first time he'd had to bend over to pay the rent, so to speak. Besides, he wasn't a fag or anything, but this guy had a look in his eyes like he'd just watched you jack off or something. He was hot. No, beautiful. *Really beautiful.* Like some sort of fucking angel.

Anyway, that first night was weird…the two of them in that darkened alcove, shielded from prying eyes and Simarone staring at him for the longest time—not saying anything, just staring. Then he leaned over, real close like, his mouth opening wide like he wanted to French.

Funny but Rio can't remember what happened after that. Maybe he'd blacked out. Come to think of it, a lot of his time with Simarone was kinda hazy. Maybe it was all the shit they smoked.

Whatever.

Since that first night, they had been tight. Real tight.

That's why it had tore him up when Simarone laughed about that weird guy blackmailing Rio to break into some password protect program, even threatening to go to the cops. How the hell had that blonde-haired, Hugo Boss-wearing dickhead known about all the shit Rio had lifted? For the life of him, he just didn't see what was so goddamned funny about it.

Then again, Simarone had grown real serious when he heard the rest of the story, that raspy chuckle of his ending rapidly. No, he sure wasn't laughing when Rio told him what happened next. Shuddering, the young man recalled the moment when he realized that there are worse things than doing time for shoplifting.

It had been well after midnight when that fashion-victim freak had first cornered him coming off the elevator of the underground parking lot and made his "offer you can't refuse" speech. It left Rio shaken and stunned silent, staring at the bundle of hundred dollar bills the guy threw at his feet, his parting words of "we'll be in touch" echoing in the empty cement area.

Anxious to get the hell outta there, Rio had grabbed the cash and hot-footed it around the bend and one level down to his battered Jeep Cherokee, stopping only at the sight of this couple making out against the side of a truck. Yeah, they were really going at it—the girl grabbing wildly at the guy's back, almost screaming, and he moaning like a cat in heat. Then the guy turns around, real slow like, and damn if it's not the same dude that Rio had just been talking to! Only now, he looks different.

Way different.

Yeah, now the fair-haired model is glaring at Rio, clearly pissed, his weird gold eyes glazed crazily and he's snarling like a fucking wolf, his long, straight teeth dripping with a thick red liquid that could only be blood.

Jesus! Rio didn't know exactly what the hell he was looking at but it sure as fuck wasn't Santa Claus.

Well, after Simarone heard that, he just turned and walked away, all silent and sullen as he does from time to time, leaving Rio with no one else to turn to.

Christ! He'd even gone to a priest who, in his oh-so-gentle and patronizing church manner, suggested that Rio's "perceptions were stemming from some internalized hostility" and that he should "seek some sort of professional help."

Yeah, right. Like talking to some shrink was going to save him from a bloodsucker!

No, that scientist-writer lady at the university had been his last hope and the only one left who could help him. He would have to find her and try again.

Coming to an abrupt halt, Rio stared at the heavy black doors and the circular fringe of tattered dark material that crowned them, gothic red lettering atop bright orange and yellow flames, the only color on the otherwise dismal canopy. Already, he could hear the driving beat of the bass beyond the club's entrance, muffled as it was.

As he stood preparing himself to go in, he felt the heavy, gnawing pain in the pit of his stomach increase and he fought another wave of foreboding terror. Trembling, he closed his eyes, remembering that he had no choice. The voice on his answering machine, echoing strangely as it had in the parking lot that night, had left no room for doubt.

Be there, or be dead.

With a shaky hand he reached for one of the door handles, a long, thin brass pitchfork that bore the name of the rave club. It read Dantes. Pulling it open, he stepped inside.

Immediately, Rio was faced with a decision. Up or down. To his right was a cheaply carpeted set of stairs that wound down, around and out of sight. Directly in front of him were three narrow steps that led up to a small quiet area. Stepping in, Rio was right away struck with the atmosphere of the intimate space that had the unexpected, informal feel of a rumpus room.

Worn leather and fabric couches had been placed flush against three of the walls. People lay, lounged or leaned against them, casually congregating in groups of twos and threes smoking and drinking, some talking, some more intimately involved. A tiny bar overseen by a young handsome boy sat unobtrusively off in the corner, and save for the odd person bumming a match, the juvenile barkeep stood inactive and looked bored stiff.

Quickly glancing around, Rio saw that the guy wasn't there. With a brief nod to the large black bouncer that was placed rather sentinel-like at the fork that split to the two tiers, Rio made his way down the other way, the music growing louder as he went.

The lower level, not much bigger than the upstairs, held a couple of booths just to the left of the grungy petite stage, on which a three-man band rocked and raged. On the opposite side was the bar, the sunken dance floor in between broken only by a smattering of small round tables. Everywhere people were undulating and pulsing to the music, the room one large mass of sweaty, writhing bodies like some sort of music-induced sex pit—their reflections caught in a huge mirror that covered the entire back wall. Just around the corner, a locked door marked PRIVATE added weight to the hushed rumors that the club contained an exclusive viewing room that allowed VIPs to visually eavesdrop on people via the two-way glass.

Moving through the rippling crowd, Rio navigated his way towards an empty table that was nearly concealed by shadows in a dark corner at the end of the bar, distracted by the escapades of a trio of frat boys as he went.

"Oooh, shooters! Over here!" one lanky student yelled, waving frantically in an attempt to flag down the pretty, scantily clad waitress that had a bevy of multicolored test-tube-like containers strapped to a thick leather belt that she wore around her bare midriff, a tube top and miniskirt completing the ensemble.

"Six please!" his buddy shouted at the girl, passing along one of the two blue concoctions she handed him to the third member of their posse.

"C'mon, drink up," the ringleader urged, raising his drink high in the air, his eyes meeting Rio's. "Cheers, buddy!"

Rio smiled weakly as he stepped around the boisterous threesome, halting abruptly to openly gawk at two women that now sat at the table he was headed for. Physical opposites, one was a dangerously gorgeous brunette, her shoulder-length hair framing her pale face in soft, dark waves that blended in with her head-to-toe outfit of black leather. The other sported a short spiked copper do offset by a super short satiny halter dress of sparkling white that was practically the identical shade as her skin — of which there was plenty exposed.

Uncrossing and crossing her legs in a Sharon Stone-esque maneuver, she dipped one long white finger into the long-stemmed glass in front of her that contained what appeared to be red wine and, raising it to her blood red lips, sucked it suggestively.

Tearing his gaze away, Rio looked over at the Dominatrix-attired, raven-haired beauty, feeling his legs threaten to give out under him as he heard a low, seductive voice reach him even over the evocative pulse of the bass guitar's sonic waves that melded with his own heartbeat.

Come here.

Mindlessly, he felt one foot moving in front of the other as he approached the table.

Sit.

In a muddled state, Rio complied, taking the chair in between the hot babes, his sight shifting from one unnatural, beautiful face to the other. In a flash the redhead was on him, literally, one cool bare arm gliding up his back to encircle his shoulders, her fingers reaching out to twist and twirl strands of his hair while her free hand clasped his wrist oddly, as if she meant to restrain him. He looked at the pallid, incandescent face that drew close, his breath quickening at the gray catlike eyes that seemed to throb, the unusual color and texture within reminiscent of polished gun metal.

A cool, moist pressure on his right ear jerked him around, the other babe now suckling his earlobe as she reached inside the front of his shirt to massage an ever-hardening nipple. Waves of foggy rapture washed over him and, panting, he felt his head fall back, a soft moan of both protest and pleasure escaping him as his eyes fluttered shut, only vaguely aware that the two beauties were enthusiastically licking each side of his neck. Deeper and deeper he sunk into the swelling realm of unconsciousness, myriad feminine voices overlapping each other, beckoning him, enticing him.

Then without warning it all stopped — that sweet swoon caused by the women's hands and lips on his skin, the abrupt return to reality leaving Rio to drift groggily out of his euphoric state and uncertainly sit upright. Still dazed, he moved a skimming glance over the packed space, bewildered to discover that seemingly things were as they had been all along — people dancing, laughing, talking — with none the wiser of his heavenly encounter with the two exotic creatures that flanked him. Perhaps he had dreamt it.

Exhaling a shaky breath, Rio turned his attention to his female companions, who had become like living statues, rigidly immobile as they glowered at something across the dance floor — their tantalizing painted mouths pulled back into silent snarls. Repeatedly tracing the course of their ferocious glare and curious as to the intended object of such intense loathing, Rio was baffled to conclude that their black-lined eyes weren't fixed upon any particular individual but rather the large mirrored wall at the rear of the club.

Then, her face melting into an expression of clear disappointment, the brunette leaned forward, sliding a piece of paper towards him.

"Tomorrow night. Eight o'clock," she said sharply.

Rio took the note and looked at it, his lips moving as he read the address.

"I don't get it," he said, confused as he looked up. "What's this?"

"Your little hacker job—remember?" the leather princess sneered sardonically.

"What?" Rio cried out in disbelief. "I can't just waltz in *there*."

"We'll get you in," the slinky redhead snapped as she leaned forward into the soft light from the wall sconce beside them.

"And make sure you get the job done properly," the brunette purred, her low voice dripping with sarcasm, her eyes hardening as they dug into his.

Gasping, he scrambled back, his chair spilling to one side and upending him on the dusty wooden floor. Taking no notice, the two women rose in unison and gingerly stepped over his sprawled form, their arms sliding easily around each other's waists as they made for the dance floor.

Getting to his feet, Rio watched the retreating duo as they began swaying erotically against each other, hips and shoulders swiveling hypnotically, alluringly, in slow, seductive circles while hands snaked up arms and slithered down backs, moving closer and closer together.

Titillated by the odd combination of arousal and fear, Rio hastily headed for the door, striding past the mirrored wall as he left. He was unaware of the dark-haired woman with kohl blue eyes behind it that was watching the pair of female goons sent by their Dark Master to meet the young man. Looking down, she opened the silver locket that hung around her neck.

It had been a long time, certainly long enough, but still he remained imprisoned in the black, blistering pain of her disappearance. He would never be free of her on his own. She saw that now. She would have to release him herself. Smiling, she tenderly touched the picture within the ornate silver adornment, her finger delicately moving over the golden eyes to trace the blonde strands of hair of her beloved Jack.

* * * * *

Someone was singing.

Well, humming, actually.

What was that? It sounded like one of those sweeping romantic tunes by George Gershwin that united the hero and heroine in an old '50s musical. She tried to open her eyes but the throbbing ache in her head flared up in protest every time she tried, the lights that surrounded her, dim and flickering as they were, only amplifying her pain.

Still she persisted and, grimacing, peered out from between swollen, red-rimmed eyelids. Blinking hard several times, she tried to bring the misshapen objects around her into focus and bit by bit, they took shape.

Overhead was a remarkable antique lace canopy, the expanse of its intricately embroidered ivory dome giving way to softly curving gossamer sheers that hung in a series of panels around the massive circular bed. The ornate detailing on the embossed mahogany bedposts alone spoke of the centuries-old workmanship on the dark, luscious wood.

Lifting her head slightly, Chancella looked around her, suppressing a sudden cry as a hard shooting pain darted through her face and neck. Through the flimsy fabric of the sheers she could see that she was in some sort of a huge, rounded room, the dimly lit area apparently trembling, the eerie effect due to the shimmering light from the multitude of candles placed about.

Directly to the left of the bed was an ornate night table, also of mahogany, its top covered by an elaborate doily on which stood a gorgeous stained glass lamp. Glass beads hung from its burgundy tassels to glitter magnificently in the candlelight, as did the crystal bud vase that held a single rose, the satiny red petals just beginning to open.

Just opposite were two dark velvet wingback chairs facing one another, separated only by a small round table that held a sterling silver tray containing two crystal glasses and a tall decanter filled with a sparkling amber liquid. Beyond the cozy, conversational sitting area, she could see the immense stone fireplace that rose to the ceiling, its crackling, dancing flames within doing little to warm the large area.

Off to the right sat an old-fashioned wooden desk and chair, the dark shape barely visible in the dim space. Behind it stood a massive bookcase that appeared to contain an impressive collection of literature. Even from this distance, Chancella could see the scores of leather-bound books within the confines of the wall-length structure that stopped only to give way to a large paned window through which the evening stars twinkled brilliantly in the royal blue sky beyond.

Only the walls, with their dark gray brick and mortar, seemed out of place, their sullen bulkiness creating the distinct flavor of a medieval dungeon, despite the appearance of the vibrant Renaissance paintings and elaborate wrought iron candelabras that were randomly placed on the bleak, chalky finish.

Straining to sit up, Chancella gasped at the unexpected clanging of metal, the clatter immediately followed by the cold, unrelenting feel of shackles pressing mercilessly against her wrists and ankles. Glancing down the length of her body, she whimpered at the sight of the restraints that, fastened to each of the four bedposts, confined her. Somehow she knew that her steel bonds were more for effect than necessity.

Maneuvering her body, she managed to rise up on her elbows, high enough to see over the heavy footboard and beyond to the vast Oriental rug that covered the immense area, the rich multicolored pattern serving to hide the cold cement floor beneath.

Louder and stronger the voice hummed now, its rich lowness reverberating around the room. Out of the corner of her eye, Chancella first caught the movement. Jerking her head around, she twisted at the ensuing pain and held her breath at the sight of a figure as it moved, without a noise, to the fire, reaching down to stoke the flames, the persistent hum finally breaking into song.

Night and day, you are the one –

The fact that she had guessed Gershwin correctly gave Chancella little satisfaction for she sensed the being's identity before he slowly turned to face her, her heart leaping into her mouth as her worst fear was confirmed, his pale gold eyes gleaming with a callous pleasure.

"Frightened, darling?" he purred as he sauntered towards her, that familiar one-sided smirk filling her with dread.

With a lean hand, he reached out to pull back the sheer, allowing Chancella a better look at her captor. He bent under the canopy and allowed a supernatural hand to drop down on her shin, teasingly following his ascent as he moved closer to her and the massive headboard that stood directly against the heavy stone wall. He sat down on the edge of the bed beside her, the mattress shifting under his weight, causing her hip to slide and press against him.

"Jack," she scarcely sputtered out from between dry, trembling lips.

It was an accusation, not a question, her voice soft and small like a child's at the terrible recollection of the events that had preceded this moment.

"Actually, it's Jacariaith but I dropped a few symbols when I 'dropped' my old life," he announced with an offhanded wave of his hand. His eyes locked with hers as he pursed his lips together in a brief, sexy suggestion of a kiss. "It was a new beginning so what better than a new name? Besides, 'Jack' is so much more me, don't you think? Although I have been mistaken once or twice for Lestat if you can imagine that."

"Lestat?" she exclaimed.

"Then you've heard of him," he stated flatly, one thick dark brow arching aristocratically in question.

"The vampire Lestat? Why, of course! But, he's...he's... "

"What?"

"A fictional character," she cried. "He's not *real*."

Under different circumstances, the look of shock that momentarily lit upon Jack's face would have been amusing, brief as it was. Quickly, it was replaced by the steely look of a sly menacing glare.

"Is he not?" was all he said.

Despite her racing heartbeat, Chancella set to analyzing her captor, trying to gauge his sincerity. Her limited exposure to him had already revealed his penchant for sarcasm and cruelty.

Scrutinizing the narrow, slightly upturned nose, delicate, almost feminine mouth and wide almond-shaped golden eyes, Chancella could find nothing redeemable on the masklike face that, incidentally, bore little resemblance to the roguish, adventuresome wild child of the now infamous novels. Mirroring her thoughts, Jack offered his agreement on the lack of similarity between the two.

"You're quite right. I don't know how people could ever confuse us. After all, the only things we have in common are blonde hair and a terrific fashion sense."

And a lust for blood, Chancella thought to herself, cringing under the burrowing weight of his knowing stare.

"We *all* have that," he responded sharply to her unspoken barb.

And then his gaze fell lazily, almost absentmindedly, from hers and became transfixed on her mouth, the golden glow of his eyes suddenly blazing with a ferocious fire. Cocking his head to one side in a bizarre mimicry of fascination, he continued to stare at her, his lips drawing back slowly into a silent snarl.

Involuntarily, Chancella recoiled, her legs and buttocks tensing as she inched herself up towards the headboard and away from the beast who, increasingly hypnotized, hovered over her.

Then in a move too fast for mortal eyes, he clasped Chancella's trembling face between his cold hands and pulled her to him where he proceeded to methodically tongue her nose and mouth in long slow deliberate licks, her violent thrashing and near hysterical shrieks unheeded.

Chancella squeezed her eyes shut, trying to block out the inexhaustible fear that brought on the furious trembling of her body. She squirmed at the slick, cold feel of Jack's tongue and lips on her face, the pain of his nails as they dug into her face and hair, the spine-tingling snarls that gurgled from his throat.

Please make him stop. Please. Stop.

Then he did, although Chancella was certain it was not because of her inner pleas. Ceasing and holding her out at arm's length, Jack proudly assessed his work.

Momentarily confused, Chancella brought an unsteady, manacled hand up to her face, the feel of her moist flesh calling to mind Jack's brutal backhand and the blood that had covered her nose and mouth. A raging, irrational anger flared within her and she hastily spat out the words, her voice, once more, shaking with the threat of hysteria.

"Get off of me, you goddamned animal!"

The sheer hostility and volume of the words hung in the air, the remnants of the last few syllables echoing around the dungeonlike space, the silence that followed seeming to grow louder with each passing moment. Imprisoned by both his grip and gaze, Chancella was only aware of her body as it continued to vibrate fiercely with an anger-tinged fear and the raspy, uneven sound of her own breath as the two stared wordlessly at each other.

Then Jack, regarding her coolly, amazingly complied.

Releasing her, he rose and moved back to the fire where he stood for a long while gazing into its frolicking depths, his hands clasped casually behind his back. No movement or sound came from him for such a length that Chancella unintentionally began to relax, her heart rate and tensed muscles slowly returning to normal.

When he finally spoke, the sound was almost inaudible and there was something in his voice, a resigned, melancholy tone that abruptly caught Chancella's attention.

"Animals? To be sure," he said quietly after the pronounced period of stillness. "And goddamned? Absolutely. Each and every one of us."

The room suddenly felt colder, hushed as it was, save for the crackling of the logs on the fire, the snapping augmented in the aftermath of his declaration.

Chancella held her breath and tried to anticipate his next move. Would he turn and lunge at her again, ripping her to shreds in an animalistic frenzy? Or worse yet, turn on that irresistible supernatural charm that his kind was known for, which, up until recently, she had only read about. She cringed at the possibility of that unstoppable sexually charged magnetic appeal pulsing between them, forcing her to fall limp and helpless at his feet while his eyes glowered with a sick immortal satisfaction.

The power of suggestion whispered to her and as she watched him, his back turned to her, she became distracted by the way the tight black leather pants accentuated the firm curve of his buttocks and seemed to cling to his thighs.

He glanced over his shoulder at her and for one awful moment she thought he had read her mind again but she was immediately relieved, for his expression, although stoic, was not without the slightest tinge of misery.

"Even Valian."

The name brought her up with a jolt, the clatter of her metal restraints echoing loudly in the silence of the room, and she fully expected to see that cruel, sadistic smile once more on Jack's lips but she was surprised by the opposite; a deep, pronounced frown.

"Valian?" she repeated softly.

He turned to face her and smiled knowingly, the gold depths sparkling with conviction.

"He got to you, didn't he?" he announced.

"I—ah, no! No!" She adamantly denied the claim, screaming vehemently against the proud, contradicting feeling that bubbled inside her, threatening to boil up and overflow.

He only nodded as if in understanding.

"Fewer are more charismatic than Valian," he said sadly. "Would you believe me if I told you that we were brothers once?"

"What? How?" Chancella exclaimed. In her wildest dreams she couldn't reconcile Jack's crazed, cruel tendencies with the gentle and mesmerizing Valian. At the thought of him, a myriad of conflicting emotions flooded to the surface and Chancella struggled to make some sense of it all.

As much as she hated to admit it, Jack was a vampire. The real deal. And if he was, then maybe, just maybe, Valian was too. And yet, if the two were acquainted, how could she be sure that this wasn't some sick ploy that the two of them had cooked up?

"So you know him then?" Chancella murmured.

"I thought I did," Jack said quietly. "Or better yet, I knew him for a time. But he changed."

His eyes then burned with a cold hard hatred, the light champagne hue within darkening to that of burnished gold.

"He betrayed me!" he spat ferociously. "Betrayed all that we stood for, all we believed in, all we aspired to. And yet I was willing to overlook his choice, welcome him back with open arms, forgive him—such was my love for him. I even prayed, day and night, that God would have mercy on his soul. But then he took Arianna." His face nearly glistened with the sheen of intense hatred. "From then on, I prayed for him and his then-immortal soul no more. Rather I hoped for its eternal damnation!"

"Who's Arianna?"

"She was what the soft-hearted would call my true love," he sneered with a sadness-edged sarcasm. Chancella was shocked at how the glitter of intense loathing that brimmed within the strange light eyes shifted to the soft glow of devotion. "Indeed, I loved her more than life itself, a truth that became painfully obvious to me after she was taken away, lured to the dark side by Valian, for only then did I realize that my mortal life was not worth living without her!"

He paused then, an anguished expression replacing the look of fury that had so completely dominated the pallid face before he began again, speeding on in an emotion-fueled flurry of words.

"For many a day and night I suffered with that reality, so drowned in my grief that I could see no way out, no light at the end of the tunnel. All I could feel was the agony of the truth...she was out of my life, dead to me, at least as I had known her. While she had an eternity to live, I had but a few decades of an excruciating existence without her that would, indubitably, feel like an eternity. Where I once had everything in the world to offer her, now I had nothing, no way of winning her back. Her beauty and power would go on for an eternity but I would, all too soon, wither and fade away. I couldn't bear it— any of it!"

Chancella felt herself recoiling at the intensity of the hatred that pulsed from Jack as he spoke, flinching as he, without warning, reached for the crystal decanter before him and whirled, firing it with a dramatic flare into the fire. The high-pitched shattering of glass shrieked loudly before abruptly ending.

When his voice began again, it had regained some degree of control and he slowly turned, his gaze fixed on the floor.

"Then, one day, after months of dismal, blinding yearning, the fog cleared enough for me to entertain the notion of a solution and that was the turnaround, for the idea, when it came, came quickly. That's when I knew with absolute certainty that the only way I could get Arianna back in my life and repay Valian for the unspeakable wrong he had done to me was to become one of them! Why, it was so simple I was surprised I hadn't thought of it earlier. As you humans say—if you can't beat 'em, join 'em."

He looked at her then and Chancella swallowed hard, unnerved by the cold triumphant expression on the unnatural face.

"For the first time in a long while, I felt the unmistakable uplifting sensation of hope, even though I hadn't heard a word from Arianna since her turning. I abandoned everything I had once held dear and set to finding a willing demon to make me as he was. To my great wonder, it wasn't as hard as I thought. I came upon the villainous being in a bar one night—my Dark Master—just waiting to prey on the disillusioned and lost souls that frequented such an establishment.

"I think I may have quite frankly flabbergasted him when I walked up and asked him to make a vampire, but more than that, I realize now in retrospect, I fascinated him. The combination of my death wish and determination charmed him and since then, not a day has gone by that I don't thank my lucky stars that he agreed to do the dastardly deed."

Jack looked off, a decidedly reminiscent air clouding his eyes.

"The actual turning is, as they say, another story. But very soon afterward I was swilling the dark dream, as it is called, sucking the spirit out of every mortal I crossed paths with and what an existence it was, but that too is best saved for another time.

"What I will tell you is that from this new beginning, I set to accomplish two goals — the only things that mattered to me in my newfound immortal life...finding Arianna and making Valian pay for taking her from me. The first has eluded me for almost a century and for reasons unknown to me, to this day my beloved continues to remain hidden from me. Contrarily, my lust for revenge against Valian has presented several opportunities to me through the years but none that would cause near enough pain for my particular liking."

He stopped then and eyed her resolutely. "But then, you came along. You see, for the past century, Valian has yearned for a release from his eternal life, struck by some ridiculous sense of morality, and it would appear that you hold the key. The only key. And now," he laughed out loud, "I hold you."

"But —"

"Enough! I'm ravenous," he announced brusquely, striding determinedly to the door.

"But what —"

"Shut up! Shut up!" he bellowed, his booming voice smarting Chancella's ears and she scrambled to raise her hands to her head to protect them, the clanging of the shackles blending in with the echo of his shouted command. In a flash he was at her side, grabbing her by the hair and yanking her up to a sitting position. Next he drew close to her face, his whispered threat hard and menacing in her ear and she trembled with fear at the monster that held her in his ghoulish grip.

"From now on, you will do exactly as I say, or I promise I'll do things to you that will make your most horrifying nightmares look like fairy tales. Understand?"

Chancella could only stare wordlessly into the cat yellow eyes, the pupils seeming to pulse with a strange fire. Fight as she might, she started to feel the hypnotic effect of his vampire gaze on her mortal will, her resolve melting into a luscious pull towards the soft parted lips, which moved to release the seductive sound of his voice.

"Say you understand," he murmured.

Her head was still brutally caught in his strong clutch, his hand entangled amidst the flow of her shoulder-length hair that had long since fallen from the tight constraints of a bun to hold her at an awkward, painful angle. The harsh movement had loosened her robe and it now hung open to reveal her. Jack took his time surveying her, his gaze lingering over the plains and valleys of her naked body. With his free hand he cupped one of her breasts and with a surprising tenderness caressed it erotically.

"Don't," Chancella choked out between gasps filled with conflicting emotion.

"Say it or I'll snap your neck like a twig," he cooed, the satin in his voice a horrific mismatch for the barbaric threat.

"I...I understand," Chancella stammered out.

"Good."

Abruptly releasing her, he turned on his heel, and striding from the room, slammed the door. Seconds later, Chancella could hear the click of a key in the lock. She struggled with trying to free her wrists and ankles out of the restraints but, weak and exhausted, she soon fell back on the bed.

If Valian was indeed a vampire with a life wish, as he had said, then Jack's plan should work and Valian would be coming for her.

The only question was when?

Chapter Five

ᔓ

Simarone rolled over and sat up, his bare feet touching the cold floor. The early morning light of dawn had not yet made its way into the bachelor apartment but he could feel its imminent approach.

Slowly turning his head to one side, he silently watched Rio as he slept. Only the arm that covered his face and a portion of his leg were exposed from under the tangled covers, the two freshly made bite marks on his inner thigh glistening with red.

Piercing his tongue with a still-extended eyetooth, Simarone let the blood spill into his mouth before leaning over Rio's slumbering form. Gently he licked at the cavities that were compliments of his vampire kiss, his bloodied tongue delicately probing the small encrusted holes to facilitate their healing, careful not to reopen the wounds.

Lifting his head, he watched the miraculous effects of his vampire blood on Rio's human flesh, first soaking up the thick red fluid only to merge the tattered edges of the gashes until only two small indentations remained. Within a few hours, they too would disappear.

At the feel of Simarone's lips on him, Rio stirred, his hand reaching down to stroke Simarone's hair, a soft appreciative moan escaping him.

Opening his eyes, he looked at Simarone with a hazy, content expression that gradually faded to a distinctive frown.

"What's wrong?" Simarone asked, a well-defined hand coming up to push back a single strand of hair from Rio's eyes.

He could see that Rio was troubled. The usually bright and easygoing earthy child had been uncharacteristically tense and quiet for some time now but before he opened his mouth, Simarone knew exactly what the problem was.

There was no need to ask.

"Forget it," Rio spat, the petulant tone causing Simarone's eyebrows to raise in question. "What do you care?"

Simarone drew closer to him, the warmth of Rio's body failing to permeate his ever-present chill.

"I care," he said awkwardly. "It's just that I—"

"What?" Rio prompted.

"I don't know how to tell you this."

Simarone dropped his head, piquing the other's interest, for as long as Rio had known him, Simarone had never been one to be evasive.

"Tell me what?" Rio persisted, the irritation registering in his voice.

The room filled with the heavy, drawn-out sound of Simarone's sigh followed by an utter stillness that seemed to stretch on indefinitely.

"What?" Rio demanded forcefully, his whispered question causing Simarone to flinch.

"His name is Jacariaith," he said finally, quietly, then adding to clarify, "the guy from the parkade."

"You know him?" Rio asked in astonishment.

Simarone only nodded, his eyes fixed on the ground.

"How?" Rio asked.

"I met him once," he said almost imperceptibly. "A very long time ago."

"And?"

"You don't understand," Simarone whispered, the words, slow and plodding, falling from his lips in a disjointed, faltering way as if each syllable was an exertion that physically pained him.

Rio could only stare at him blankly. Increasingly uncomfortable, he moved away from Simarone's icy form.

"What the hell are you talking about?" he snapped.

"Rio," Simarone began hesitantly, not wanting to and yet unable to stop what he had now set in motion. "This scheme you told me about—you can't get involved. The guy is trouble."

"I can handle it."

"You don't understand."

"Understand what?"

"He's a—vampire."

"Yeah right."

"I'm serious, man."

Dead serious, he thought sadly, the pun not even remotely funny in light of what he was about to say.

Rio could see from the stern expression on Simarone's face and the obvious pain in the normally sparkling brown depths of his eyes that his friend wasn't joking.

"Vampires are real," he repeated, the sarcasm dripping from his voice, watching in amazement as Simarone nodded his agreement. Slowly, the conviction of his words hit Rio, causing the half-smile to slip from his face.

"But...how...wha...what do you mean? *How* do you know?"

Simarone took the equivalent of a deep breath in and, fearing Rio's reaction, fixed his gaze on some far-off point on the horizon, squinting ever so slightly as he answered.

"I know because I am one."

The forced laughter that pierced Simarone's ears sounded harsh and jaded, Rio's mocking countenance blurring before him. Perplexed, Simarone blinked repeatedly, startled by the realization that his eyes had filled with tears.

"You're fucking crazy—you know that?" Rio all but screamed at him as he got off the bed. "You've smoked too much pot!"

Simarone rose and grabbed him by both shoulders, shaking him violently as his passionate plea rang out into the previously calm space of the tiny room.

"Listen to me! It's the truth and you know it. Just think about it. All those nights when I had to go out and leave you alone. Remember? You always asked me why I wouldn't stay."

"I thought you were going to score some E."

He loosened his grip as he implored Rio further.

"For Christ's sake, Rio, if it wasn't for me you would've bled to death all those times you nicked yourself shaving, you stupid klutz."

Rio's face alone spoke of his vague recollection, the murky air of a struggling memory slowly dissolving into one of disbelief.

Then horror.

The soft adolescent lips parted, the bottom lip quivering steadily as he tried to speak and yet no words would come, his eyes widening in a fear-laced astonishment.

He began to back away.

"But, but you said it was a joke," he managed to stammer.

"It's no joke," Simarone softly answered, his full lips pulled down into a tortured grimace.

"You...you said it was a weird fetish," Rio cried, the desperation edging into his shrill voice.

Simarone tried to smile.

"It is. Sorta."

Rio began to shake his head from side to side, first sluggishly, a slow-motion twisting that progressively gave way to a furious thrashing.

"No way!" he yelled. "It can't be! You're fucking lying."

"Rio," Simarone moved towards him. "C'mon, man, don't. I know it sounds crazy but ya know, it's not so bad. I mean," he shrugged almost feebly, "it could be worse, right?"

"What?" Rio howled, his eyes growing dark with pain. "How? How could any of this possibly be worse?"

Simarone's face fell.

It could be much worse and before long they would probably see how, for with his declaration Simarone had just broken the first and most important Dark Commandment.

Never reveal your true nature to any mortal.

The very fact that mankind regarded vampires as beings of fiction allowed them the freedom to walk the earth unchallenged and unhampered. Through the centuries, disbelief has been their greatest ally. So great was their dependence on the myth of their kind that if others learned of his confession, both Simarone and Rio's lives would be in danger.

"I don't know," he moaned ruefully. "I'm so sorry. I—"

Rio watched him, his own tears now flowing freely.

"Sorry?" Rio echoed incredulously. "Why, Simarone? Why didn't you tell me before? Why now?"

Simarone's voice took on an odd shrillness that made Rio wince. With leaden determination he spoke, choking out the words that clearly hurt him.

"I didn't know any other way, man. I dug you, dug being with you, and couldn't take the chance of telling you what I really was. But now this plan that you got involved in—the only way I can help you is if you know the score. Besides," he looked up, his eyes wide and earnest with sincerity, "I don't want to lie to you anymore."

Simarone ignored Rio's snort of disbelief.

"You gotta believe me… I wanted to tell you before. I just didn't know how. I guess I was…scared."

The admission seemed to bewilder him, an alarmed, incredulous expression flashing in the angst-filled eyes, as if it had been a great while since he had felt a sensation or emotion even vaguely resembling fear.

"Scared? You? Of what? You're a goddamn murderer!"

Rio's outburst wounded Simarone deeply but the profound emotional slash was immediately hidden behind a mask of fury.

"Scared of what? Of this!" Simarone roared, motioning wildly. "Of this very thing. Of you not being able to handle this, not able to get your head around it and then distrusting me and hating me!"

He threw his head back then and groaned out loud, giving full voice to emotion, the anguished caged-animal sound of frustration causing Rio to cower. When he next regarded the shaking mortal, the gentle words that came from him were filled with a sad despondency.

"But most of all, I'm scared of the look that you have on your face right now. I don't want you to fear me, Rio. *Ever.* Please," his voice quavered oddly. "Please, don't be afraid of me."

Rio remained motionless but his response, although tentative, was not what either expected.

"I don't know what to say," he began. "I mean, I trusted you. I thought we were friends, you know?"

Rio struggled with the fresh emotion that was forcing its way to the surface, searching and yet hesitant to utter the words that resounded in his head.

"I...I loved you, man," he whispered under his breath.

A soft gasp escaped Simarone as the words hit him hard and he turned away quickly from the other's entreating gaze. He had never heard those words in his life—from human or immortal—and he didn't know which hit him harder...the declaration itself or the fact that it had been stated in the past tense.

Stunned into a dour silence, he turned back at the sound of Rio's mournful tone.

"None of this makes any sense."

There was a note of finality in the way Rio said it. As he started to leave, the gentle pressure of Simarone's hand on his chest made him stop. He looked up then into the smooth, darkly handsome face and for the very first time, Rio clearly saw Simarone's fangs, not teeth but the unmistakable daggerlike shape of his vampire canines, their hard white enamel gleaming in the dim light.

"How could I not have known?" he asked the silent sullen space.

"I made sure you didn't," Simarone mumbled dejectedly, unwilling to meet the questioning gaze that followed. "I blocked you."

"Huh?"

Simarone looked him square in the eye then, his hands moving in slight, non-descript jerks as he tried to explain.

"It's a mind meld kinda thing, a blurring of the memory so that you wouldn't remember some of the stuff you saw when you were with me."

"Stuff?" Rio reiterated, a fresh surge of anger igniting within him. "Don't you mean truth, Simarone? Isn't that it? You saw to it that I wouldn't see the truth!"

Simarone wordlessly nodded, the chocolate brown of his eyes lessening to dark tan as he continued to stare at the now seething youth before him.

Rio's face grew increasingly enraged and his lips pressed together in a thin, tight line. Simarone watched cheerlessly as Rio's emotional roller-coaster ride took yet another turn and denial set in, hard and heavy.

"Yeah? Well, I don't fucking believe it—any of it!" he screamed as he abruptly pushed past Simarone and hastily threw on his clothes. "You and your fucking Halloween dentures can go to hell! You're all crazy—do you hear me? I don't believe it! I don't believe it!" he yelled as he raced from the apartment, a resounding "Go to hell!" echoing down the empty hallway.

Standing up, Simarone pulled a pair of jeans on and without bothering to do them up, padded over to the worn easy chair that sat opposite the window. Flopping down, he casually slung one leg over the armrest and stared out into the night sky. The moon glow played across the striking face, briefly illuminating the sad coffee-colored eyes.

Go to hell?

He was already there.

* * * * *

Hunched over the dimly lit countertop of the lab, Nick frantically began leafing through the various books, hastily scratching down some final notes on a thin writing pad that lay within reach, unconsciously checking his watch every few moments. His meeting wasn't until ten o'clock but already he had the sinking sensation that he was behind schedule.

Glancing at the half-open briefcase, he gave it the once-over, speedily assessing its contents. There appeared to be everything he needed—several syringes, a small array of vials and plastic beakers, several long stretchy elastics to isolate a major artery, cotton gauze, duct tape, ultraviolet bulbs, thick heavy cords, numerous sturdy leather straps and a good supply of atracurium besylate.

By God, he thought to himself with a growing mixture of excitement and fear, this was it. Once that hot shot computer nerd that Jack had secured figured out Chancella's secret password and broke into the system's formula database, he would be off and running. Chancella may have hypothesized her way to success but he was going to one-up her in the sweetest, most ironic way possible, for where she merely surmised, he would prove, and by using her own theories. Jack had guaranteed him a specimen but after that, the rest would be up to him. He'd have one and only one shot at infamy.

Snapping the locks shut on his attaché case, he quickly bounded from the lab, making little or no effort to conceal the fact that he had been there. Retracing his steps down the silent hallway, he made his way out onto the street where he flagged down a passing taxi and hurriedly climbed inside.

"Where to?" the cabbie asked over his shoulder, frowning as his fare ignored the NO SMOKING sign and lit up. A pronounced exhale quickly followed by a cloud of smoke preceded the answer that came from the darkened backseat.

"Ferry's Landing."

* * * * *

Simarone stood and did up the fly of his jeans, hastily throwing on the crumpled red shirt that had lain on the floor. Shoving his bare feet into loosely laced hiker boots and grabbing his jean jacket, he stepped out of the dingy apartment and bounded down the three flights of stairs to the main landing.

Out on the street, he closed his eyes, his wide nostrils flaring to take in the night air and its co-mingled scents. Everywhere was the particular fragrance of life, from the dust of the pavement, the overpowering stench of the city fumes and gases, the soft perfumes of both nature and man's invention and teasingly intertwined with it all was the faint, subtle smell of blood.

A sudden ear-splitting clatter arose in the alley beyond the narrow avenue, the noise a painful, deafening clanging to Simarone's hypersensitive hearing. With wanton desire, he watched from afar as the swarthy, young homeless derelict rooted through a filthy garbage can, the hot aroma of the street kid's body and blood filling Simarone's nostrils and bringing hot tears of painful need to his eyes.

Instinctively he licked his lips, his wet tongue making several loops around the diameter of his full soft mouth. He continued to stare at his prey, and without deciding to do so, he began to head in the direction of the unsuspecting youth, invariably slinking across the empty roadway.

Closer now, Simarone halted abruptly, scrutinizing the way the girl's light hair hung long and unkempt down across her small shoulders as she dug passionately through the soiled papers and empty cans. Simarone's eyes now glittered malevolently in fascination, briefly hypnotized by the erratic movement of the kid's torso and the way she leaned forward, waist deep, into the trash can, stood up to examine her findings and then dived back in again.

Without a sound, Simarone crept up to her, soon close enough to feel the humid heat coming off of her body. For a split second, he contemplated leaning over and whispering in the teenager's ear but decided against it. Toying with his victims had never been Simarone's style. In fact, most of them never knew what hit them.

His vampire teeth were now fully lengthened and protruded rather obviously over the swell of his bottom lip, as if waiting for that glorious moment when they would be called into action. A dizzying swell of desire rushed over him as he reached around and clasped the teenager from behind, his head involuntarily drawing back so as to deliver the added weight of the fateful blow while his strong arms held the youth motionless, helpless in this supernatural embrace. With a hard, brusque motion he lurched forward, driving his teeth into the soft side of the girl's neck. He struck right at the place where it extended to the top of her shoulder, his lips quickly closing around the ripped gashes on the tender flesh and the fount of hot liquid that poured from them.

Only a soft indecipherable murmur came from the kid, both hands reaching up to grab the arm that imprisoned her, the knuckles on the skinny, dirty fists turning white with their futile exertion. Then, just as quickly, they dropped to her side, the young body slumping backward against that of her attacker.

It all took less than a minute.

Pulling back, Simarone experienced the immortal equivalent of panting—a winded, pained breathlessness that always follows a feeding. His closed his eyes, allowing the sensation of the blood coursing through him to work its soothing magic on his tattered soul.

With a slow, unhurried movement he licked the dead girl's neck, sealing the fresh wounds.

Just then, unexpectedly, the scent wafted across him, light and vague as a distant memory but nevertheless unmistakable and he jerked around, his slain victim sliding down the length of his body to fall crumpled and lifeless at his feet. The street, empty and black, stood silent and menacing before him, the promise of danger lurking in its many dark recesses.

Again it came, that distinct aroma drifting by him on the wings of the wind and he smiled at its familiarity.

Ancient blood.

Unmistakably, it was the blood of one of the oldest of their kind but more than that, it was the blood of the one who had made him.

"Simarone."

The gentle, low voice reached his ears first, turning him about face where he had to smile at the approaching figure and the familiar gait, so practiced and assumed so as to appear human.

That was one lesson Simarone had learned at the hands of his Dark Master. Their vampire mannerisms were always just the slightest bit out of sync with their human counterparts, and if not careful would arouse suspicion and draw unwanted attention. Most humans didn't notice, but there was the occasional person, highly perceptive for their species, that would pick up on these little miscues. As a vampire, he must always *act* human. And none was better at it than the figure that now stood before Simarone.

"Simarone," the figure said again, almost in reverence, the warmth and the love within the word itself speaking volumes.

The two vampires embraced for a suspended moment, like two long-lost brothers cherishing an unforeseen, overdue reunion. Nine and a half decades had come and gone since their paths had last crossed and yet, the passing time that had once stood like a great, insurmountable barrier between the two of them suddenly seemed like a distant irrelevant memory.

Simarone pulled away first and looked up, searching the beautiful face of the one who had been more of a parent to him than either his eternally absent, dope-smuggling father or cheap showgirl mother had ever been. Relieved, he smiled at the unmistakable gleam of affection deep within the emerald depths of the other's eyes.

"I've been thinking about you, Valian," he whispered, the unusually powerful bond between Master and progeny impervious to age, race, sex and, as was recently made evident, time.

"Yes, I know," Valian answered. "I heard."

"Is that why you came?"

Valian stared at him wordlessly, ignoring the question, a rare look of something akin to concern quickly superseding his former expression. Then in a sad, non-accusing tone, he summed up Simarone's dilemma in one quiet brief statement.

"You're in love."

Simarone only looked away, unable to meet the steady gaze of his blood relative. He had never meant to fall for Rio. The boy was to be an appetizer one night, just like the scores of young men and women before him. Nothing more.

But Rio had an openness and an honesty that Simarone hadn't seen in decades. Hell, if ever, and it had most unexpectedly captured his heart. There was no doubt about it. Rio was the one.

Simarone could only shake his head.

"I didn't plan it."

"Who does?"

Simarone lifted his gaze from the ground and looked into the serious green eyes. Valian continued softly.

"We can no more choose who we fall in love with than we can choose when and how we're going to die."

Simarone grinned broadly.

"Yeah, but I did," he announced proudly. "Choose my death, I mean."

"No, Simarone," Valian shook his head sadly. "You only think you did. The truth is you were tired of running and you chose to hide, hide in an existence that like every other has its pros and cons, hide from a reality that you could no longer bear." Valian shrugged resignedly. "It was the same for me."

"But I wanted—"

"I know what you wanted and I gave it to you, but do not be fooled. There are not many more answers in this life than were in your last. Only some random illuminations. In the end, you will come to realize that you have not eliminated the anguishes, only exchanged one set for another."

"Jeez, Valian, what's up? You make it sound like it's not worth it."

Valian remained silent. His plan for mortality was something he had never dreamed of sharing with Simarone. How could he tell this beautiful, angelic youth brimming with fire and hope and dreams, this wondrous bohemian child of his own making, blood of his blood, soul of his soul, that he was pursuing the end of his journey, seeking to accomplish the unthinkable? Were there enough words in the world to make this soulful dark angel understand?

Thankfully, Simarone indirectly steered their conversation back to his problem.

"You know what? Maybe you just need to fall in love."

"Is that it?"

"Believe me, man, it's a whole new world when you love somebody. This aloneness can be unbearable."

"Really?" Valian replied, squelching the temptation to sound mocking.

"Yeah. You can't imagine what it's like not wanting, no, *dreading*, waking up each night."

Valian didn't answer. Only the look in his eyes spoke of his understanding.

"But in the strangest way, this one person has made my life worth living. Until I met him, everything was empty. He's so full of life and hope and innocence."

Just like you, Valian thought sadly to himself.

"Now, there's no emptiness, no futility, no hopelessness. I have a reason to get up each night—I have a purpose."

"And that is?"

"To love him. Simply to love him," he said almost gleefully. "I'm telling you, it's like heaven."

"Heaven?" Valian raised his eyebrows in disbelief. "Come now, Simarone. Don't be a fool."

"I know it sounds crazy but it's true. Love makes everything worthwhile again. It's yours if you want it. You just have to take the chance."

Then with his dark eyes twinkling, he added as an afterthought. "You've just forgotten what it's like."

"Simarone, I can assure you that I remember the sensation of love."

"Do you? Really?"

"Yes, of course! What are you insinuating? I have loved people in my life."

"Loved—that's past tense. What are we talking? Two hundred years ago? Who do you love *right now*?"

Valian fell silent. He wanted to blurt out his parental declaration and shout "You! I love you, my beautiful child!" but he firmly pushed down the urge.

As if reading his Dark Master's thoughts, a virtual impossibility for an offspring, Simarone spoke.

"And don't say me. I'm not talking about family—"

"Which we are," Valian interrupted to which Simarone immediately agreed.

"And will always be. No, I'm talking about the big L. The make-you-weak-in-your-bloodsucking-knees kind of love. Not to mention… "

Valian let a slow frown spread across his face as he waited, fully anticipating the other's train of thought.

"When was the last time you dropped the reins and let your heart lead the way?"

"What?" Valian gruffly asked.

"I mean it, man. You're a control freak. Love is possible but you gotta let go. I mean, I couldn't believe it the first time I felt myself responding to Rio. I thought all that was dead to me."

"Pardon the pun," Valian said softly, repressing a sarcastic smirk. Simarone ignored him.

"But I went with it," he lowered his voice to a whisper, "and I'm so glad I did because I learned that it's not only possible for us but way better than I could've imagined. More powerful. When you drink while you're in love—"

Valian held up a lean hand.

"Please, Simarone, I really don't want to get into an in-depth, blow-by-blow description of your romantic exploits. You're in love. Great. I'm happy for you, but—"

"But?"

"With a mortal, it's more complicated."

Simarone clasped Valian's cool, smooth hand, a seldom seen look of desperation darkening the usually open, bright face. "I know. What do I do?"

"I think you know."

"I can't," Simarone whispered, a sudden shiver shaking his shoulders. "I can't do it."

The words drifted away as did the light that had shone in his eyes when he spoke of Rio. Simarone knew all too well his Dark Master's answer to his dilemma. Besides breaking the code, there was an even more compelling reason for not getting involved with a mortal. Simply put, they can't handle it.

With the very rare exception, the human psyche is unable to bear the reality of their kind. It's just too much for them. Therefore, the most merciful thing a vampire can do if they ever show the misjudgment of becoming emotionally involved with a mortal is to disappear.

No trace.

No explanation.

And yet, Simarone couldn't even bring himself to imagine it, for after a virtual lifetime of searching, he had finally found the morphine for his pain.

As a mortal, his fatherless existence had haunted him incessantly, the gnawing ache of rejection whispering into every moment and every aspect of his life. He thought he could outrun the agony when he stepped into the dark life, but the truth was Rio was the only one who had been able to fill that anguished void within him, silencing it simply with his presence. The flower child's fragile, beautiful spirit, an artist's soul, filled with genuine wonder at nature, animals and music, soothed him and was, in return, no longer abused nor neglected but found solace, security and an unlikely synchronicity in Simarone.

Often as they sat side by side at the opera (one of the many things Rio had introduced him to), their knees barely touching, Simarone envisioned the two companions as the physical embodiments of the bittersweet moan of the cello and the soft meandering voice of the piano; Two separate entities that alone were quite beautiful but together made an astoundingly rich duet—each complementing what the other lacked while compensating for the other's shortcomings.

And now the tapestry of love, blood and friendship that existed between them had merged them so that they were no longer two separate entities but rather two offshoots of one soul.

In a silent agony, Simarone realized that the impenetrable bond between him and Rio would not allow him to walk away.

Ever.

"Both your lives are at risk now," Valian barely uttered, then imperceptibly bit down hard on his tongue in an attempt to restrain the gush of strong emotion that rushed up and threatened to spill out. He closed his eyes at the warm taste of the rich liquid that filled his mouth. Swallowing the blood, he glanced away, secretly hoping that his offspring couldn't smell his fear.

"I can't protect you from the choice you've made. I would if I could." He cleared his throat and looked down at the ground, daring not to lift his head lest the godforsaken tears that threatened to fill his eyes would spill over and course down his pale cheeks. "You know that, right?"

Simarone's voice, when he spoke, was soft and reassuring and there was a brief tangible sense of a kind of humanesque role reversal—one where the child, so often comforted by the parent, steps forward to soothe their elder.

"I know."

Leaping back, Valian reached both hands up to his head in obvious pain as bright, incongruous flashes of pictures suddenly filled his mind's eye, harsh, stark images of Chancella, bloodied and unconscious in the arms of Jacariaith then screaming and crying as she struggled against her metal imprisonment.

Valian winced as the visions played repeatedly in his mind's eye—Jack's barbaric blow to Chancella's delicate face, her head snapping back, the gushing of the brilliantly red blood flowing over her lips and chin, his demonic form straddling her naked body as he savagely lapped at the blood on her face.

"I have to go," Valian said hurriedly, straightening up.

"What is it?" Simarone asked, sensing his kin's intense agitation but unable to see the reason for it.

Valian reached out and embraced him quickly before pulling away, kissing him lightly on the lips as one hand moved up to lingeringly caress the side of the questioning, youthful face.

"We'll talk again. Soon."

With that, he was gone.

Chapter Six

Nick sat alone in a rented tan Plymouth, drumming his fingers anxiously on the steering wheel. Agitated, he lit a fresh cigarette off of the one in his mouth, his third within the past hour, and as the smoke filled the dark interior, he crushed out the finished butt in the overflowing ashtray. For the umpteenth time, he ran a visual scan of the eerie abandoned complex for any sign of potential witnesses — more from nerves than necessity for although people knew of its existence, few seldom visited.

Blackwell Island, as it was once called, was still surrounded by a granite seawall that created a distinctively medieval flavor to the now historic area. Back in 1828, the island housed the city's major correctional and public health institutions, including a charity hospital, the penitentiary of the day, a workhouse and the ancient, handsome brick and freestone building that stood like a vast, sprawling estate before him — the Lunatic Asylum. The latter had long since been closed and abandoned, but rising out of the deserted compound was the eye-catching octagon tower of the forsaken mental facility and longtime lair of Jacariaith Valescoise.

And how appropriate was that, Nick thought to himself with a shudder of disgust. No one was crazier than that un-dead Calvin Klein-wearing psycho. God he hated that guy! Still, their forced affiliation would have to be tolerated, for the sadistic monster now held the bait that would lure the elusive Valian — his specimen — out into the open.

What was that? Nick leaned forward, peering intently at one of the windows on the far side of the tower. Was it a flash? He stared hard at the clear glass, concentrating so intently that his vision began to blur. He could see a faint light glowing softly out of a couple of the tower's windows but so far no sign of Jack, the woman or his case-study-to-be.

Sighing, he returned his attention to the blazing reddish-orange tip of his nearly finished smoke. Shit! Was this really going to work? He had argued with that pompous ass that he should be up there, ready and waiting, but his "ally" had insisted that Nick's human scent would tip their quarry off.

So as it stood, he would just have to wait for a "sign from heaven" as it were to rush up with an invariable suitcase full of atracurium besylate and nail the poor unsuspecting bastard while Jack restrained him.

Wasn't it a stroke of luck, Nick mused, that Chancella had so recently ordered the restocking of the powerful tranquilizer? Indeed one could say that fate was on their side. For after learning of Jack's plan in depth, Nick had to agree that the two wouldn't have a hope in hell of subduing the likes of Valian without it.

Once again, Nick reached for the near empty pack. Damn, he hated all this cloak and dagger crap. He would be so happy when he had the creature, safe and sound, in the lab where he could finally start on the road to notoriety.

Snorting, he set to light one smoke off another but instead jumped at a high-pitched roaring wail that seemed to erupt from across the barren space.

Hurriedly reaching for the door handle, he knocked his knuckles against the dashboard and sent the lit cigarette flying, along with a firework fan of red sparks.

"Jesus Christ!" he yelled, ignoring the dropped smoke and scrambling from the car, skidding out onto the pavement.

Turning towards the building, he hesitated, the animalistic cry spilling out from somewhere high overhead to shower down into the deserted area and echo hauntingly throughout the concrete yard.

The scream, if that's what it was, was filled with the most unbearable sound of anger and pain, the waves of an almost mournful tone rising and falling on the wind repeatedly.

Nick took a step forward. Then back. He stopped. What should he do? Damn that Jack!

A long moment passed in which he stood rooted, frozen with indecision. Then abruptly, he moved past the open car door to reach inside and, gruffly snatching his briefcase, raced for the entrance to the asylum.

* * * * *

Rio banged away at the keyboard in the muted light, nervously glancing over his shoulder from time to time at the two wraithlike beauties that had been sent along to "help" him. Like two WWF rejects, their revealing outfits of shining black rubber accentuated every curve and muscle in their angular, taut bodies as they lounged indifferently against the wall, flanking the exit door to the high-security lab.

"I need more light here," he said sharply, starting at the sudden and silent appearance of the redhead to his right, bending down close to whisper in his ear.

"Negative, *twink*. We aren't going to let everyone know we're here, now are we?"

Shaking his head, Rio leered at her, her cold gray eyes flashing with an uncanny fire. Fuck, he hated it when she called him that—even if the slang term, meaning a young hot gay guy, was a compliment of sorts. The way she said it sounded like a swear. Jesus, where the hell did Jack get these babes anyway? The dark attired, sunglassed duo looked like a movie hybrid of *Debbie Does Dallas* and *The Matrix*. To boot, their superhuman strength was not only decidedly unfeminine but downright freakish. And if that wasn't enough, the redhead had the most unnerving habit of clenching and unclenching her fists.

Constantly.

BEEP!

For the second time since he started, Rio heard the annoying sound of the computer refusing entry. Hell! What was taking so long? He could crack any goddamn program within an hour with his eyes shut! This couldn't be any more difficult than some of the systems he'd hacked into before.

His fingers moved like lightning over the keypad, the rapid fire, nonstop fluttering of the keys being depressed similar to the pounding rhythmic sound of distant rain on a windowpane.

"Shit!" he yelled, as yet another blocked admittance beep sounded in the quiet area. Damn it, he couldn't concentrate. Simarone's words kept repeating themselves over and over again in his head. That crazy dickhead had really screwed him up good with his "I am a vampire" and "I dig you, man" crap. Fucking junkie!

Ferociously he pounded away, his fury and confusion fueling his determination to break the code.

For hours he worked, sweating profusely, his head pounding under the strain, the weak illumination with which he had to work threatening to exhaust his eyesight.

Then at last, the speakers burst forth with the most beautiful sound in the world, the harplike cascading arpeggio that always accompanies opening a protected program.

"Got it!" he yelled.

The broads were immediately at his side, undoubtedly to ensure the top secret formula was correctly copied onto several backup discs.

"Forget the initial research info. We're only interested in Dr. Tremaine's mortality serum," the brunette ordered.

"Yeah," the redhead concurred, "make sure you get the components right or there'll be hell to pay." Her luscious red lips pulled back into a horrific scowl, the contorted expression filling Rio with dread.

"Do it!" the brunette shouted at him, shoving him roughly to face the computer screen once again.

Again he tapped away uneasily at the keyboard, commanding the transference of information from the hard drive. After a lengthy download time, he turned and handed the set of four discs to the redhead.

"That's it," he breathed deeply. "All of it."

Unsmiling, the two then escorted him out to the black Cherokee with darkened windows that was out front.

"Get in," the brunette ordered.

Rio halted as a sick, heavy feeling stirred in the pit of stomach.

"Nah, it's okay," he said lightly. "I can walk from here."

The redhead put a forceful hand on his back and shoved him towards the door.

"It wasn't a question, twink."

Once inside the immediate click of the Jeep's automatic door locks sealed Rio's fate, his heart sinking at the sound. Leaning forward, he pounded on the black glass that separated the backseat from the front but to no avail. With an increasing desperation he frantically tried each of the locks but as expected, he couldn't budge them.

On they went, heading out first over the Brooklyn Bridge then north on Interstate 278 for a time, finally hooking up with Interstate 495 where they drove for an eternity. The gentle rolling hills of the inland soon gave way to flat stretches of sand and soil just as the moonlight threatened to dissolve into the first feeble rays of dusk.

Totally disoriented, Rio stared out the black windows at the barren, arid terrain as the SUV came to a slow, gritty stop on a deserted gravelly road and the locks snapped open. Where the hell were they anyway? The fucking Mojave Desert?

Without waiting to find out, Rio hotfooted it out of the backseat and took off in a random direction, the dirt from his impassioned sprint kicking up to envelop him in a smoky cloud of dust. Blinded, he continued to move forward, more hesitantly now, his arms stretched out before him, only to be painfully caught in the not-so-romantic embrace of the brunette who alternately pushed and dragged him back to the vehicle where the redhead was waiting for him.

Thinking to himself, he grimly reasoned that this particular threesome wasn't going to be of the fun variety. But in one respect he had been wrong…it wasn't going to be a threesome at all.

Without warning copper-top hauled off and cold-cocked Rio alongside the head, her heavy, open-handed blow sent the youth flying several feet away, knocking him to the ground. Struggling to his hands and knees, he didn't see the kick that was coming, catching him deep in the tender fleshy part of his midsection. Gasping, he rolled to one side, clutching his ribs.

Glancing up through the dust, Rio looked up at the brunette who leaned, rather unaffected, against the side of the vehicle, a pronounced lack of emotion on her waxen face. She spoke in a strange mechanical fashion, the words surreal as they drifted out from between her painted lips as, slowly and uncertainly, Rio struggled to his feet.

"Rocky Balboa over there likes to get her hands dirty, make it personal. Me? Not so much."

The next series of blows fell expertly into a combination that would've urged oohs and aahs from the mouth of Mohammed Ali. A stiff Southpaw uppercut jerked Rio's head, lining him up for a stinging right jab. This was immediately followed by a stunning left hook, then the youth flung back against the shiny black SUV with the full force of a punishing right cross.

Sliding down the side of the car, Rio lay sprawled alongside the front tire, blood pouring freely from his nose and the corner of one eye, matching the length of the thin trickle that oozed from his left ear.

Working his way up onto one knee first and then shakily to his feet, Rio saw the moonlight catch the brunette's extending vampire teeth, slowly tilting her head back as if the movement itself accelerated their growth. Slack-jawed and beaten, he tried to put his hands up in a futile attempt at self-defense but they couldn't move. Nor could he.

"C'mon, you guys," he spat out from between bloodied lips. "Don't do this. No one has to know about any of this."

"That's right," the brunette snarled as she slunk towards him. "And they ain't gonna, either."

She lurched forward in an incredibly fast move, her teeth slicing through the most tender part of his neck, only centimeters away from his jugular vein, her hard forceful mouth quickly wrapping around the deep gash.

Gasping, his hands flew up to ward off the redhead who had, likewise, fastened herself to his opposite shoulder, the blood from her bite bubbling up and flooding down over his chest.

Then, all of a sudden, Rio was eating dust, literally—his eyes, nose and mouth filled with the dry soil that, seconds earlier, he had stood on. Pushed flat to the ground by an unseen force, he couldn't see a thing but his ears conveyed a scene that he could scarcely interpret.

Struggling to his knees, he pawed at the grit that covered his face as he listened to the racket. His eardrum, perforated from the force of the redhead's left hook left all the sounds muffled and garbled.

Then, just as suddenly, silence.

Rio continued to clear his cloudy vision, wiping at the unemotional tears that had sprung forth to cleanse his eyes.

Slowly the scene before him began to take shape and what a gruesome view it was. The two females lay sprawled on the blanket of dry soil, their dark attire almost grey with the dust that covered them. Each now had but a bloodied, serrated stump for a neck, the torn, shredded flesh giving away to loose tatters of clawed skin with amazingly little blood on the ground where they lay.

Panting, Rio stumbled to his feet, his eyes glued to the grisly sight. A small movement to his right registered and he whirled about, crying out, hardly prepared to defend himself against the blood-hungry animal that had undoubtedly created this savage massacre, but the next gasp he uttered was one of recognition, not fear.

Wordlessly, Simarone walked over to him, his mouth oozing red from the fresh blood of the attack, his eyes still blazing with the thrill of the kill. He reached out a gentle hand to Rio's face, pretending not to notice how his mortal companion, visibly horrified, recoiled from him.

Simarone stopped the movement in midair, his eyes locking with Rio's for a long moment, sending wave upon wave of silent comfort and reassurance over the flabbergasted youth before continuing forward, reaching out to tenderly touch Rio's chin and turn his face to the side. In silence he regarded the river of blood that poured down from the Rio's ear.

For the second time that day, Simarone set out to heal his partner's wounds. Drawing a reluctant Rio into a loose embrace, Simarone cradled Rio's head in one hand as he once again pierced his own tongue with his razor-sharp teeth. Delicately snaking his profusely bleeding tongue as deep as possible into Rio's ear, the rich ancient liquid that oozed from it ran down into the damaged canal, repairing the ruptured membrane nearly on contact.

Rio swooned at the combination of pain and pleasure that washed over him. His fingers tightened on Simarone's leather jacket, relieved at Simarone's strength and the feel of his arms tightening around Rio's shoulder and waist, holding him up as he lapped at the gashes on his neck.

The words like a distant, drug-induced journey sounded softly in his head, one internal utterance melding with another, whispering sweetly and gently and lovingly somewhere deep inside him.

I love you, man. I love you.

Rio fell with full force against him then, unable to stand any longer, but Simarone caught him and held him tightly. His head falling back further, Rio looked up into the dark, exotic eyes that beheld him with the tangible radiation of concern and was surprised by the startling trail of tears down Simarone's cheeks. Shimmering streaks of silver in the moonlight spilled over the fringe of the thick dark lashes and coursed down Simarone's pale skin, leaving unnatural metallic tracks on the whiteness of his cheek. Mystified, Rio reached up to trace the glittering tracks on Simarone's pale flesh. His touch brought a wince to the dark angel's handsome face and his lips drew back in a grimace of hurt and pain.

Then finally, softly, Simarone spoke.

"Do you believe me now?"

* * * * *

Within the hour, faint, distant screams began to make Chancella's skin crawl, her pulse threatening to be heard at the realization that the horrific sounds of terror were getting closer.

Louder and stronger the pleas and cries grew until Chancella was certain they were outside her door.

Her heart sank at the click of the lock and the door swung open to reveal Jack casually dragging in a young male, barely twenty, with dyed pink hair and a series of steel studs through his nose, eyebrows and just below the swell of his lower lip. Beyond that, his face, bruised and bloodied, was a mask of pain and fear, and Jack, holding him quite effortlessly at arm's length, smiled warmly as they entered the chilled area.

"This is… I'm sorry, I didn't catch your name."

"Piss off!" the youth cried in a soft Cockney accent, flailing unsuccessfully against Jack's iron grip, his tattooed arms swinging violently about.

"Tsk, tsk, tsk," Jack nodded in mock disappointment. "Young people have no manners nowadays. Oh well, it is of no matter. I simply wanted to you meet this young 'gentleman,'" he sneered, "for his fate is also your own."

Like a cat toying with a mouse, he batted the boy around the room for a time, allowing him just enough time and strength to get to his feet before he would backhand him again, sending his worn and brutalized body flying through the air. All the while, Chancella's pleas for mercy went unheeded as she strained violently against her metal restraints. When it was apparent he had nearly beaten all of the fight out of the punker, Jack clasped him close to his body, bending his neck back at an awkward level.

"Do you know what it's like to be drained of blood?" he whispered almost seductively into the boy's ear, his hissing voice audible above his heavy panting and raspy breathing. "Some say you can actually feel your life slipping away."

"Stop it!" Chancella shouted, tears filling her eyes at the sight of horror on the teenager's face. "Don't do it!"

"Ah, but do it I will. First to him. And then to you. Now watch and learn. Animals, you call us? You have no idea."

With that, his eyes now a sickly yellow color, widened and blazed as he drew back his head and lunged forward, halting directly at the whispered stream of words that poured from the adolescent's mouth, a momentary look of shock flying across the youth's contorted face. The boy's eyes were now tightly closed and his voice rose dramatically, faster and faster, the words easily reaching Chancella's ears now…he was reciting the Our Father prayer.

"Stop that! Stop saying that!" Jack bellowed before driving his awful teeth into the soft flesh between his victim's neck and shoulder. The young man screamed and struggled further, bucking wildly in the death embrace of his tormentor, the snarling, howling sound from within Jack's mouth muffled but still remarkably loud.

He began to rock the youth, ever so slightly, back and forth. Helplessly the kid clung to the cold hard body that was pressed against his, his short black nails digging into the silken fabric that covered Jack's back. The latter's animalistic growls soon shifted into sounds not unlike those of human pleasure; barely audible moans and heavy breaths that almost drowned out the whimpers that caught in the boy's throat.

Chancella wept—hot, angry, scared tears as she watched in horrified disbelief. Then she gasped and recoiled quickly, her head striking the headboard behind her as Jack's eyes flew open, that demonic gaze peering out from over the youth's shoulder to lock with hers—those yellow orbs crazed with a commingled expression of pleasure, pain and hatred. Tearing her gaze away, Chancella looked at the boy, who from her vantage point no longer appeared afraid but rather peaceful, his angular, painted face melting into an expression of relief almost as if he had just sat down after a very strenuous and long walk. For a time he remained so, this look of near serenity lighting his features until finally, open-mouthed, his head fell back and he was dead.

Jack pulled away, his lips smeared with the boy's fresh blood, and he dabbed at the thin, slow line trickled from one corner of his mouth.

"Young blood," he smiled, his teeth baring the color of his latest attack. "There's nothing like it. But—" he purred, tossing the corpse carelessly to the side, Chancella wincing at the sound of his head hitting the floor, "I'm still hungry."

Chancella couldn't help but notice the warmth and color now present in his usually pale complexion as he crept towards her, his eyes not having yet regained their assumed human appearance. Alien and demonic, they stared at her from beneath his bushy dark eyebrows.

"Your turn."

He leapt at her then, flying an incredible height through the air, only to land nimbly on top of her, the merry, elfish manner in which he had sprung at her terrifying her as much as anything.

Screaming, Chancella withdrew even farther against the cold, heavy headboard but Jack was on her, his cold, heavy weight flattening her body where the chains and shackles rendered her spread-eagled to his assault.

"Now don't worry," he slithered closer to her face, drawing back her hair to reveal the vein that throbbed in her neck. "Just a couple of nibbles. I promise it won't hurt."

Then his daffodil-tinted eyes slowly looked up, the lids all heavy and hooded with desire, and he made a small shrugging motion with one shoulder before scoffing.

"Okay, I lied. It's going to hurt a lot."

He snarled, a ghastly, inhuman shriek, and lunged for her, his teeth digging hard and deep into the tender flesh of her throat. Frightened as she was by the animalistic sound that had broke loose from his throat, Chancella somehow suspected that it was more for effect than anything else for clearly, nothing thrilled Jack more than terrifying his victims.

The jolt of the initial pain surged through her body and engaged every nerve ending, as if the wound itself was being endlessly torn, or so it felt, one long throbbing gash that seemed to run from the top of her head to the tip of her toes.

Chancella screamed and tossed her head, her naked body flailing against the creature that suppressed her, but his hands held her in such a way that her efforts were futile. At first, all she could feel was the two agonizing lesions themselves and how they seemed to pulse—her heartbeat a loud, booming drum beating its anguished, feverish rhythm along the torn shreds of the holes in her throat. But as Jack closed his mouth tighter around the gashes, the nerve-titillating feel of his moist mouth on her quickly eclipsed the pain. A shiver ran down her spine and she felt her body break out into sensory-charged perspiration and gooseflesh at the sensation of his rhythmic sucking. The stab of sexual desire jolted her, the sweet liquid honey of desire coursing through her body and coming to rest and throb everywhere. Slowly her heartbeat became a distant sound and she began to feel the surrealistic sensation of floating.

"No," she panted, squeezing her eyes shut.

Jack raised his head, his eyes gleaming with a pronounced look of victory.

"You don't like it?"

Chancella shook her head, fighting the trembling that threatened to contradict her.

"Maybe you don't like it *there*," he emphasized the last word, motioning to her neck. "How about here?"

He shifted down slightly and bit full force into the soft flesh of her breast. Chancella howled at the rip of agony that shot through her. Once again, she felt the pain-pleasure cycle run its course—the initial jolt of pain mercifully reduced to an ache as the sweet, warm moisture lulled her into a dangerous complacency. Fighting waves of unconsciousness that rose and fell like waves on the sand, she lay weak and listless, moving only slightly in response to the alternate waves of torture and bliss that raced through her.

On and on Jack continued down her body, moving first from one breast to the other, than from one thigh to the next. Taking just enough from each freshly made fount to whet his appetite but not to satisfy it nor to drink her dry.

As he lay surveying his handiwork, the five oozing gashes charted along the length of her body, he dipped his head slightly to peer at the obscure region between her legs, contemplating the sight of his next nibble. A decidedly malevolent grin spread across his face and he chuckled as he leaned forward, spreading his lips wide to reveal his extended wolflike teeth, prepared to dig them into the most tender flesh on a woman's body.

"Get off of her."

The softly spoken command that seemed to come from above was so soft that Chancella wondered if she had imagined it. Still, her eyes fluttered open and she groggily peered over the form of Jack, who straddled her naked body, but her vision, so badly blurred, revealed nothing but the steady flicker of the fire.

Jack unflappably lifted his head to look over his shoulder, a decided smirk failing to offset the hatred that burned within, his voice dripping with a cold hard sarcasm.

"Why tie me up and call me Daisy. What in the world are you doing here?"

No sooner had he spoken than Chancella saw a blur of movement and felt her cruel captor being ripped from atop her. Watching through the foggy haze of blood loss and fear, Chancella watched as Jack stumbled backward a bit before regaining his footing only to stand motionless to her left, seething at someone or something across the room.

Following his gaze, Chancella felt a fresh surge of tears accompanied by a palpable sense of relief as she regarded the most beautiful sight in the world to her—Valian. He stood, looking for all his part as her own personal savior, his sleek black hair and porcelain skin nearly glowing in the candlelight, as did the white cotton of his shirt and those angelic emerald eyes, now shimmering with an emotion that Chancella couldn't readily identify.

For a time the room was silent and then Jack spoke in a quiet, subdued voice.

"It's been a long time, Valian, but I can't say I'm surprised. Like a dog searching for its lost bone. I knew you'd come. You're so predictable."

Valian remained silent, his eyes locked with Jack's.

"You're pathetic," Jack's voice suddenly boomed, shrill and angry. "You've wasted decades hiding in the shadows, bemoaning your existence and taking pity on those beneath us on the food chain. Your Hamlet-ian, tragic philosophies about love, life and morality are laughable!"

"Indeed? But funny thing, Jacariaith, you don't seem even the slightest bit amused," Valian retorted. "In fact, you appear quite angry. Why is that? Perhaps your fairy-tale life is lacking something?"

"Don't play games with me. You know exactly what's missing in my life because you took it away!"

"Ah, is that what this is all about? Arianna? Come now. I'm afraid you have remembered your sweetheart differently that what she really is, keeping your inaccurate memory of her housed up in the dark recesses of your memory where truth and reality can never touch her. Besides, it's been almost two centuries. Don't you think it's time you faced the truth and awakened from your foolish daydream? Give it up, Jacariaith."

"It's Jack. And I will never give up avenging the memory of her and me...of what we could have been," Jack stopped, clearly caught in a struggle between what he felt inside and what he was prepared to reveal.

"Yes, but never were," Valian coolly prompted. "Memory? Don't you mean fantasy? The dream that you and she would one day be together?"

"What would you know? You never felt anything for another soul in all of your miserable existence," Jack spat out, his eyes once again brimming with a palpable fury. "In fact, I'm not sure that you're even capable of it!"

Valian's chilly expression spoke volumes while he, himself, said nothing for a long while and when he did speak, his voice was dangerously low.

"Let me ask you something, Jack. Why did you think Arianna refused your impassioned offer to denounce everything you were just to be with her—hmmm? Why did she leave you and run straight to me?"

"*Run* to you? What the hell are you talking about?" Jack shouted, the volume of his voice causing the tiffany lamp on the nightstand to shake, leaving the tinkling sound of the glass beads in the wake of his incredulous question.

"Once again, my friend, I fear you remember things or perhaps in this case, believe things, as you would have them be. The truth of the matter is your beloved Arianna came to me."

"Oh, this is a new low—even for you! Arianna would never have loved the likes of a lost soul like you!" Jack screamed, taking a long stride towards Valian but stopping abruptly to glower at him. The two beings were now within a couple feet of each other and where Jack was clearly incensed, Valian watched him with that same sympathetic look that had graced his face since he arrived.

"I never said she loved me. Only that she came to me."

"You're lying!"

"What possible reason would I have for that?"

"How about just for the fun of twisting the knife?" Jack nearly winced when he spoke the words, the clear combination of hate and pain shining in his eyes and contorting his face.

"Please, Jack, I beg you to listen," Valian responded softly, the sympathetic sound in his voice causing Chancella to struggle up on her elbows to see him more clearly. Where Jack was facing her full on, Valian had turned slightly and she was unable to see his face. Chancella tried to rise up even further but she soon fell back, exhausted and sweating from the exertion, her heart pounding wildly in her temples. Closing her eyes, she breathed deeply, trying to remain alert as she strove to absorb all the details of the two men's past.

"As always, your arrogance rules your thoughts," Valian carried on. "Whether you choose to believe it or not, my nights are not filled with you and ways in which to inflict the most pain."

"That's only because the deed is done. You can't do any worse."

Valian fell silent, staring nonemotionally into the golden depths of Jack's eyes, the overtly wounded expression within interlaced with the blazing fire of hatred and anger. A raging eternal silence fell between them but when Valian finally spoke, his voice was soft, almost gentle.

"That was never my intention but I again implore you to seek the truth."

"What truth?" Jack irately snapped.

"The reason behind Arianna's decision to leave her life with you and embrace the darkness, shunning both you and the light. Ask yourself that, Jack."

The stunned silence that followed was deafening. Jack only shook his head, his face a masked of tortured denial. Valian continued.

"And what of today? Where is she now when she knows you are looking for her? It is only in those answers that you will find the peace you seek, my friend. Not in lashing out against me."

"Is that right?" Jack sneered.

Chancella peered out over the edge of the bed and although she couldn't make out his face, she was certain she saw him nod his agreement.

"It is."

"Perhaps you are right on one count," Jack conceded as he began to turn away from Valian. "Maybe Arianna owes me an explanation, but all the reasons in the world can't change one thing."

"What's that?" Valian asked.

"You stole my one chance for the life I wanted and so I intend to steal yours."

He lunged forward, once again on Chancella, and with one fluid motion he dipped his head down and bit harshly into her neck. Chancella moaned deeply.

"Jacariaith!"

The ear-splitting boom of Valian's voice filled the room, instantaneously shattering the tiffany lamp on the night table. Through an increasing haziness, Chancella watched as Valian, his face an unrecognizable heart-stopping mask of fury, contorted with a demonic rage and flew through the air, his raven hair blown back as he lunged at Jack.

Drifting in and out of a groggy inertia, she could barely reconcile the handsome, sad-eyed man who had stood only moments earlier near her with the inhuman wild animal that was thrashing about, locked in a supernatural battle of wit and strength.

Unable to move, and feeling the seductive call of unconsciousness, she fell into a partial dream state, with only an auditory account of the incredible event unfolding around her. Crazed, indescribable cracks, thuds and crashes rang out from every direction as the elegant dungeon-come-sitting room was reduced to a pile of rubble that cluttered every possible inch as if a tornado had swept through the suddenly hushed area.

Unable to move from the imprisonment of chains and exhaustion, Chancella lay blearily staring at the canopy overhead, unsure as to how much time had passed. She felt as if she had woken and fallen asleep, and was now left with the unnerving feeling of not knowing what was real and what was not. A deafening silence pressed in on her and a sluggish desperation began to grow inside as she wondered how she would free herself, now that she was apparently alone. The haze of unconsciousness threatened once again and just as her lids fluttered shut, she saw the cool calming sea within mint green eyes through the mist of her near delirium.

Only vaguely in her feverish state could she detect the moist, gentle pressure, the rhythmic, tentative lapping that unbeknownst to her was cleansing and healing each of Jack's bites as a single word was repeated over and over again in her head.

Rest.

Then she was floating. No, flying. No, floating. Being carried — her hair blowing in the wind as it shrieked and howled in her ears. She was cold. Then warm.

Then nothing.

Sweet merciful nothing.

* * * * *

The main entrance to the Lunatic Asylum was impenetrable. A frantic scurry around to the side of the building revealed the same of the locked double doors.

"Damn it!" Nick snapped. Maybe that bloody Jack could fly directly up to the tower but how the hell was he supposed to get in?

He scrambled up the attached fire escape, hesitantly stepping through the debilitated window, careful not to cut himself on the ragged shards of glass that, from the outside, served as some sort of barbaric picture frame to the barren state of the room he entered.

The cell was empty save for a flea-ridden, soiled twin mattress that lay strewn in one corner, the entire area still containing the faint odors of urine and chloroform.

Passing quickly through, Nick headed down the hallway towards the continuing sounds of the commotion, his hands pressed tightly to his ears. A bizarre sound that could only be described as a mutated combination of a freight train, a hyena and a grizzly tore at his human eardrums , intercut with a partially rhythmic banging.

On Nick pressed towards the horrifying clatter, grimacing and running, his mind trying, in vain, to conjure up the scene that would produce such noise. The unbearable clamor rose to such a volume that he felt he could not go on, the din ascending to an unimaginable pinnacle, the nerve-tingling icy sound of smashing glass high above it all. Then just as abruptly as it started, it stopped.

Coming to a sudden halt, he stood panting, his ears ringing in the aftermath of their aural torment as he stared at the closed door opposite. He knew the commotion and what had made it had come from behind that door and yet he could not move.

With a strong surge of fear-fueled irritation, Nick leapt forward and barged through the massive entranceway, sucking in his breath at the unfathomable mess that had once been Jack's bedroom of sorts. The savagery and violence that had befallen the circular space was impossible to digest and Nick could only gawk in stunned silence at the sight before him.

The cement floor, once concealed by the intricately patterned rug, was now covered in an indecipherable scattering of wood, cement, fabric, velvet, chiffon, glass and what was that? Nick squinted. Rose petals? The only items that remained in place were a couple of paintings that hung on the wall, but sadly no longer intact was DaVinci's *The Last Supper*, so shredded or clawed that one could barely distinguish the faces of Jesus and the twelve apostles. Too, the large circular bed stood barren in the center of the space, like some lone survivor of a tornado. The metal shackles that ran from its headboard lay open and empty amidst the ivory satin sheets.

Across the way, the enormous wall unit had been ripped from its moorings and every one of the books from within destroyed and littered around the room. Even one of the large paned windows had been destroyed, large pieces of glass and wood littering its tattered frame. The dangling shreds shifted slightly with the heavy movement of two hands that gripped the edge of the gigantic window, and with a great anguished cry the body they were part of was hoisted up and over onto the floor of the desecrated room.

For a time the thing lay there, his torn and battered body barely concealed by slivers of silk and leather, the frayed remnants of his clothing. Up then, he stood and hobbled forward, the disheveled, bloodied figure of Jack, his face horrifically unrecognizable. One side was swollen and bruised so badly it appeared to be almost charred but the other was worse, drawing gasps from the mortal that stood in front of him. Shredded and hanging in raw, bloodied strips, his flesh seemed to have been clawed by a wild animal and his nose had apparently been dislocated over to the area where his cheekbone should be. Only his eyes remained as before, their cold yellow orbs fixed with a tangible loathing on Nick's face.

Swallowing hard, Nick looked away, unable to meet the seething vampire's gaze. A long time passed and when he ventured a glance once more at the mutated form of his immortal ally, he winced, feeling the intense heat of Jack's anger and hatred directed solely at him. When Jack finally spoke, there was still the sound of the animal in his supernatural voice as he spat out the words that dripped with a bitter obviousness.

"You're late."

Chapter Seven

ℰ℧

Valian placed Chancella gently down on the dark leather couch of her office just beyond the lab. He wondered if she slept often on the worn chesterfield as he pulled the fuzzy blanket that lay crumpled at one end over her slumbering form. Studying her face, he noted the pale, drawn complexion and light, shallow breathing. She had lost a fair bit of blood and would require several hours of sleep to reproduce it all.

An irrational pang of compassion surged through him, and without thinking he reached out and gingerly stroked an errant strand of hair that had fallen across her face, smoothing it back into place. His hand remained, his flesh absorbing the delicious silkiness. It had been centuries since he had enjoyed the tactile sensation of a human without it being a precursor to a kill. He relished the moment, barely resisting the temptation to repeatedly run his fingers through the auburn tresses that had fallen loose. He smiled. Somehow he knew that the ever-proper, reserved doctor would be flustered by the wild and windblown state of her appearance, even if she looked better this way.

But then, distressed by this human digression of sorts, Valian turned from his mortal temptress to survey the tiny space, noting how everywhere were telltale signs that clearly revealed the mass of contradictions that was Chancella.

Behind the small metal desk, on the three-tier bookcase was a gothic-looking bouquet of dried black roses, artistically mixed with baby's breath and German statice alongside which stood an impressive figurine of Michael the Archangel. Standing as an informal bookend for a series of books on death and dying was a rectangular candle in a pewter and bronze holder that bore the Oriental symbol for eternity. An antique picture frame surrounded the image of a stunning black stallion under which the name Diablo was written and beside that, a portrait of a snow-white cat entitled Angelica.

The scores of books that filled the structure were an invariable dog's breakfast. Books on Thai cooking stood side by side with the theories of Einstein, while S & M manuals shared space alongside the teachings of the Catholic Church. The works of Picasso and Mary Shelley were opposite the philosophies of Freud.

Likewise a case containing innumerable items spoke of Chancella's eclectic taste in music, for in only one glance Valian recognized the faces of old friends Rachmaninoff, Jim Morrison and Billie Holiday gracing the covers of their CDS.

Again he smiled.

A scientist with an artist's soul. What a struggle her life must be, he mused, what with her heart and her head continuously vying for supremacy.

Glancing back at Chancella, his attention was drawn to the book that lay upside down on the little table beside the couch. Turning on the lamp that stood at its center, he turned it over where it immediately flopped opened to the dog-eared page entitled:

A Season in Hell: Poems by Arthur Rimbaud.

Sitting down on a nearby wooden chair, Valian began to read the words of the sixteen-year-old genius, the first selection marked with a red asterisk in the margin.

Once, if my memory serves me well, my life was a banquet where every heart revealed itself, where every wine flowed.

One evening I took Beauty in my arms — and I thought her bitter — and I insulted her.

I have withered within me all human hope. With the silent leap of a sullen beast, I have downed and strangled every joy.

Unhappiness has been my god. I have lain down in the mud, and dried myself off in the crime-infested air. I have played the fool to the point of madness.

Now recently, I thought to seek the key to the banquet of old, where I might find an appetite again.

"You will stay a hyena, etc..." shouts the demon who once crowned me with such pretty poppies. "Seek death with all your desires, and all selfishness, and all the Seven Deadly Sins."

Ah! I've taken too much of that. I pass you these few foul pages from the diary of a Damned Soul.

Valian's gaze moved slowly from the words on the page to the face of the one who lay sleeping before him. She was indeed beautiful in her mortality, but there was something deep inside her that was calling him, drawing him into the sweet chameleon that she was.

There was an uncertainty within her determination, a passion beneath the intellect, a trembling under the strength and a profoundly enticing vulnerability under the stoic crust of her resolve. Like a magnet he felt the irresistible pull of his desire to break through her barriers, so long erected and honed to keep her safe. More than anything he could recall in recent history, he wanted to shake her to her very core, releasing her mind, body and spirit from their current prisons and in doing so, release himself.

A vision played across his mind's eye and he trembled at the imagined sight of her head thrown back, her delicate face nothing but a beautiful canvas on which rapture and euphoria lived. Tears of joy and pleasure streamed constantly from her eyes while he, Valian, held her close and bathed her body in the sweetest, most ardent kisses and caresses.

With a jolt, Valian came out of his daydream, stunned at the sensual breathlessness that usually follows drinking blood. What was this madness? How could this be? Damn Simarone and all his fool's talk! He had planted a seed where there had been none before!

And yet, even as the thought came to him, Valian knew it was a lie.

The seed had always been there. It had followed him from his past life into this one and now, for the first time in centuries, was starting to grow.

Staring at the one individual who could help him on his quest, Valian resolutely quelled the feelings even as they continued to rise up, stubbornly shunning the long-dead romantic notions that, if he had a pulse, would have surely quickened it. He had to remain focused, but like some tug-of-war between, literally, love and life, Simarone's words came back to whisper hauntingly in his mind.

Love makes everything worthwhile. It's yours if you want it. You just have to take the chance.

* * * * *

Jack burst into one of the rooms, howling ferociously. His pale yellow pupils were offset by the whites of his eyes that were now blood red, and the crazed, demonic expression on his face would turn any mortal's blood cold.

"Lewis!" he bellowed, the ear-splitting, strangely tinny scream filling the dingy room and ricocheting off the bare walls.

The inhuman sound filling his ears, Nick whirled on his heel and sped out of one deserted space in search of another, hotfooting it down the hall of the asylum until he reached a dead end. Frantically he began trying the doors along the length of the hallway and immediately gained access to an old office where he scurried behind a tall metal filing cabinet. As he crouched there, hidden from view, he watched as Jack, hot on his trail and like a drug-induced bender of some angst-ridden rocker, had burst in and began systematically trashing the room.

Ripping the small '50s black and white television and attached rabbit ears from its place, Jack sent the entire contraption soaring through the air with inhuman force. Connecting with the far wall, it disintegrated into a pile of metal fragments, the clatter and crystalline sound of glass breaking competing with his hyena-like shriek.

Following was the TV stand itself. Then a cobwebbed oval lamp hurling across the length of the space managed to crash through the side window, whereas the faded and stained orange couch traveled seemingly effortlessly through the distant barred window, shards of glass and twisted metal ringing out into the darkened yard below.

"Lewis!" he yelled again.

Throughout his tantrum, Jack could smell Nick's human blood, now tainted with the pungent scent of fear, and for that very reason knew that the object of his fury would taste especially good.

He also knew exactly where the weaselly little gnat was hiding, but had decided to give the damnable fool a show he wouldn't soon forget! Tossing his head back, he howled madly. Nick's soft, sporadic whimpering was lost in the roar, only audible in the aftermath of Jack's shrieks.

That and the sound of movement, too faint for human ears, easily reached Jack and revolving about, he positively prowled over to the area where he sensed Nick's tremulous form.

"Come here," Jack commanded, the timbre of his voice shifting into a low growl.

"I'm-I'm sorry, Jack," was all Nick could muster, his shaking, sweating shape bringing a smile of unfathomable evil to Jack's face. "I don't know what happened. By the time I got there, he...he was gone. I guess our timing was off."

"I'll tell you what happened," Jack whispered, casually striding toward Nick, clenching and unclenching his jaw in a pronounced mannerism of human anger. "You messed up. And you know what that means? I'm going to mess *you* up."

"No, no, please," Nick cried, backing away, his hands spread out before him. "I can explain. I'll make it up to you. We can still get him."

"Shut up!"

Without warning, Jack lunged at Nick and, whirling him about, threw him full force across the length of the room, his body smashing into the wall. Roughly hoisted to his feet, Nick struggled at the feel of Jack's hand as it roughly grabbed his hair. Repeatedly his face was slammed into the window, leaving fresh blood to spurt from his lacerated mouth and nose.

Grabbing the arm that Nick held out to protect himself, Jack twisted it abruptly, driving it up between Nick's shoulder blades in back, the sickening snap of bone breaking echoing loudly in the now empty room.

Screaming, Nick fought hysteria as he squirmed, desperate to break free from the incensed monster before him.

"Please," he panted, teetering on the brink of unconsciousness and squinting through the constant stream of blood that poured into his eyes. "The lab. We, we can go to the lab."

"What for?"

"The formula. It's there. Only there. If your vampire friend is as determined to become mortal as you say, then that's where they will be. I guarantee it."

"Of course, that's where they'll be. The doctor's sweet blood has already told me that."

"Yes, yes," Nick said eagerly, nodding enthusiastically as he tried to smile.

"So then what do I need you for?" Jack asked, grabbing Nick's hair and savagely jerking his head back, baring his teeth as he bent down towards Nick's exposed neck.

"Wha...wait! Wait! Ah—ah—you can't get in. Not without me."

Jack stopped, arching a fine aristocratic eyebrow in question.

"No?"

"You couldn't get past the security guards—they're everywhere."

"I could just kill them...like I'm going to kill you," he said calmly.

Nick swallowed hard, his bottom lip quivering frantically.

"Not without the access codes. Every floor is blocked and locked by a steel entrance door in which a four-digit code must be entered. They change the codes weekly and every floor has its own number."

"But you're forgetting something. I don't use doors."

That stopped Nick cold for a second but thinking on his feet, he took another fear-fueled stab at it.

"But wait, no, besides that, this plan will work better—it really will, because you and Valian have some kind of history—right?"

"So?"

"So, this time, he knew it was a trap. I mean, he must've known that you weren't luring him here for tea, right?"

"What is your point?" Jack asked crossly.

"There is no such history between Chancella and myself. Believe me, she will never see us coming. She trusts me."

"Ah, yes," Jack sneered bitterly as he gradually released Nick. "Trust…the best appetizer to an entrée of betrayal."

* * * * *

When Chancella awoke, she was dumbfounded to see where she was. Unclear as to how she had gotten back to the lab, she blankly gazed about her small office, her sight immediately caught by the lamplight, glinting off something across the way. Her curiosity aroused, she got up and began walking in the direction of the twinkling item, squinting hard to bring the item in question into focus. As she drew nearer, she deduced that it was merely the light reflecting off the gold lettering on the spine of a thick book snugly wedged amongst others in the tall book case just opposite.

Chancella stopped short as she read the label, *The Big Book of European History*, the remnants of her conversation with Valian the night before echoing in her head directly after.

"My father was Spanish. When he was crowned King, he turned his back on my mother and me."

Removing the hardback, Chancella made her way back to the sofa and, sitting down, began searching for Spain in the index.

When she found a corresponding page reference, she flipped frantically to the appropriate place and feverishly began reading. As expected, she could find no sign of any family name de Mortenoire but of course, why would she? Valian had said that was his mother's name, unless, of course, he had made that up too.

For heaven's sake, she scolded herself. What was she doing? And yet, without rhyme or reason, she found herself reading on.

Without a proper surname, she didn't really know what she was looking for but still she continued, leafing leisurely through the thin pages, her eyes taking in paragraphs and pictures of European architecture and geography, until her heart suddenly skipped a beat at the section entitled Spanish Royalty.

Flicking through scads of bios and portraits, her gaze only glancing from one face to the next, she searched for some clue, some thread that she could grasp onto that might validate Valian's story.

Turning another page, she gasped aloud, her eyes widening in shock at one sketch in particular. The artist's charcoal rendering of King Philip V of Spain was, for all intents and purposes, a drawing of Valian. Granted the eyes were a little narrower, and the subject in the portrait had a thick bushy moustache but the long straight nose, full pouting mouth and chiseled jaw line were remarkably like that of the faux doctor-turned-vampire.

Blinking her eyes repeatedly, she checked and rechecked the date of the King's reign written under the portrait but no matter how many times she tried to clear her vision, the numbers remained the same — 1700–1713.

How was it possible?

Despite the uncanny resemblance and the butterflies of intuition that fluttered wildly in the pit of her stomach, the picture before her couldn't possibly be Valian's biological father for that would make Valian...a long, slow chill ran down Chancella's spine, causing her to shudder violently. She tried to keep the words from sounding in her head and yet they came, soft and eerie like the cry of a ghost...*over three hundred years old.*

Slowly her gaze returned to the drawing. The likeness was undeniable.

Wait a minute! She mentally turned on her heel to abruptly challenge herself. She *had* to approach this rationally.

In all her years of scientific study, many a time she'd had to apply eleventh-century Franciscan theologian William of Ockham's basic principle, better known as Occam's Razor, that states, "All things being equal, the simplest explanation tends to be the right one."

Despite some fairly convincing evidence, this was no time to abandon logic.

Holding hard and fast to her scientific ways, she asked herself...what was more likely? That a real live vampire showed up on her doorstep to offer himself as an inhuman guinea pig on which she could oh-so-conveniently prove her serum? Or that a sad, lonely individual with a bag of tricks stole a name from an old history book and created an illusion so complex and intricate that he, himself, actually began to believe it?

Ignoring her honed sixth sense that screamed in favor of the former, Chancella had to allow that the latter scenario was more than likely the real one.

Even more sadly, she had to recognize that her own desire, both as a woman and a scientist, had played a part in overpowering her rationale.

But what of the inexplicable? The cut on his hand? His supernatural speed and strength as exhibited during his joust with Jack?

Back and forth she started again, as she had done since this all began, indeed, just as she had always done in all areas.

Question over accept, know over sense, think over feel.

Then suddenly and without any kind of warning, a miracle of sorts occurred. The ferocious vacillation stopped, that anxious, desperate questioning quit and a quiet, almost serene peace filled her soul. Divine intervention or something quite like it stepped in and Chancella, for the first time in her life, abandoned her analytical ways and listened to her heart and in that moment...she knew the truth.

Returning her gaze to the photo, she smiled a tentative, almost shy grin as a soft low voice broke into her secret thoughts.

"You are correct. *Finally.*"

The hint of light sarcasm in the last word caused Chancella to turn and face Valian, her eyes locking with the cool green gaze that beheld her and as he next spoke, he only told her more of what she already knew.

"That was my father."

Chancella could only nod. Suddenly she became acutely aware of his closeness to her and yet, unlike before, she was neither uncomfortable nor afraid. Reading her thoughts, he continued.

"I told you—you have nothing to fear from me. I have sought you out only for your assistance. You're the only one who can help me. I promise I won't hurt you."

"I just never—"

"What?"

"Never really believed..."

She let the sentence fall away. Throughout her life there had been scads of things she never believed in—justice, faith, love—just because she had never seen them firsthand. Now she wondered if she had been wrong to doubt the existence of some of those things.

Maybe all of them.

"We all lose faith, Chancella," he said, his gentle voice nearly caressing her. For a suspended breath, they stood looking intently into each other's eyes and just like in the restaurant the night before, Chancella had the sensation that they were floating while the room swirled around them, the sweet dreamlike spell broken only by the sound of Valian's voice. "But, now, will you help me? I beg of you."

"I will," Chancella answered, heaving a deep sigh of relief at the return of her irrepressible curiosity. With all the theatrics behind them, she had to admit that she was absolutely dying to find out what Valian was made of. Literally.

"Okay, let's get started," she said directly as she led the way into the lab, and after securing her hair back up and off her neck, she reached for her white coat. "First things first. I'm going to need a blood sample."

Chancella led Valian over to a small desk in the corner of the lab and motioned for him to take a seat.

Everything about Valian had become fascinating to Chancella and now as she watched him she noticed the pronounced, particular manner with which he rolled up his shirtsleeve. It was as if he was imitating the movement for the first time and wanted to get it just right.

"The way you move," she began uncertainly, not quite sure how to phrase it. "It's somehow…different."

"Yes," he immediately agreed. "It is often the one thing that gives us away."

"Gives you away?"

"As non-human."

He fell silent but when he raised his head and saw the expectant look on her face, he carried on, trying to explain the unexplainable.

"Vampire gestures are fraught with bursts of kinetic energy, making our movements appear—" he looked off, struggling with an analogy that would make Chancella understand. Then his expression suddenly brightened. "As mosquitoes do to you. Only faster."

"Really?" Chancella gasped as she envisioned the flighty, jerky course of the miniscule insect.

"It is a constant struggle to animate ourselves accordingly, purposefully creating mannerisms and slowing them so as to blend in with your kind."

Another thought seemed to strike him then and he smiled.

"Actually, in a roundabout way it's quite fitting that we have to deliberate our physical movements for in all other areas we savor the moment. You see, the life of a vampire is a purely hedonistic adventure — all the senses leisurely drinking in the titillation of all that surrounds us."

"Gosh, that sounds wonderful," Chancella said as she peeled off the paper casing from the syringe. "The world is so busy these days, one rarely has the time to 'savor' anything."

"Ah, but the world and all it has to offer, all its many experiences were meant to be relished and enjoyed in a lingering fashion. To rush," he concluded with a definite sense of conviction, "is a sin."

"A sin?" Chancella echoed in disbelief, astounded at the potential of getting into a moral debate with a vampire.

Valian read her mind and that lazy, spell-casting smile appeared once more on his face.

"There are many kinds of sins."

"No kidding," was all Chancella could muster as she tied the long stretchy elastic on his upper arm before slapping gently in the crook of his elbow, the cool glossy texture of the milky white flesh threatening to distract her.

"What are you doing?" Valian questioned, his eyebrows knitting together in an almost comical imitation of incomprehension.

"Looking for a vein."

He then made a slight motion with his wrist, almost too small to notice, the movement producing the emergence of a thick blue vein just under the surface of the pearlized skin on his arm.

"How's that?"

Chancella nodded in obvious appreciation.

"Perfect. Now, hold still."

She habitually reached for a cotton puff and dabbed it on the alcohol dispenser.

"It prevents infection," she offered in response to his questioning look.

He stared blankly at her for a moment but soon, Chancella felt her lip twitch in response to the half-smirk that slowly spread across his face, the two sharing a smile at the futility of the procedure.

Taking the needle, she snapped the glass tube into the back of the syringe. Pressing delicately on the procuring artery, she laid the needle tentatively against his skin and then gently eased it in just below the surface.

Her eyes flew up to his and as she anticipated, he regarded her coolly and without emotion.

"Did that hurt?" she asked out of habit.

"We don't feel pain."

"What do you mean you don't feel it? Not at all?" she asked in amazement.

He made a funny slight movement with his lips, nearly pursing them as if mulling something over.

"Well, we do, but not in the same way as you."

"I don't understand."

"I know. Unfortunately, there's no way to make you understand. I can only try to use words that might give you some sense of it."

"So use some."

"Make no mistake. We feel pain but the emotional response is totally merged with the physical one, creating a uniquely multi-sensory experience."

"So...what does that feel like?"

"Umm..."

Chancella found herself giggling at the sound of indecision.

"Frostbite. Fire. Yes, yes, something like that. I think that's it."

"You've lost me."

As he began to explain, Chancella glanced down and watched as the blood from his vein spurted into the empty clear test tube, shooting down its length to slowly fill the narrow cylinder.

"Those words are generally thought of in terms of a physical sensation, but try to imagine their emotional equivalent combining with that physical sensation and you have some indication of the way we register pain."

"So you feel nothing with your body?"

"On the contrary. We feel everything. Only not exclusively externally. Our perception has changed from a strictly physical reaction to a binary fusion of the external with the internal, a tactile with the emotional."

"Humans are like that."

"No they're not," he said directly.

"Of course they are!" she argued. He adamantly shook his head.

"No, at any given moment, mortals either feel something on the outside or on the inside. Your systems are not set up to compute simultaneous sensation. Not at the same time."

"That's crazy. There are many situations in which a human being registers stimuli both physically and emotionally."

"Such as?"

A heavy silence fell between them.

"Grief," Chancella pronounced proudly. "Profound pain caused by the loss of, say, a loved one, is felt both internally and externally. Your body aches as much as your spirit does."

"That may be the perception but the reality is that in that case, the pain is felt emotionally, not physically. Your body aching, as you call it, is more from a lack of sleep or not eating than from an actual physical response to the cause of your grief."

"Oh, c'mon! I don't believe it!"

"Believe what you wish. It will not alter the fact that vampires are unable to detect any sensation—not only pain—unilaterally. For us, this whole business of 'feeling' has moved to a higher plane, an alleviated state of consciousness if you like, but it is not without some casualties."

"What do you mean 'casualties'?"

"Some impressions of the world have been heightened, but others have lessened and then, there are those that are lost all together."

"Which ones?" she urged, removing the blood-filled test tube and capping it before gently snapping a second into place.

"The epicurean pleasure of feasting or partaking of various stimuli from alcohol to the latest drug is gone. Not only does the mere thought of ingesting food as you think of it not appeal to us, more than that it is repulsive."

"So you never fantasize about a steak or some deep-fried shrimp or a piece of chocolate?"

Chancella laughed out loud as Valian screwed up his face.

"What is that expression? Oh yes! Gross!"

"But don't you get hungry?"

"All the time."

"But not for food."

"Right."

"Other tactile delights such as hot baths, cool rain on your face and massages are greatly diminished but nevertheless still enjoyable."

Chancella waited, his eyes regarding her coolly.

"What about other experiences?"

"Which other experiences are you referring to?"

"Well, umm, something perhaps more intimate in nature?"

Chancella could feel her face flushing and she secretly scolded herself, surprised that she had to remind herself that she was a scientist and Valian was nothing more than a case study. Granted, a very enticing case study who was undoubtedly reading her mind at this very minute.

"Do you mean sex?" he asked flatly.

"Yes," she replied, lowering her eyes to insert yet another test tube into the base of the syringe that was still protruding from his forearm.

"What about it?" he deadpanned.

Eeeeeesh, he was making this hard.

"Well, is it the same?" she asked in a somewhat flustered manner. "As a vampire, I mean."

"No, well, I don't know."

He stared at her for a long moment and then a beguiling smile lifted the corners of his mouth and creased the skin of his cheeks as deep dimples set in.

She returned his gaze for a long moment, uncomprehending his meaning, before he humored her with an enlightenment of sorts.

"The fulfilling and stimulating experience of human sexual contact has, for the most part, been replaced by drinking the dream but the *sharing* of blood is said to far surpass any human occasion of love and pleasure. However it seldom occurs."

"But it is similar to the human experience of —?" she asked uncertainly.

"Lovemaking?" he finished for her. "Different, I expect. Better, I assume."

"But we're talking about two different things," Chancella said in frustration. "I'm referring to a physical expression of love."

"So am I," he said with a degree of surprise. "For a vampire, there is no greater proof of one's commitment. But it is extremely rare."

"Why so?"

"Because by nature, we are what society would call loners. Seldom, if ever, have we even the desire or need to merge our souls with another in any way, least of all through a physical exchange."

Chancella persisted.

"But don't you get lonely?"

"Of course. It is, as they say, the nature of the beast, but unlike some humans we do not use this sort of intimacy to alleviate our own loneliness, but rather to truly merge our spirit with another."

"But you do have the choice. I mean, you *are* able."

"To express love physically?" he asked. "In *our* way — most definitely," he agreed resolutely.

A period of quiet followed and then Chancella started in again, almost timidly.

"Do you think you will? I mean, do you want to?"

The sexy smirk that had intermittently graced his face throughout their flirtatious dialogue disappeared and the sea foam green eyes twinkled with something very close to ardour.

"With you?"

"Excuse me?"

"That is what you meant — you are inviting me to your bedroom, are you not?"

"Ah—no! Not at all! I just wondered what your position was."

"What my position is?" he asked teasingly.

Chancella laughed out loud, not even caring that Valian must've, by now, noticed her blush but this time, she was not embarrassed, only riding the wave of titillation. Besides, she mused, he thought her blush was *ravissant*.

"You know what I mean," she scolded him. "Now be serious! Despite your tendency to go it solo, is it something you aspire to?"

"Mmmm—aspire to? No. If I felt the desire—absolutely," he said with a smile but then just as quickly, "however I can't imagine ever feeling the desire."

Astounded, she worked to clarify his last statement.

"What are you saying? That you've never, how did you put it?"

"Shared blood."

"Yes, shared blood. You've never shared blood with anyone?"

Valian wordlessly shook his head no.

"But what of those you make? You take blood from them and they from you."

"Yes, but not simultaneously. To share blood means to take and give at that same time and in doing so, creating an unending circle of giving and receiving."

"And you've never done this?"

He smiled then, a slow almost hesitant smile that seemed to be bordering on shyness.

"Not yet."

"Wha—well, why?" she blurted out in amazement. "You must've come across many attractive lady vampires in your travels," she looked down, dabbing absentmindedly at the pinpoint of blood on his forearm from where she had withdrawn the needle. "I mean, as a vampire you can only—"

she struggled with the words—"share blood with another of your own kind—right?"

He regarded her a long quiet moment.

"Wrong. I can choose my lover just the same as you can."

Chancella's heart rate doubled as Valian's glittering green eyes locked with hers and for one long moment she had the idiotic feeling that he was going to lean over and kiss her and even more surprising, she sensed that she wouldn't pull away.

Gathering her wits about her, Chancella reached for a piece of tape to put over the minute mark. At the feel of his cool hand gently enclosing hers, Chancella looked at him again.

"It's okay," he said softly.

Glancing down, Chancella marveled at the sealed, flawless skin where the tiny hole had been seconds earlier.

Fighting a kind of giddiness, Chancella wordlessly moved over to another counter where she placed a spot of Valian's blood on a slide. Reaching for her glasses, she bent over and eased it under the microscope.

Valian leaned back, stretching out to casually cross one leg over the other as he crossed his arms over his chest, studying Chancella as she worked.

"Do you ever let your hair down?" he asked, noting her ever-present bun.

Chancella laughed without lifting her eyes from the microscope.

"Do you mean literally or figuratively?"

"Both," he said flatly.

Straightening, she turned to face him, arching her back like a cat and rotating her shoulder to relieve her tired muscles.

"Ah, well, let me see. Yes…and sometimes. How's that?" she smiled.

Valian nodded solemnly as if absorbing and filing away the information for a later date.

"How do you do it?"

"I beg your pardon?"

"Let your hair down—for jocularity purposes."

"Jocularity?" she repeatedly incredulously. "You mean fun?"

"Fun. Yes."

"Oh, I don't know," Chancella squirmed slightly, feeling somewhat uncomfortable as if all of a sudden she was the one under the microscope. "I like to read."

"Read? For fun?"

"Well, yes, no, you know what I mean," she said a little flustered.

"Not exactly."

"Well, I like to cook."

"Wild," he said, jokingly.

"Okay then," she started defiantly, "what do you like to do for fun?"

A slow, sexy smile spread across his face, once again bringing color to Chancella's face.

"Never mind," she said quickly. "I don't want to know."

"You might be surprised," he countered.

"Oh, I'm sure of it."

He sighed deeply and then without any kind of prompting began talking in a thoughtful slow manner as if he were thinking out loud.

"I've grown bored with most mortal follies. Reading is too redundant—everything is the same, just using different words, and I've traveled enough to last one lifetime, never mind several. I guess you could say I don't take pleasure in much anymore."

"Oh that's dismal. Surely there is something that brings you a kind of…peace."

"Peace?" he repeated almost incredulously.

"Yes, tranquility, serenity, peace."

He nodded, his face lighting up with an immediate comprehension.

"Ah yes. The blood does that."

"Besides that. Something else."

"There is nothing else."

"Think back," Chancella firmly persisted. "When you were mortal. There must have been something, at one time or another. You must have felt it from something."

Valian frowned for a time, struggling back through the decades to another place, another time and then a look of momentary contentment played across his face.

"Water," he finally said.

"I beg your pardon?"

"Yes, water," he smiled, a full, open expression playing across his face at the recollection. "I used to love the sound of it splashing against the shore, the musty, salty smell of it and the feel of it as it rocks a ship side to side like a mother rocks a child. Yes, I found a kind of 'peace' when I was near water."

He turned to regard her with a new look — one that softened the continual frown and often blankness within his eyes.

"What about you?"

Chancella didn't even have to think.

"In discovery. I always feel good when I'm learning something new."

"Is that why you became a biologist?"

"What is this? Twenty questions?" she laughed.

Valian only regarded her wordlessly, waiting for her response to the question. She had the unnerving feeling that he could wait all night.

"Well, not exactly. I started out as an English major, if you can believe it, but for some strange reason I veered off into sciences after my first year."

"What strange reason was that?"

She looked at him then, taken aback by the notion that he knew what she was about to say before she said it, making every utterance irrelevant and repetitive.

"I lost a good friend to a very rare disorder," she said frankly, feeling her throat tighten with emotion. "My *best* friend to be more precise. She wasted away at the ripe ol' age of twenty-two and there was nothing, not a goddamned thing the doctors could do. Well, I just couldn't get my head around that. There had to be some way, some manner in which to treat it. I wouldn't accept any less."

"So you set out to find 'the cure'?" he offered quietly.

"Yes."

"And did you?"

"I found one. I think. For Clara's disease, I didn't but along the way I veered off and in the interim, I think I may have opened the door to prolonging life, maybe even permanently so. Of course, some feel that there is something Frankensteinish about it all. It's as if I'm playing God."

Valian didn't answer but Chancella thought she detected the slightest trace of a frown on his still face as he looked away.

Returning her attention back to the microscope, Chancella jumped.

"Oh my God!" she suddenly shrieked, her head jerking up from the eyepiece. "This is the most amazing thing I've ever seen. Come here, look. I've never seen anything like this."

Valian whimsically watched her before silently obeying her. He stared down through the eyepiece at the flat circular cells that pulsed under the powerful magnification.

"What am I looking at?"

"You are looking at yourself!"

Valian eyed her skeptically.

"So?"

"So?" she nearly bellowed as she pushed past him to look once again at the magnification of his blood. "Oh, you just don't get it. Cells move, I mean they are on the go all the time but yours are stationary. They're completely still except for this bizarre little oscillation, a throbbing. It's as if they each have their own little heartbeats. It's like they're dead, but alive."

He stood very near her, regarding her silently, a bemused expression etched clearly onto the beautiful face suddenly darkening into a grimace as the sweet soft scent of her humanness wafted across him. Valian stiffened and moved away, a slow languid recoiling from their semi-prone position. Sensing the change, Chancella looked up from the microscope.

"What is it?" she asked.

Wordlessly, he began backing away from her, his eyes locked unnaturally with hers.

"Where are you going?" Chancella called after him as he reached the door to the lab.

"Valian—" she half-asked, half-stated.

"I need to go out," he brusquely announced, Chancella perplexed by the sudden look of exhaustion on his face. Uncomprehending she moved towards him.

"Wha...what?" Chancella stammered, confused. "Now? Where?"

Valian looked at her in a direct, solid gaze, his face, as usual, unreadable. He said nothing.

Chancella returned his stare for a few long moments before the reason for his sudden change in mood hit her.

"Ahhh," she glanced away and then down, feeling a swift rush of discomfiture. "I get it."

The two had been holed up in the windowless lab since 8:00 last night, and while she had munched and snacked here and there on her 'energy' stash of chips, cookies and pop, Valian had nothing.

How could she have been so stupid?

After twenty-four hours, it was clear where he was going.

The click of the doorknob turning brought Chancella's head up with a snap and her heart pounded as a question, perhaps *the* question of her career, hovered hesitantly on her lips.

"Valian?" she called weakly, hoping that he didn't decipher the crackle of fear in her voice.

He turned and regarded her blankly.

"Can I go with you?" she barely whispered.

Valian didn't answer, only stood watching her vacantly from the doorway.

"Would it be okay?" she tried again.

"Why?" he finally spoke, his voice thick and heavy with need.

She shrugged once more, feeling the heat of embarrassment coloring her face. "I don't know, I just want to—"

"Watch?" he offered, his face impassive. "Why?" he asked again, his eyes glittering with an indecipherable emotion.

"I—" She couldn't finish the sentence because the truth was, she didn't know why. Perhaps it was the scientist in her that wanted to observe this phenomenon of a creature on the hunt. Maybe she still couldn't really believe Valian was a vampire until she witnessed him feeding with her own eyes. Or maybe, as a woman, she wanted to learn about and share in every aspect of his life. Whatever the reason, she felt a strange, magnetic need to accompany him on this late night, and what would surely turn out to be ghastly, trip.

Her eyes locked with his and still she could not speak even at the feel of the swirling presence of his mind within hers as he sought to learn her thoughts.

"I don't think you'll like it," he announced matter-of-factly, as if it were Modern Dance or Impressionist Art he was introducing her to for the first time.

"I know," she demurred, fighting the urge to sulk. "I just—
"

He watched her closely, noticing how her breath had quickened and her increased heartbeat, which now pounded in his ears, made her breasts rise and fall at an accelerated rate.

"As you wish," he said quietly as he moved to go.

Chancella quickly threw off her white lab coat and, grabbing her suede jacket, followed Valian out of the lab.

Chapter Eight

ଓ

Under different circumstances, the hypnotic sound of water lapping against the ship, and the silvery hue of moonlight casting a magical glow on everything, would have been decidedly romantic. But considering the gruesome reason for their post-midnight adventure, Chancella felt an increasing sense of dread gnawing nonstop in the pit of her stomach.

Too, it didn't help that Valian's previously gentle and accommodating manner had changed. Now, sullen and brooding, he stood wordlessly beside her, his eyes constantly scanning the shoreline, searching...

Chancella couldn't for the life of her figure out how Valian had managed to get the operator to agree to their private, moonlit jaunt across the water. She was going to ask but on second thought decided against it. In fact, he had seemed positively annoyed when she suggested they take the ferry. Maybe he had guessed that she wanted to see the water work its soothing magic on him firsthand. However it would seem to be true for despite Valian's surly state, Chancella sensed that her immortal companion, on some level, relished the quiet that surrounded them.

For a long time they stood like that, staring out at the black water as they made the slow trip to Fire Island.

When she could stand it no more, Chancella softly broke the stillness with a tentative question.

"Mind if I ask you something?"

"Go ahead," he replied unenthusiastically.

"Why?"

His eyes drifted up to her face and locked with hers but he didn't answer.

"Why do you want to become mortal again?"

"Why do you think?"

"I don't know. I mean, from where I stand you've got a lot of things that people want."

"What things?"

"Oh gee, let me think," she replied, not even trying to hide the gentle mockery within her response. "Power, strength, freedom, eternal life — stuff like that."

"True, these qualities have their use but until you've experienced it, lived it, you can't possibly know."

"Know what?"

"That life becomes pointless, truly futile, after a time. There are a few seasoned, wise-beyond-their-years mortals that have come to this conclusion, but for the most part, seventy or eighty years on the planet doesn't bring about this kind of revelation. It takes centuries to really absorb that the more things change, the more they stay the same."

"Yes, but just think of all you've seen!"

"Precisely. I've seen decades of history repeating itself. Man killing man and for what? What are wars except one side trying to force the other side into doing or not doing something? And how creative your injuries to each other have become — the ways and means as varied as people themselves! Be it blackmail, exclusion, gossip, adultery, rape, murder — each one brings the same end result — death to the spirit."

"But we're not all like that," Chancella cried in astonishment, trying to reason him out of his impassioned black mood. "What about you when you were a mortal? What were you like?"

"No different," he stated flatly.

"What do you mean?" Chancella stammered, imagining the worst possible scenario of his former human existence. "You mean you were—"

"I was like everyone else, saints and murderers alike—a lost soul trying to find his identity, purpose and meaning to the universe in this random chaos called life. Ironically, after three hundred years I have come full circle, back to the same conclusion."

"And what's that?"

"That we are all fundamentally alone, drifting aimlessly through a series of random mishaps and tragedies."

Chancella gawked at him.

"Oh, Valian, don't say that. What of God? Had you no faith?"

"Are you trying to be funny?" he snapped sarcastically. "God? Where is he? I see no sign of him. And faith? Faith is a contrived concept, introduced by the religious organizations of the world as an emotional Prozac. When life dumps all over you and you are being abused and torn and pushed to the limit, have faith. It's their way of controlling a worldwide riot against the injustice and unfairness in the world. And to a certain extent it works. The Bible-thumpers of the world are only repressing what the villains and criminals of the world are expressing."

Valian carried on with an increasing vigor and enthusiasm, the passion and conviction of his words fueling him as the volume of his voice rose.

"God and faith? I believe in neither," he asserted defiantly. "If there was a higher power, His rationale for allowing these atrocities doesn't fit my concept of what such a deity should be. Besides…we make our own destiny. That is, of course, with the exception of the victims—their paths are not by their own hand."

"That's not true. No matter how terrible the situation, we can always turn it around."

"Is that so? Could your friend with the illness turn it around? Could you?"

Chancella fell into a sudden silence, her eyes smarting with tears. When Valian spoke next, his voice had grown soft and sad.

"For as far back as time goes, the desperate, lonely and disillusioned have been taking out their pain and frustration on their unsuspecting and undeserving victims. In the words of Eric Draven—'victims, aren't we all?'"

Chancella remembered the line from the hit gothic movie *The Crow* but was surprised that Valian had seen it. Indeed, just as Jack had claimed about himself, Valian was turning out to be full of surprises.

"I understand their plight—the criminals—for their torment is incredible but make no mistake...I denounce their methods. Where's the sense in unleashing your hostility on someone or something that has nothing to do with the problem? No, I reserve my fury for one who has the power to stop such injustice."

"You mean God? I thought you didn't believe in him?"

Valian's eyes flashed.

"I believe in him. I just don't *believe* in him. Not anymore."

"But you once did?"

Valian turned away from her, ignoring the question.

"No God I can imagine would allow such things. It has taken me several lifetimes to realize that man is on his own and sadly, as time goes on, he only becomes more of what he is—a primitive, violent, self-serving animal driven by instinct and need, not rationale and love."

"Primitive animal? Driven by instinct and need? That's funny coming from you."

"Is it really?" he cocked one aristocratic eyebrow as he glared at her intently. Chancella swallowed hard, her heart pounding under his hard scrutiny. "I am only, on the exterior, what we all are in the inside. And unlike so many others, I chose my path and now I wish to choose another."

"What do you mean, chose it?"

Valian sighed and looked away.

"It's a long story and one that would only grow longer in the re-telling."

"I think we have the time."

Valian hesitated but Chancella gently urged him to continue.

"Please. I want to know how it happened. I want to understand."

"Why?"

Once again, Chancella found herself at a loss for words. She didn't know the answer. She only knew that she wanted to know everything. Valian regarded her in silence before looking out over the water, the breeze stirring his dark hair across the sharp plain of his cheekbone and into his eyes. Chancella bit her tongue and quickly averted her eyes, pushing down the overwhelming desire to brush the silky dark strands from his sight as she had wanted to that first night.

"I don't know where to begin," he nearly whispered.

"Start anywhere," she smiled. "Just start."

"I was lost—really, truly," he began softly, gazing off, his voice dipping so low that Chancella had to strain to hear him. "Searching endlessly, but in the end, my search was in vain. Whether I was looking in the wrong place or in the wrong way or for the wrong reason is now all irrelevant."

He sighed deeply, a pained expression darkening the beauty of his face. "I was exhausted. Perhaps it was the lack of acknowledgment from my father, maybe the death of my mother and just the commonplace uncertainty that every man feels at one time or another. Whatever the reason, demoralized, hopeless and unspeakably lonely for my thirty-three years, I set out to end it all."

"You mean kill yourself?" Chancella whispered, shocked at the intimate disclosure.

Valian turned to face her, the slightest hint of a sad smile tugging at one corner of his full mouth.

"That's generally what that means."

Unwilling or unable to hold her eyes with his as he spoke, he looked off again and continued his story.

"I was going to put a stop to the wasteland of cold, dark emptiness that permeated my days and nights and yet, it would seem that fate, if there be such a thing, had other plans for me. As I reached for my trusty knife, that cold winter night in Andorra, hell-bent on slitting my own throat as I crouched deep in the forest, a voice called my name."

Transfixed, spellbound, Chancella stood motionless, hanging on every word, astonished from time to time at how the details, as rich and intricate as they were, failed to illicit any response in the speaker.

"But it was no ordinary voice but one like a memory that drifted, faint and ghostlike, speaking to me simultaneously from within and outside, surrounding me, caressing me. Whether it was female or male, I could not know, only a haunting yearning and yet a quiet wisdom came from within the sound.

"I jerked upright and wildly looked around, for my pride was such that I wanted no living thing to witness what I was about to do.

"Again it called to me like the sweet warbling cry of the thorn bird on the wind, its voice lifted in the most beautiful of songs, a fatal song that precedes its self-induced death."

At the moment, Valian turned, his eyes locking with Chancella's, a soft fire blazing within the sparkling green depths while his face remained stoic.

"And then she was in front of me, a creature I can scarcely describe for she was like none I had ever seen. Her hair, like spun gold, floated down around her slender shoulders, trailing down the length of her back to lightly graze the curve of her bottom. Her ivory chiffon dress gave the distinct impression of being in a dream for each movement of hers brought a delayed slow-motion response from the flimsy delicate fabric as it undulated and floated about her body.

"And yet as pale and tender a shade it was, it seemed vibrant in relation to the alabaster hue of her luminous skin. And how odd a skin it was, glowing with the strong steadiness of any oil lamp found in the stables, the moonlight almost ricocheting off its porcelain finish.

"But nothing in this world could have prepared me for the eyes that beheld me, indeed, held me captive in their gaze, for they were excruciatingly beautiful—truly. I felt pain as I looked into their violet depths, all the purples of the forests and gardens swirling within and I began to feel dizzy and on the brink of unconsciousness and yet I had to know, before I fell, what this creature was.

"'Are you an angel?' I whispered, frozen with a mixture of fear, amazement and desire as the thing approached me. What a wonder that was to behold for her legs seemed not to move and yet as surely as I am telling you, she steadily approached until she was beside me. Bending down in a strangely unnatural movement, she knelt in front of me.

"'To some. To others, a devil,' she replied, the soft feminine tinkling of her voice mixed with a masculine huskiness, 'but for you, tonight, an angel I am.'"

Chancella's throat had long since gone dry and now she worked hard to swallow, her eyes locked with Valian's as he took her even further.

"Young and virile as I was, a sudden throbbing began in my loins and my heart beat ferociously as I felt the age-old lure of the flesh spring forth. She smiled knowingly then, a barely perceptible parting of her lips that managed to reveal her startling white teeth.

"Not unacquainted with the pleasures of the flesh, I desperately wanted to lunge at her. I wanted to devour those lips with my own, bury my face in the strands of golden hair and touch and consume every inch of her heavenly body with my mouth, endeavoring to merge my body with hers."

As he spoke, Chancella fought to remain as unemotional as Valian appeared to be, but her entire body trembled with a heightening physical arousal as he divulged the remarkably intimate details of his turning. Heaving a deep, unsteady breath, she secretly prayed to the God that Valian had so hotly denounced, hoping that her winded breathing, obvious in the increased rise and fall of her chest as well as the telltale flush of desire on her face, would go unnoticed.

With the exception of the rare flicker within the dark green of his eyes, Valian carried on, stating the pulse-quickening facts as nonchalantly as if he were reading a grocery list.

"And yet, I was uncharacteristically paralyzed, frozen with a fear that left me trembling and immobile. She knew this and I felt the swell of passion surge once again as she leaned in, her face so close to mine that her lips almost brushed mine as she spoke.

"'Do not be afraid, my beautiful one. I will not hurt you. Rather I will give you pleasure beyond your wildest dreams and moreover, an end to this pain that burns within you.'

"With that, she kissed me, the soft, moist feel of her lips on mine causing mine to involuntarily open. She pushed me down onto the soft moist earth and began systematically working down the length of me, her incredible strength pinning me down and rendering me helpless as she ravaged every possible spot on my writhing body."

The distinct clink of metal on metal rang out sharply as Chancella's hand flew up to tightly grip the steel railing, the metallic clang coming from the contact of a ring on her index finger with the latter. Swooning, she felt her knees threaten to give way underneath her as she clung to the cold, wet barrier for support, her knuckles white with effort.

The noise had halted Valian's reverie and now he regarded Chancella pointedly, his lips spreading into a knowing smile, the movement revealing a sexy pair of dimples. Suddenly aware of a raging thirst, Chancella moistened her lips with the tip of her tongue, her heart almost stopping at the change in Valian's expression from bemusement to desire, his eyes dropping from hers down to her lips only to drift lazily back again. Chancella couldn't breathe. An eternity seemed to pass in which they stood, silently communicating, a palpable fire running the circuit back and forth between the two, over and over, like an electrical wire that had been looped to ignite itself.

For a split second, an insinuation of a frown crossed Valian's forehead, a shadow of confusion across his face. Then mercifully, he looked away, releasing them both from the unpredicted spell. Clearing his throat, he carried on.

"I do not know how long she toyed with me but the play of her hands and lips on my body seemed to last an eternity and yet any time I made a move to sit up I was pushed rather forcibly down and held captive. I was very near the point of pleading for both, the release of her grip as well as release of my passion, when I felt the strange sensation of two knife points piercing the flesh just above my heart.

"Exclaiming, I jumped but the weight of her body on mine kept me horizontal and I began to feel the intense throbbing pain give way to yet another wave of rapture—a different kind in which my very soul was being fondled and kissed and urged to release. I think I arched my back as my heavenly visitor, unbeknownst to me, sucked the blood from my body, and yet, I was delirious with a slowly creeping grogginess that seemed to spread further through my veins with every pull from her hungry mouth on my flesh.

"Just as the coma-like complacency reached its pinnacle and I was drifting off in a blinding, blazing bath of warm sunlight, I was threaded back, pulled from my sweet delirium where the feel of warm moisture on my mouth and a soft gentle voice urged me to the present.

"'Drink, my sad Prince. Your pain is over. Your anguished days will cease with the swilling of the dark dream. Open your mouth as if it were me you were consuming for I tell you most surely, it is. You are drinking me, my love, and every power I have will soon be yours.'

"Though I could not fully comprehend her meaning nor predict the consequence of the action I was about to take, I did understand one thing—'Your pain is over. Your anguished days will cease.' I needed no further enticement."

Valian stopped then.

"What was it like, that first time?" Chancella whispered.

"At first, I disliked the strong metallic taste but within mere seconds my starving body metamorphosed and I loved it, even craved it. With every swallow I could feel my veins swelling and my life returning, but more than that was the intimate, internal interplay with the source of this elixir. I was touching this angel of darkness *inside*. So much more than the external physical pleasures of the body, this was the inexplicable sensation of our souls touching, reaching out from within our bodies to merge and dance, swirling around each other in an unimaginable spiritual intercourse."

"Did you realize what was happening?" Chancella asked.

"Not at first but at the touch of her hand on my hair, my eyes fluttered opened and it was then that I saw that she was cradling me much as a mother does a child, and I, likewise, was fastened lovingly to her breast. Even so, I could barely bring into focus the shape of her face as wave upon wave of our soul sex filled my senses whilst her blood filled my veins."

"Then what happened?"

"It stopped and I plummeted harshly down to earth. But the need to return to that sacred place time and time again was now permanently entrenched, tattooed, if you will, into my veins and I had become what I am now and do what we all do, chase and swill the dark dream. That is my existence."

"It doesn't sound all that bad," Chancella offered weakly with a thin smile in an attempt to lessen his gloominess.

"You don't think so?" Valian nearly glared at her. "Watch."

By now they had reached the shoreline of Fire Island. Getting off, they headed to Cherry Grove, one of the more lively beaches on the sprawling sand-dune-like oasis, and walked for a time along the well-populated coastline that became less inhabited as they went until, finally, it appeared they were alone.

"Stop!" Valian suddenly hissed, his arm shooting out to prevent her forward movement.

"What is it?" Chancella whispered, peering intently into the flickering dimness ahead.

Directly after, Chancella could just barely decipher a soft crackling sound mixed in with a low chuckle and murmured conversation. Chancella tensed as she peered around the halted form of Valian. Not a hundred feet away, two men were circling a young girl who was sitting alone in front of a crackling fire.

"Murderers," Valian whispered softly as he crouched down behind a pickup truck that had been driven and parked near the water's edge. Slowly he began to creep forward. Mimicking his movements, Chancella followed close on his heels.

"What?" Chancella gasped, clearly alarmed. "How can you tell?"

"I can smell the blood on their hands."

"But—"

"Sssssh!"

"Hey, whatcha got there?" one of the intruders said, pointing to the book the girl was reading. He was short and stocky, his tight T-shirt and jeans revealing his bulging biceps and thighs, a mean, challenging look glinting within the beady dark eyes.

The girl looked up, clearly startled, and glanced warily from him to his friend, a somewhat taller version of the first with a torn jean jacket and a red bandana tied around his head. Smiling nervously, the girl started to fumble in her pocket, the jangle of keys breaking the silence.

"Oh, just some book."

"Yeah? You like to read, huh?"

The girl, now rising to her feet, refused to look at either of the two menacing males in the eye as she stuffed the novel into a canvas bag and anxiously folded up the blanket she had been sitting on.

"Mm-hmmm."

The intimidating twosome began to slowly close in on the girl, the second man pulling out a flask from inside his jacket and taking a long swig from the metal container.

"What else you like to do?"

The girl, now visibly shaken, didn't answer but only continued hurriedly packing up her belongings.

Chancella shot a nervous sideways glance at Valian, who squatted perfectly motionless beside her, his face and form obscured by shadow until he shifted slightly, the movement briefly illuminating his eyes and the spark of fury within them.

"Huh?" the first man urged as he reached out and stroked the girl's hair. Gasping, she tried to evade the stranger's caress but stumbled back, the contents of her newly-packed bag falling at her feet.

"C'mon, don't be like that. We just wanna have some fun."

"Yeah, you like having fun, don't you?"

The girl started to scream but the stockier one of the two lunged at her, covering her mouth with his hand as he dragged her towards the water's edge, his buddy following to jeer and shout encouragement.

Throwing her to the ground, the one convict grabbed her flailing arms as his friend pinned her body to the ground with his own. The first man released his hand from her mouth only to produce a switchblade from his pocket, the moonlight glinting off its long steel edge.

"Now you shut up or I'll slit your throat wide open."

The girl grimaced, turning her head away, the shine of tears on her cheeks sparkling in the light from the fire.

"Yeah, hey, I wonder what that would feel like?"

"You're about to find out."

Both the two men and Chancella jumped at the snarling threat and turned in unison in the direction of Valian's voice, their eyes widening at the blur of movement that erupted from behind the vehicle.

Chancella stiffened at the rush of movement from her side, watching in a kind of awestruck horror as Valian pounced on the second man, the bandana-covered head yanked back as a flash of fangs was quickly followed by a peculiar gurgling scream. Within seconds the guy's body slithered down the length of Valian's to fall lifeless at his feet, his face smeared with wet sand.

"Fuck me!" the remaining man cried, letting loose of the girl's arms to take off in the opposite direction.

Finally free, the young girl scrambled backwards on all fours, like some sort of retreating inverted crab, her movements impeded somewhat by the sand as she tried to make it back to the fire and her things. But like Chancella, she was mesmerized by the events as they develop.

By now, Valian had turned, his eyes clearly burning with an incensed, infuriated fire as they locked on the rapidly departing form of the remaining assailant. Another blur of motion preceded his catching up to the coward, a wry smile breaking the smooth surface of his pale face as the man, in a crazed, drug-induced bravery, waved the knife in Valian's face.

"C'mon, motherfucker!" he spouted. "Let's see what you can do!"

Valian, his face still and stern, said nothing but only languidly walked towards the man.

"Yeah, that's it. Just keep coming, ya cocksucker. Yeah, it's a whole 'nuther ballgame now, ain't it?"

Seemingly impervious to his taunts, Valian steadily approached, stopping within a foot of the stoned individual. In fact, he didn't even flinch as the man lunged forward and sunk the blade of the knife deep into Valian's chest. Dumbfounded, the man started to back away, the handle of the knife still protruding from Valian's chest.

Chancella screamed, horrified, as she bolted forward but Valian's strong warning stopped her.

"Stay where you are."

Without taking his eyes off the retreating youth, Valian grabbed the knife and pulled it out, letting it drop to land on the sand with a thud. Gap-mouthed, the man continued to back away, his lips trembling.

"What the fuck are you, man? Wh…why are you doing this?"

Valian halted, openly glaring.

"I just wanna have some fun," he mimicked the other's earlier taunt to the frightened female. "You like to have fun — don't you?"

Then in a blaze, Valian dove forward and harshly pulled the man close.

Stunned but mesmerized, Chancella stood watching in a hushed astonishment as Valian set to kill the violent criminal. From only a few feet away, she observed the way Valian held the man so tightly so as to render him helpless, his lean white hand coming up to firmly tilt the struggling victim's head back and to the side. The movement, though rough, was not violent. There was a quiet, nearly purposeful manner in the way Valian spread his lips, his own head tilting back to reveal his bloodied canines, elongating even further. Then with a sharp, sudden movement, he drove forward to embed his teeth in the flesh of the ex-con's throat — his loud gasp filling the night air.

From her vantage point, Chancella couldn't help but feel there was an almost sensual insinuation within the embrace of death as she was seeing it and no sooner had the thought formulated in her mind then Valian shifted slightly, his eyes opening to regard her over the shoulder of his victim. But unlike Jack when he had glared at her while he had drank from the poor punker he had dragged into his lair, deep within Valian's eyes was an unusual desire that quickly translated into a longing, a request, an *invitation*.

Entranced by the call, Chancella barely felt her feet move one in front of the other as she walked towards the entangled pair, her eyes locked in a mesmerizing manner with Valian's. Closer she moved and still he held her with his eyes even as he held his victim, draining the life from him. She stopped finally, so close to him that she could reach out and touch him.

And she did.

The adrenaline pumped so wildly in her system that she was nearly drugged and was quite totally numb. And yet, she could feel her hand lifting, as if in slow motion, to move up and over the criminal's back to stroke the luscious length of Valian's dark hair. The one-time single movement, drawn out and soft as it was, carried with it so much more than words could ever say.

With a sensual breathlessness Valian released the man, but never Chancella's gaze, even as the dead figure fell to the ground and her hand, as if glued, remained delicately fixed on his silken tresses. A spot of fresh blood threatened to swell over the curve of his bottom lip and trickle down his chin.

As Chancella became aware of it, she couldn't stop her fingers from moving across the jut of his chiseled cheekbone to tentatively touch the drop of crimson liquid with her index finger. No sooner had she done so than she felt Valian's cool grasp as he tenderly moved her hand towards his mouth where he slowly sucked the blood from her finger, his eyes never leaving hers.

"Your chest," she said shakily, somehow finding the strength to shift her view from his remarkable face to the torn hole in front of his black satin shirt. "Are you all right?"

In response Valian merely eased her hand, still clasped loosely in his own, down the front of his body and lightly urging her fingers in through the gaping, ripped fabric, he guided her along the smooth, fully healed flesh.

Breathlessly she returned her gaze to his incandescent emerald eyes that now glowed with such intense warmth, she feared she might faint.

Mercifully, the girl who, now crying softly, had "flipped" and crawled on all fours towards her truck, broke the trance. Reaching it, she crouched beside the right front tire, working hard to catch her breath, a slow look of dread seeping onto her face as her eyes once again found Valian.

Chancella turned to him but gasped at the empty space beside her. When she glanced back at the girl, she started at the sight of Valian crouching down beside the terrified teenager and staring intently into her eyes, his pupils seeming to radiate a warm calming light.

Gradually, the girl's expression softened and the dread left her face. Bending down even further towards her, Valian placed both his hands on either side of her face so as to entirely cover her eyes with his palms. For a long moment he held her so, her breath slowing from its quickened state to such a regular, even pace one might think she had fallen asleep. When he withdrew his hands, the girl's eyes gradually opened, a bewildered look upon her youthful face.

"Wha...what happened?" she asked uncertainly.

"Nothing," he replied gently. "You fell asleep reading. You should go home now."

Valian stood up and stepped back, nodding slightly as he offered her his hand.

Cautiously she accepted it, her gaze moving between Chancella and Valian before she gradually moved to the driver's side of the vehicle and, unlocking the door, shakily climbed in. Firing up the engine, she threw the stick shift into drive before speeding away.

Chancella came up beside Valian.

"What did you do to her?"

"There's no sense in her being a victim as well," he said softly. "I just made sure she didn't remember any of this."

"You can do that? You can make people forget you?"

Valian wordlessly nodded. Without thinking, Chancella surged on.

"But why? Why would you do such a thing?"

"It's better than the alternative. It's got to be one or the other."

"Oh."

She let her head drop down on her chest, the sudden overwhelming weight of misery filling her heart and if she wasn't careful, this ridiculous gloom would spill over and down her cheeks in the form of girlish tears. What ever was the matter with her, she wondered, at the same time knowing full well what had struck her so. The thought that she had only a few more days with Valian and then he and every miraculous aspect of him would be wiped clean from her memory forever distressed her terribly. And much to her own amazement, it wasn't because of the valuable data and research information she would lose from this once-in-a-lifetime immortal "specimen." Looking up, she eyed him dejectedly, preparing to ask him to make an exception with her, but his immortal telepathy beat her to the punch.

"Chancella, don't. Please."

"Don't what?" she prompted bitterly as he turned and began walking down the beach.

"Are you going to do that to me when we're finished?" she yelled out, not even knowing if that would be a possibility for him then.

"Are you?" she called after him. "I don't want you to. I want to remember all of this."

He wasn't listening. Or maybe just not answering.

"I want to remember this," she repeated even louder than before as she ran to catch up to him. "I don't want to forget you, Valian!"

* * * * *

When they next entered the lab, the soft shade of lavender in the night sky spoke of the impending dawn. They hadn't spoken the entire trip back, the awkward, raging silence growing unbearable.

"I thought tomorrow I might continue this work at the cabin," Chancella started in lightly. "I have a little place on Lake—"

"I know where it is," Valian responded, his mental prowess once again amazing her. "'til tomorrow," he said, moving towards the door.

"What? You're leaving?"

"I've got to go," he stated matter-of-factly.

"Of course," Chancella said, somewhat dejectedly. "But Valian?"

He turned, watching her expectantly.

"You know what you said about making the choice to become a vampire? Do you regret it?"

"Not in the least. Those first few years as a supernatural being are so new, so exciting and you are truly consumed by everything that you can think of nothing else. So many things come as quite a shock—things that I now take for granted took some time to get used to."

"Like what?"

"The gifts you spoke of earlier—telepathic ability, strength, speed, the ability to fly. It took me a long time to discover all of my dark gifts and then years after to hone and control them. Then there is the task of masking your identity and blending in with humanity. I guess it's an entire process and one that kept me busy for the better part of a century. More than busy—it distracted me."

"But you aren't distracted any more?"

"No. Now I find myself very much in the same situation as when I chose the path in the first place. My life, as it is, no longer holds any interest for me."

Chancella looked perplexed. Reluctantly Valian continued.

"Mortality allows me an end. A finality. You see, I thought living forever would give me some insight or at the very least some means of coping but in the end, this journey has turned out to be nothing more than a diversion."

"So, in essence, you're planning to kill yourself again," Chancella said bitterly, fighting to keep her voice from rising.

Valian only regarded her in silence, a sad look of defeat on his face.

"Is there nothing in this world worth living for?" she demanded in a desperate tone.

"If there is, I haven't found it."

"Oh Val," she looked away, "don't say that. There's so much! Why, think about—"

"What did you call me?" he sharply interrupted.

She stopped distracted by the question, unable to remember. He answered for her.

"You called me Val."

"Did I?"

"Say it again."

She shook her head in confusion.

"What?"

"Say my name, like you just did."

"Val—"

She said it hesitantly, softly, her eyes dropping from his eyes to his lips as she felt an indescribable pull towards him. Without thinking, she reached up and let her fingers delicately touch the fine, ivory cheekbones before moving over to play through the luxurious depths of his hair.

Cocking his head to one side, he studied her, his curiosity at her apparent attraction soon replaced by another emotion and one he couldn't readily identify. Mystified, he allowed her to continue stroking his hair, examining her face as he examined the turmoil that was blazing inside him.

Her skin was so beautifully luminous and delicate, like all mortals, but hers hypnotized him like none other he could recall. And her scent. He inhaled deeply, drawing in the distinctively human smell of flesh, blood, hair and perspiration—all intertwined with the perfume with which she cloaked her body every morning and the sweet subtle fragrance of being a woman.

Suddenly dizzy, he reached out, his hands grasping her delicately on either arm.

"Val," she repeated softly, uncertainly, her knees weakening at the feel of his hand on the small of her back gently pulling her closer.

Lazily his gaze fell from the bright sparkling hazel eyes that, filled with desire and an unspoken question, were locked on his. Down over the straight, narrow nose to the soft, pink lips that were parted in invitation.

Slowly he began to lean forward, the outlandish thought of kissing her reeling him in. It had been over two hundred years since he had locked lips with a mortal, or even had any desire to, but as he descended on her welcoming mouth, he felt a long-time slumbering sensation deep within him stir and awaken.

He leaned closer, their lips almost touching, and then with a ferocious growl he pushed her abruptly away.

"What do you think you're doing?" he demanded angrily.

Shaken, Chancella stared open-mouthed at him.

"Nothing. I, I..."

"Don't go getting any romantic notions about me, Doctor," he spat out crisply. "Have you forgotten what you have just seen?"

"No, of course not, but I thought we—"

"We?" he bellowed. "There is no 'we' and there never can be!"

"How do you know?"

"Do I have to remind you what I am? I'm no better than those butchers I intercepted earlier tonight."

"That's not true!"

"It is! I am a killer! Pure and simple. It's what I do. It's who I am and although I seek to change that, blood is as necessary to me as air is to you. It's in my nature. You would be wise to keep that in mind."

Confused and angered by the feelings of tenderness and desire that she had awakened in him, he stalked from the room but her words followed him, causing him to stop dead in his tracks.

"Yes, but it's not your only nature," Chancella called after his retreating form. He turned slowly then and looked hard at her, his murky green eyes glowing oddly in the light.

"There is goodness in you, Valian," she offered meekly, standing tall under his hard and unwavering gaze. "I can feel it," she added with a barely perceptible shrug, as if in explanation. "You have a good spirit."

"Don't be so sure," was all he said before he stormed out, slamming the door behind him.

Frustrated beyond words, Chancella grabbed the first thing she could get her hands on and hurled it at the steel exitway, the empty glass beaker shattering into a million pieces to shower down upon the light tiled floor.

With a particularly exasperated huff, she retrieved the dustpan and brush from the cupboard and proceeded to the sight of her vented fury. Fine! she thought smugly as she sharply collected the remnants of the smashed container, sweeping the tiny shards of glass agitatedly onto the plastic pan. If Valian wanted to be eternally alone—so be it. She didn't need this. Resolved to put her foolishly emotional thoughts to bed, once and for all, she continued cleaning up the decimated measuring cup, totally unaware of the violent tussle that was taking place on the street below only blocks away...a struggle that ended with Valian's drugged form being dragged rather unceremoniously into Jack's silver Corvette.

Chapter Nine

∞

Nick whistled gleefully as he prepared a batch of Chancella's "life" serum as he sardonically referred to it. He bustled hurriedly about the secret "experimentation" room that was nestled deep in the bowels of the decrepit facility Jack called home. The hidden labyrinth of passageways that led to the remote area had gone undetected since the building was first built. Far below the eleven-story edifice, white-capped waves crashed violently against the cragged rocks that all but engulfed the island hellhole-turned-haven. Shooting a quick glance over his shoulder, Nick grinned at the near-unconscious figure who had been strapped, rather unceremoniously, to the cold gray research slab that had more than once doubled as an autopsy table in the asylum's dark history.

Despite his total disdain for Jack, Nick had to give his eternally arrogant ally credit, for after all, through this entire ordeal he had repeatedly worked his dark magic to supply Nick with whatever tools and assistance he needed. Now as the latter stood peering down the length of Valian's bare torso, he gaily realized he was on his way to fame and fortune.

"But first," Nick whispered softly as he dipped his head under the bizarre shape of the recently installed ultraviolet light fixture, "I want to have a little look-see."

Leaning over the quietly moaning form, Nick surveyed the smooth white plane of Valian's exposed chest, trying to determine where best to insert the tip of the steel-bladed apparatus he held. Hesitating ever so slightly, Nick shot a transient look at his subject's face and in that split second Valian opened his eyes, the pulsing mossy depths serving to freeze Nick's scalpel wielding hand in midair.

"Go ahead," Jack urged from somewhere behind them. "Gut him like a fish."

"I don't want to 'gut' him," Nick snapped, his total disdain for Jack's bloodthirstiness readily apparent. He deeply resented the interference in his work, most especially from the leather-clad individual who was perched, inhumanly, along the top of a tall filing cabinet.

"I want to *study* him," he clarified crisply. "There's bound to be a lifetime of answers in his blood, in his organs, in his tissue. I need time to examine it all!"

"Yeah, whatever," Jack answered smugly.

Ignoring the steady gaze of his specimen, Nick placed the instrument's tip against the taut, smooth skin of Valian's chest and pressed, feeling the blade of the scalpel slice beneath the pearlized flesh. Dragging it downward, he made a two- to three-inch incision, a burst of thick burgundy blood immediately rising up and spilling over the sharp edge to trickle down over Valian's right ribs and begin to form a small pool on the flat surface underneath.

Though Valian winced he didn't make a sound.

Withdrawing the tool, Nick peered closer at the gash he had just made. The blood directly around the wound began to sizzle to some extent, frothing and bubbling as if boiling. Then slowly the gash began to close, starting at the far end and sealing all the way up as if the cut was being drawn together by some sort of invisible zipper.

Nick let out a low, soft whistle — a radically different sound than his earlier trilling.

"Holy shit."

"Yes, remarkable," Jack concurred dryly, looking away in disinterest.

Now all that remained of the gash was the trail of dried blood that had oozed from it. Raising his eyes to Valian's face, Nick stared into the vague depths.

"How'd you do that?"

"It's magic," Jack hissed sarcastically before his voice dropped to a dangerously low pitch. "Now, enough fucking around. How about you do what we're here for?"

"Jesus, what's the hurry? It's not like he doesn't have all the time in the world. We'll turn him into Mr. Mortality in due time, but for now leave me the hell alone so I can examine this supernatural phenomenon."

Within a flash, Jack was at Nick's side, his throat tightly clasped in one strong, pale immortal hand.

"Do you dare to contradict me?" Jack threatened, whispering almost seductively into Nick's ear as he held the struggling form as easily as one might hold a skittish kitten, his cold preternatural tongue flicking out to flit back and forth over the tiny nick his long thumbnail had produced just under Nick's jawbone. "I have had enough of your petty impertinence. Why, I've a good mind to slit your throat from ear to ear and drown myself in the blood that pours from the wound!"

"No, stop—please—I'm sorry, I'm sorry. I'll do as you ask," Nick sputtered out, whimpering as he shook violently within the confines of Jack's one-handed grip.

"You bet you will," Jack growled as he abruptly sent Nick flying the length of the room to crash, with a clatter, into the near empty bookcase opposite.

Cowering, Nick watched him uncertainly as he raised a quavering hand up to touch the minute grazed area on his throat.

"Now," Jack said impetuously, before strolling back and hopping without effort up on top of the tall filing cabinet and back to his panoramic vantage point in that cavalier manner that was so typically his.

Straightening his lab coat, Nick got to his feet and shakily headed back to the table. Reaching into a nearby drawer, he withdrew a thick elastic band, which he tied tightly just above Valian's left elbow before moving to the cupboards across the way.

"What are you doing?" Jack demanded hotly.

"He needs to be knocked out before the serum is administered."

"What for?"

"To minimize any physical or mental stress."

Jack grinned ghoulishly.

"Give him nothing."

"But—"

"Do it!" Jack yelled, his voice booming in the silence of the space.

Nick frowned, wanting to argue the matter further. Experimenting on a conscious specimen was, to say the least, inhumane and he felt a momentary flicker of a nausea-tinged morality hit him as he stood poised over the imprisoned test subject but he knew better than to contrary Jack again.

Filling a syringe with the cloudy white liquid, he injected the serum into the thick protruding blue vein in Valian's forearm, his eyes flying to the latter's face, anxiously awaiting the appearance of any reaction.

At first, nothing seemed to happen and Nick grew perturbed staring at the restrained vampire's face, all the while feeling Jack's hard gaze digging mercilessly into his back. Then slowly, Valian's eyes rolled back in his head and his body began to tremble, not so much a pronounced shudder but more of a quiet vibration, from head to toe, increasing in intensity and progressing steadily into that of something not unlike an epileptic fit.

Thrashing wildly, his arms and legs strained violently against the series of tethers that held him tight as a horrific, low sound began deep in his throat, rising in pitch and volume until the entire room shook with the sound.

Unlike Jack, who sat motionless, staring blankly at Valian's twisting, writhing form, Nick began to back up, his face contorted with disgust as he moved away from the examination table that was bouncing heavily with Valian's involuntary spasms that rose and fell in intensity for the next several minutes.

Finally, after what felt like an eternity for them all, the seizures subsided, leaving Valian exhausted and near unconsciousness.

Wiping at the perspiration that had first appeared as shiny beads on his forehead, soon trickling down either side of his face, Nick panted heavily, steadying himself against the far counter.

"Jesus," he mumbled faintly.

Jack, who had been oddly silent throughout, shut his gaping mouth and, regaining his seldom lost composure, jumped down, landing on the floor with a thud to clap his hands together with one loud resounding smack.

"Woo!" he yelled. "That was good! Hit him again."

"What? Are you crazy?" Nick exclaimed, the words out of his mouth before he had weighed the wisdom, or lack thereof, behind them.

"Give him another shot," Jack said sternly.

"Now I'm not questioning you," Nick began, his hands spread out in self-defense before him, "but you got to understand something. Injection for cell reanimation must be timed correctly. If given too close together, they will cause a permanent reversal of cell reanimation, making any future hope of restoring life to the cell null and void."

Once again the face of the Devil seemed to be staring out at Nick as he heard Jack's scathing reply.

"Yes, I know. That is, after all, the point. Now do it."

* * * * *

The following night Chancella drove out to her cabin on the lake as she had said. Although she had purchased the property as an escape from the hustle and bustle of city life as well as the demands of her work, the small, three-room cedar chalet had been equipped with a fully functional laboratory.

One never knows when one might need to do some research.

Retreating to the woods would allow her a quiet space to work and perhaps some time to think but as always, her curiosity won out. Setting to it almost from the moment she arrived, Chancella got to work further studying Valian's sample and conducting some preliminary experiments on isolated blood cells of his, only to be surprised when, well after two a.m., he had not yet appeared. A couple of times she thought she could sense him there and whirled around, fully expecting to see him standing, silently immobile in the shadows, unnaturally statue-like save for the glimmer of fire that blazed from time to time within the mystical recesses of those unforgettable eyes. But in each case, she was mistaken and, breathing a sigh of both relief and disappointment, she reluctantly returned to her work.

They had nearly quarreled last time and as Chancella tried to focus, she struggled against the worry that she may have overstepped her boundaries with Valian and, consequently, driven him away.

The persistent and increasing pounding in her head reminded her that she had been working too long and too intently without a break. Rotating her head in slow, full circles to loosen the muscles of her neck and shoulders, she peeled off her lab coat and, throwing it over a chair, headed out. A walk in the surrounding woods of the lodge would give her some fresh air that, in turn, would clear her head.

Grabbing the plaid flannel jacket that hung on a worn wrought iron hook near the front door, Chancella stepped out into the chilly night air, the black sky overhead dotted with a million pinpricks of light. She stood on the wooden veranda a few moments, letting her eyes get accustomed to the light, or lack thereof. Striding forward, she felt the soft moist earth cushion her footsteps as she headed into the well-trodden path that led through the dense forest of pines and spruce that served to hide the secluded cottage from the main roadway.

Not long into her late-night saunter, Chancella was startled by the unexpected appearance of someone and not, as it turned out, the someone she had been waiting for.

"Dr. Tremaine?"

The small, thin voice that reached her from behind drifted across the dark, wooded area hesitantly and was clearly laced with the sound of apprehension. Chancella pivoted and peered down along the worn trail that was only briefly illuminated by the soft glow of moonlight.

"Who is it?" she asked fearfully.

A slender figure emerged from the ghostly woodland but despite the sense of familiarity that began to tug at her memory, she could not put a name to the youthful face.

"Who are you?" Chancella asked again, warily taking a step backward as the young man walked towards her.

"I was at the lecture at the university last week," he answered gently, a shaky smile creasing the boyishly smooth skin of his cheeks but not quite making it to his eyes.

Chancella stared at the slight form blankly, her heart starting to pound at the realization that he was steadily approaching her.

"Lecture?" she asked weakly.

"I asked you for your help," he said with a small shrug of his slender shoulders. "Remember?"

Just as thoughts of the notorious horror-in-the-woods story, *The Texas Chainsaw Massacre*, darted through her mind, the memory of the young man rallied forward.

"Right," Chancella said sluggishly, recalling more specifically that the guy had been terrified at the existence of a vampire that was, what was it again? Oh yes. Blackmailing him.

At the recollection, Chancella abruptly ceased her withdrawal from the tentative-looking figure as her fear at the inexplicable appearance of the young man at her private residence was quickly replaced by curiosity.

"What did you say your name was again?"

"Rio," he said gently. Then almost as an afterthought he added, "And this is Simarone."

He motioned over his shoulder and out from behind the trunk of a particularly large spruce tree stepped a youth who was, even in the dim light of the moon, quite simply the most mesmerizing adolescent Chancella had ever seen. His smooth olive skin and innocent, androgynous beauty, tinged with an exotic flavor, gave him the definitive air of an angel—granted one that hailed from the island of Tahiti or the shores of Malta or quite possibly a bit of both. Chancella almost gasped as she noted how the sleek strands of his long dark hair kept falling with titillating frequency across his openly vulnerable face. When he spoke, his voice was as rich and warm as the soulful brown eyes that observed her and in that instant, she knew he was a vampire.

"We have to talk to you."

"About what?" Chancella asked nervously, her gaze moving quickly from one to the other. Rio started again.

"Valian."

"Valian?" Chancella bristled. "What about him?"

"He's in trouble."

"What kind of trouble?" she resisted shrieking as her heart rate kicked into overdrive.

"Jack and your friend Nick have taken him."

Chancella stared at Rio blankly for a long moment.

"Nick Lewis?"

Rio nodded wordlessly. Chancella shook her head irately in confusion.

"Taken him? What do you mean? And what's Nick got to do with this?"

Simarone spoke then, the low monotone of his voice raising the hairs on the back of Chancella's neck in an odd combination of fear and arousal.

"Your friend Nick wanted a 'live' vampire to prove your theories on but Jack—Jack just wants to hurt Valian any way possible." He finished, the words trailing off as he grimaced in a most unusual way when he said Valian's name, as if the utterance itself physically hurt him.

Distracted, Chancella turned back to Rio at the sound of his heavy sigh and listened intently as he related the whole story, starting first with Jack's "proposition," the night at Dantes and finally, cracking Chancella's computer code and his near-death experience in the desert with Jack's fledgling bitches.

Rio looked at Chancella expectantly. She had just shot a quick glance in Simarone's direction, which confirmed her suspicions he was watching her as keenly as she had been Rio, and with such a forceful, mesmerizing stillness that she found it hard to look away. In fact, it was not unlike the way Valian often held her transfixed with his eyes. Begrudgingly she looked away, smoothing an errant hair back from her forehead as she frowned. The pieces slowly began to fall into place and above it all was the gut-wrenching knowledge that Nick had set out to undermine her. Fighting back a sudden urge to cry, she squared her shoulders and, clearing her throat, fought to get the facts.

"There's something here I just don't understand," Chancella frowned, hoping against hope that she had misunderstood her assistant's involvement. "How did Nick know of Valian's existence?"

"He didn't—not at first," Simarone answered. "It was all Jack."

Chancella repressed a shudder of disgust and horror at the recollection of Jack's tongue on her body and the way his cold topaz eyes dug into her with a tangible burning hatred.

"From what I can tell, Jack guessed that your book would lure Valian out into the open, something he himself had been trying to do for decades but with no success. Unfortunately, he guessed right." His chocolate brown eyes seemed to darken and sparkle in the moonlight as he spoke.

"I see," Chancella answered softly, a spasm of guilt stabbing sharply in the pit of her stomach.

"Yeah, then once exposed, he would use me to get the serum and your friend Nick to administer it in such a way that it would create the most damage," Rio concluded.

"Stop calling him my friend!" Chancella burst out angrily. "And what do you mean, 'the most damage'?"

"We don't know yet," Simarone answered, "but Jack is determined to stand in the way of Valian's quest for mortality and he somehow must've found a way."

"Hmmm," Chancella pondered a moment before once again turning her attention to Rio.

"And Jack *told* you all this?"

"No," Rio said, motioning towards his companion. "Once we came clean with each other, Simarone pieced it together."

There was something in the way Rio had said *come clean* that revealed that he had only recently been made aware of Simarone's true identity. Even in the dim light of the moon, Chancella noticed how Rio reached out to fleetingly touch Simarone's hand and as her gaze flew up to meet the dark one's face, she immediately knew their situation.

Chancella sighed deeply, thinking back to the first time she had encountered the fair-haired youth.

"God, I'm so sorry. I should have paid more attention to you that day. Maybe we could've prevented this. But why didn't you tell me everything at the lecture?"

"I didn't know that *you* were going to be used by Jack like the rest of us. I swear to God I didn't know! I just went there because I figured you were an expert and if anybody knew how to stop a vampire, it would be you! I was so terrified of the fucking things I would've done anything to keep my distance!"

He and Simarone exchanged a lengthy look.

"My thinking has changed a lot since then," he said with an air of certainty and a slight smile towards Simarone.

"Besides," Rio continued, "I couldn't talk to you with all those people there…too many ears. It just wasn't the right time."

"And all of this because of my book," Chancella nearly moaned as another pang of remorse overcame her.

"Look, we're not here to make you feel bad," Simarone said flatly, that cool, silken voice strangely engulfing her in a sea of satin. "That's not why we came."

"So why did you?"

His eyes locked with hers then and in the faint glow of the moon, Chancella thought she could see the shimmer of tears brimming within the sullen rich darkness of his supernatural eyes.

"I know where Valian is."

"And?"

"If we work together, we can get him out."

Uncomprehending, Chancella could only shake her head.

"Rio can get us in and I'll take care of Jack, so you can get out."

"So what do I do?"

"Just be there."

"But I want to help."

"You will—just by being there."

"I don't understand."

"Chancella," Simarone began, "Valian has tried to keep it from me but I have sensed his despair all along. I know he has lost hope in everything and sought you out to put an end to it all. But the truth is that although he thrashes wildly against it, after an eternity of pain and despair, someone has given him reason to question his course of action."

"Who?"

Simarone hesitated.

"Tell me!" Chancella all but shouted. "Who has made him reconsider?"

"You, Chancella. It's you."

* * * * *

Chancella moved through the dark, winding passageway, her hands feeling along the cold cement walls as she went. She could barely make out the shape of Rio's form ahead that maneuvered along the dim labyrinth, the only solid indication of the guy's presence found in the soft scratching sound of his sandals on the floor. Somewhere behind her, Simarone was bringing up the rear but as Chancella had recently witnessed, the dark-haired youth's movements were as languid and smooth as fog and twice as quiet.

Chancella shivered, the chilled, damp air permeating her bones. They must be near a water supply for she could hear the distant, musical tinkle of water trickling down somewhere.

Bam! She smacked her head against the wall as they came to yet another dead end, Simarone's softly whispered directive arriving a moment too late.

"Turn right. This way."

With a hand placed to her scraped forehead, Chancella obeyed, continuing her blind search. Seconds later, she ran into the back of Rio.

"Geez!" she exclaimed quietly.

"Sorry," Rio offered under his breath. "It's here."

"What is?"

"The door to the secret passageway."

With a tentative hand, Chancella reached out and felt the unmistakable texture of a steel lever. She let her hand move down the hard, cold plane of the angular metal wand.

"Don't touch it!" Rio hissed. "You'll trip the alarm!"

"Alarm? This place must be a hundred years old!"

"You'd be surprised what kind of systems were installed here in the '50s and how long they can last."

"Besides, Jack would have done something to ensure his privacy," Simarone offered quietly.

His explanation was followed by a small, narrow beam of illumination from the mini flashlight Rio had used to guide them.

"Here," he directed at Chancella. "Hold this while I find the wires. Now there could be a motion detector in this, so whatever you do, don't move!"

Chancella wordlessly complied, her heart pounding so loud that she was certain that the sound itself would set the alarm off.

Seconds passed with only the sound of the odd click from Rio as he worked to separate and deactivate the security system. Chancella could feel a thin line of perspiration travel from the base of her neck, trickling slowly down between her shoulder blades. Steeling herself, she resisted a shudder.

A loud click preceded the sound of Rio's pronounced exhale.

"That's it," he whispered. "We're in."

The soft pressure of Rio's body as he backed up a step sent Chancella backing up and she was directly sandwiched between him and Simarone. Vaguely, she became aware of the latter's feathery cool touch on either side of her shoulders as he steered her delicately towards the doorway.

Turning the knob, Chancella followed Rio through the darkened space, easing the heavy metal door shut behind her, immediately squinting into the darkness. Directly in front of them was a dimly lit hallway that had all the makings of a sterile hospital ward, the long narrow passageway breaking off on each side into separate rooms, the contents of each private cell visible through large glass windows.

Tiptoeing, they moved along, careful that their footsteps on the whitewashed tile floor didn't make any sound.

Down they silently made their way along the prison-like corridor that branched off into separate dingy cells.

"What is this place?" Chancella's voice buzzed lightly in the quiet area.

"After the asylum closed in the '50s, for a time it was an underground, top secret holding bay, a catchall for the mess-ups, cover-ups and everything in between. Aliens, geniuses and freaks. Considering what he is, it's fitting that Jack lives here."

Simarone raised a dark eyebrow in question.

"Sorry, man," Rio offered to Simarone, reaching over Chancella to pat him lightly on the shoulder.

"And you're sure Valian's here?" Chancella murmured quietly.

"He's here," Simarone's voice brushed her from behind as they came to a halt in front of the last door.

Up to this point, Chancella had battled with Valian's true identity even though she had witnessed it with her own eyes, and yet she just couldn't believe that Jack and Valian were the same species. In her mind's eye, she recalled the sight of Valian leaping high in the air with such an obviously inhuman strength and speed that she could only gawk, open-mouthed in a shock-tinged awe. Or how his beautiful, ever-changing eyes could take on a horrifying glaze and intensity when he was enraged or the sensual fire of passion when he fed.

And yet none of these telltale proofs filled her with the sense of dread or terror that Jack did. So obviously and deeply excited by the horror which he struck in each one of his victim's hearts was he, that abhorrent, perverse pleasure he took in baiting and trifling them blazing in his cat yellow eyes. Even the pure, animalistic act of feeding played over and over again in Chancella's mind and she shuddered at the recollection of the spurting blood and tearing flesh brought on by his crazed frenzy.

No, though she fought against the rationalization, she couldn't help feeling that although Jack and Valian were in one respect the same…in another, they couldn't be more different.

The loud snap to her right indicated that Rio had disarmed another alarm and with the last barrier freed, the trio entered the secret back room where Chancella stopped short, her heart jumping at the sight before her.

The room was uninhabited except for Valian, who was hunched over on a large table, his arms encircling his legs which he drew up close to his chest, his head hidden beneath their cover. Several dozen thick leather straps that had been used to confine each one of his limbs and four even thicker straps that ran across his torso had been broken, some literally ripped from their bearings. A gigantic overhead circular lamp, as used in operating rooms, had been fitted with single ray attachments, stretching out in all directions like some sort of high-tech octopus.

From each appendage as well as its circular center were fitted the high-voltage ultraviolet lights that created an invariable labyrinth of lethal light around Valian's imprisoned form. Staring in disbelief, Chancella knew, as did Valian, their intended purpose. One wrong move into but one of the myriad of soft purple rays and his flesh would first sizzle, then bubble and blister until finally igniting into flame.

Her heart twisted at her sight of his forlorn form, the distress coming in strong tangible pulsations of pain and a bitter shame.

As if her thoughts were silently communicated to him, he slowly raised his head, her eyes locking with his — now a faded shade of khaki, their light hue all the more accentuated by the redness of his eyelids. Clearly the lights were hurting him, even from a safe distance. His normal pale complexion was now a sickly gray tone except for the darkened areas in the pronounced caverns under his eyes and cheekbones. The unnourished skin had begun to shrivel and dry up, the lack of blood literally starving him.

Without warning, Simarone bounded towards Valian, the latter's fiercely shouted warning of "No, don't!" failing to stop the exuberant youth.

A searing howl pierced the silence of the area as the younger vampire leapt back, his hands flying up as he fell to his knees. Covering his face, he rocked back and forth in obvious pain, a thin wisp of smoke spiraling up from between his quivering fingers.

Easing Rio gently away from Simarone's side where he had rushed to, his arms protectively encircling his lover, Chancella knelt down beside the injured vampire, murmuring softly as she lightly rubbed his shoulder.

"It's okay. Let me see."

Delicately edging his fingers away from the area that had been exposed to the lethal rays, she examined the blistering skin. The burn that covered a portion of his forehead and down along the left side of his face was now black and severely blistered, nearly corrugated as the skin had tightened and shrunk with the heat, pulling his left eye almost shut in the process. Feeling her knees tremble underneath her, Chancella worked hard to stifle her gag reflex as she attended to Simarone, ignoring the smoke and the sickeningly strong smell of burnt tissue that oozed from the wound itself.

"Gimme your T-shirt," she said abruptly to Rio.

"What?"

"Your T-shirt—hurry!"

Complying, Rio peeled off his jean jacket and whipped off the white garment and handed it to Chancella. She then raced to the sink across the way, the dirty water sputtering out in dribs and drabs before bursting out full force to douse the cotton fabric with cold water. Wringing it out thoroughly, she crouched down beside Simarone and lightly pressed the makeshift compress to his face.

"Hold this here," she ordered softly, her eyes suddenly filling with tears as she looked past Simarone's doubled-over form to lock eyes with Rio.

"I don't know how to help him," she whispered miserably as Simarone's agonized moan rose and fell in softly cascading crescendos.

"I do."

Pushing her aside, he maneuvered Simarone up to a partial sitting position and pulling him close, embraced him loosely so his head was in line with the curve of Rio's bare shoulder.

"Come on, man. C'mon," Rio coaxed soothingly, one hand tight around Simarone's waist while the other glided up around to the uncharred side of his friend's face. Tilting his chin up, Rio dragged his thumb over Simarone's lips so as to part them and then leaning in, pressed the curve of that region where his neck met his shoulder firmly against Simarone's open mouth.

"Do it, man. C'mon. Hurry," Rio said softly, tensing only slightly as he felt Simarone shift.

Spellbound, Chancella held her breath, entranced by the voluntary exchange that was about to take place.

Simarone's head fell back slightly but it was enough for Chancella to see his mouth opening wide, exposing his vampire teeth that were thickening and elongating before her very eyes, the gums around them tearing and bleeding so as to accommodate their growth.

Lurching forward, he bit down forcibly into Rio's tender flesh, his lips quickly closing around the wound but continuing to move in a rhythmic wave of suction. At that precise moment, Rio had reached out for Chancella, his fingers clamping tight around her wrist. Save for the initial gasp at the point of entry, he was silent, his eyes fluttering soft in a near swoon of pleasure and his head tilting down to gently rest atop Simarone's as his muffled moans of need and desire drifted out softly.

Overcome by the odd experience, Chancella watched in fascination, drawn in by the fantastic unity and the power of the passion that coursed between the two young men. Oddly paralyzed by the unlikely threesome, she looked at Valian, their eyes then locking with such intensity that she felt her heart would pound out of her chest in response. Confused by the bizarre mixture of sorrow, fear and desire that vied for dominance within her, she turned once more to the sound of faint murmurs to her right.

Simarone was sitting straight up now and the two young men were talking softly. Reaching forward, Simarone delicately touched Rio's face before planting a tender kiss on his lips. When he turned to face Chancella, she couldn't help but exclaim out loud.

Though still scorched, his skin had already begun a remarkable recovery, the former blackness of the charred flesh having lessened to a deep gray and the bulbous swell of the blisters shrinking considerably. His left eye now was almost entirely open, the surrounding skin having being nourished and moisturized enough to allow the movement.

Unable to speak, she stared in wonder at the sullen dark angel who was making an impossible revival and as she did so, she heard the words radiate from her very soul, resounding over and over again in her head and fervently hoped that Valian could hear them. But so much more than that, she hoped he would *accept* them.

I'm sorry for all of this. I'm so very sorry.

The words that met her ears were not what she was expecting.

"Well, well, well. You just love to play doctor, don't you? But you're working on the wrong specimen. Over here, Chance, together we can show the world what an incredible talent we are and prove, once and for all, that life can be eternal."

Starting, Chancella looked over, her sorrow dissolving into a fiery anger that melted back to sorrow again at the sight of Nick and the sarcastic smirk that covered his pinched face. Trying to still her fiercely trembling mouth, she implored her backstabbing protégé.

"Nick, why?"

"Ah, gimme me a break. You would've done the exact same thing as me if presented with the opportunity first and don't pretend you wouldn't. The chance to try out your theories for real, come on! I know you, Chancella. You and I are the same."

"Only the same species but that's where the similarity ends."

"Bullshit!"

"Nick, I know what you're saying and yes, this is an incredible opportunity, an unbelievable prospect but—"

"There are no buts! You are a scientist and as much as you want to deny it, you are dying to dissect Dracula over there just as much if not more than I am!"

Chancella lowered her eyes, a rush of embarrassment coloring her face as she softly spoke.

"You're right," she said sadly, her stunning admission drawing a gasp of shock from Rio. "There was a time when that would've been true, when the need to unravel and study and break down every little nuance of this, this being was a priority."

Her voice broke and she shyly raised her gaze to Valian's, directly taking strength from the expression of warmth within the fading green of his eyes.

"But not anymore."

"What do you mean? This *thing* is a cold-blooded murderer, a premeditating assassin of human life. If for no other reason, he should get a little taste of what he's been dishing out for years!"

"I don't care."

"Say what?"

"I said I don't care what he is or what he's done." She drew in a sharp breath. "I'm going to help him in any way I can and that means standing between you and him if necessary."

"You can't be serious!"

"But I am."

"You think another bloodsucker is going to just show up on your doorstep tomorrow? Chance, for the love of God, think!"

"Not this time," she smiled. "This time, I'm going with my heart."

Nick's face dissolved into a look of sheer hatred as he ran at Chancella, but Rio intercepted him, a wild, impassioned cry of rage rising from deep within and breaking free from his throat as he ran headlong into his unsuspecting peer, knocking him down.

"Fucking prick!" Nick spat as he struggled up on one knee. Rio, standing tall over him, didn't even let him get to his feet, he just hauled off and cold-cocked Nick flush alongside the head, knocking him out.

"Back at ya, asshole!" he sneered over his shoulder en route to taking his place at Simarone's side.

Rising, Chancella headed straight for Valian, a sudden desire to reassure him fueling her.

"Noooo!" he shrieked at the top of his lungs, the shrill, hyena-like wail threatening to break her eardrums. Her hands clasped on either side of her head, she collapsed on the floor, waiting for the piercing noise to stop. Stunned, she stared uncomprehending into Valian's terrified face, her arms slowly dropping to her sides.

"What is it?" she cried.

"Get back," Simarone warned sternly from the floor. "Don't go near him. The need is upon him and you risk your life getting too close."

"But—"

"Listen to me," Valian pleaded, his cracked low voice barely above a whisper as his eyes entreated her. "Stay away from me."

Chancella's face grew hard and unrelenting and as she spoke, she steeled herself for a following protest.

"No, you listen to me. I got you into this and I'm going to get you out."

Then with a wide, looping motion of her arm, she indicated the two that stood behind her. "No, actually, *we're* going to."

Valian locked eyes with Simarone for a long time and although Chancella couldn't know the nature of their union, she could feel the strength of the emotion that coursed between the two.

When Valian next spoke, his voice sounded almost hopeful.

"What's the plan?"

Just then, a thunderous wail assaulted the group, shaking the very floor that they stood on and shattering the bulbs of the man-made light structure that had kept Valian captive, shards of glass spraying in a million different directions.

Leaping to his feet, Valian ran unsteadily to Simarone. Pulling him swiftly up, he reached for Chancella's hand and made for the door.

"What the hell is that?" Rio shouted over the blare.

With Chancella and Simarone in hand, Valian made for the door, answering over his shoulder as they went.

"It's Jack."

Chapter Ten

ஐ

Chancella and Valian raced down the sinister darkness of the cold corridor, the sound of their feet scuffling along the damp cement floor echoing through the narrow passageway. After a very quick vote of everyone present, they had decided, mortal and immortal alike, that it would be stupid to wait and confront Jack, especially considering that the effect of Valian's repeated exposure to the serum had not yet been determined. The two archenemies' long overdue showdown would just have to wait for another time.

Or perhaps sooner than they would've liked, for as they felt their way along the hall's rough walls, desperately hoping that they would find an exit, Chancella's heart fell at the sound of Jack's sadistic call.

"V-a-l-i-a-n, where are you?"

Somewhere along the dark, twisting maze of hallways that ran through the underground labyrinth of the building, they had taken one sharp turn too many and were separated from Simarone and Rio, and now Chancella grew truly frightened at the sound of Valian's heavy, labored breath.

Stopping, Chancella reached back for Valian and felt along the jagged edge of the wall, her knuckles scraping against the sharp surface. Gasping, she jerked her hand away and although it was far too dim to see, she could clearly feel the warm moisture on her skin as fresh spots of blood poked out over the scuffed skin in miniscule polka dots that swelled into spherical red shapes. Gingerly reaching out again, her hand fumbled then closed around the cold, clammy flesh of Valian's forearm.

No sooner had she touched him than she heard another noise erupt from him, a half cry, half growl. Harshly he grabbed her, his fingers digging painfully into her flesh as he jerked her wrist upwards, her fingers and knuckles immediately bathed in the moist coolness of his mouth as he sucked hungrily on her bleeding skin.

"Val," she whispered awkwardly, peering intently into the darkness that masked him from her eyes. "Don't. Please."

The strong rhythmic pull of his mouth on her hand first lessened and then ceased altogether, following which came the scratchy sound of fabric against stone and a heavy thud and in her mind's eye, Chancella saw him sliding down to fall slumped against the wall. When he spoke, the gentle hiss of his voice sounded freakishly loud in the blackened space.

"I can't. You go on the way we've been heading. The entrance to the main building must be near."

"I'm not leaving you now," Chancella said defiantly as she reached for his arm and began pulling him up, her eyes growing accustomed to their dark surroundings.

"You're not listening," he said angrily. "I can't. I haven't the strength."

Just then Jack appeared.

"Oh now isn't this sweet? And how symbiotic! Why, first he rescues you and then you rescue him. Must be true love."

"Absolutely," Chancella angrily spat out from between clenched teeth, her heartfelt admission drawing a gentle look from Valian.

"Indeed?" Jack answered coolly. "But before you plan the wedding, there are a few things you should know about your knight in shining armor. In fact, his armor is not shining at all but rather it is tarnished and tainted with the blood of the innocent — irreparably stained and blackened — almost as much as your godforsaken soul."

"That's funny coming from you, Jacariaith," Valian smirked. "Have you forgotten the path that you yourself have chosen?"

"One must wage war against his enemies on that battleground they have taken refuge in, following them to smite and obliterate them in their elected sanctuary."

"Spare me your impassioned proclamations. You always had such a flare for the dramatic but I'm afraid it's been wasted on me."

"That's stating the obvious."

"Your pious rhetoric is best saved for the pulpit. Perhaps you can work the evils of abandoning your faith into your next sermon, eh, Jacariaith?" Valian paused. "Or should I say 'Father'?"

He nearly whispered the last word, that foreign expression once again blazing in his eyes and darkening his brow. Staring hard at him, Chancella soon identified the seldom seen emotion.

It was *pity*.

"Could I not call you the same?" Jack growled, taking a warning step forward.

"No longer. It was never the life for you and I knew it almost from the moment I joined the church but you...you were born to be a priest. Why ever would you leave your destiny?"

"You know damn well why!"

"Oh yes, Arianna. The woman you loved enough to leave the priesthood for. Only she left you before you had the chance."

This revelation of the dark and twisted history that existed between Jack and Valian hit Chancella hard. In a motion of exasperation she released him with a huff, flinging her arms heavenward in a sharp single flailing jerk as if to say to the powers that be "What more can you send us?" The movement caused her wrist to connect, rather painfully, with a cold metal lever just up over her left shoulder.

Whirling to face it, she eased herself forward, both hands now feeling against the harsh textured wall for the cold, silky feel of the metal wand. Pulling it down with both hands, she heard a slow, grinding noise and felt the wall in front of her give way and begin to move.

It seemed to take forever for the foot-thick barrier to slide its width to the side but when it finally stopped, a winding staircase only slightly better lit than the medieval corridor they stood in, complete with a metal handrail, spiraled up and out of sight.

"C'mon, let's go," she murmured, and not thinking, grasped Valian's hand once more in her own, pulling him towards the opening, and although Jack remained strangely fixed in place, his wailing threat followed them as they went.

"Yes, run where you will, Valian, but you will never be able to escape the truth of what you are and what you will now always be!"

Up five flights they wound until they were soon staring at a heavy wooden door blocking their escape. Chancella reached out and tried the knob but, not surprisingly, found it to be locked and, strangely enough, from the outside.

"I guess this is the kind of place they tried to keep people in, not out," she huffed, exhausted by the many trials that had risen to foil them along the way.

Without a word, Valian reached over and, grasping the doorknob firmly, began to turn it slowly, his worn, pale face a mask of exertion and pain. A high, squealing whine leaked from the doorframe before it shuddered and burst open, splinters of wood and remnants of the metal knob flying in a multitude of directions.

Charging out, they found themselves on the rooftop of the castlelike structure, stories high above the lawn below with only the other Amazonian buildings of the deserted compound, crowding in like curious children, to keep them company.

Jack's eerie, mournful wail drew closer, reminding them that to go back the way they came was not an option.

"You can't escape what you are and I've seen to it that you will suffer for all eternity."

A cursory glance around confirmed Chancella's worst fears—this was the only way out from the dungeon-like hell of the secret laboratory and now they were trapped. Looking at Valian, she knew they were done for.

For where once his sleek black hair glistened and shone, now it hung in limp, dry tufts. His skin, once so luminous, so beautiful to behold, too, hung in loose, sickly flabs of green and gray flesh, his skeletal form emerging in an almost grotesque shape under the starving skin. And his eyes, once things of wonder, now beheld her with a dead, solemn lifelessness, their khaki depths cold as stone.

"What are we going to do, Valian?"

He only shook his head and looked down, defeated.

The thought was suddenly in her mind and then she was by his side, urging his gaze up from the ground to meet her eyes with a gently crooked index finger under his chin. Angling her head to one side, she spoke the one word, the only word that would save them.

"Drink."

His eyes widened and he began to back away, seemingly repulsed by the notion.

"No," he shook his head again, but this time more vehemently. "I won't."

"Please, Valian," she pleaded, moving towards him once again. "Don't you see, it's the only way. He's coming and I need your help. I can't do it alone. *Please.*"

She stepped forward until they were almost touching and in a slow, seductive move, tilted her chin down and to the side to expose the curve of her neck.

"Do it," she urged softly.

Unable to resist, Valian needed no further invitation. Grabbing her roughly, he pulled her to him, the force of the movement crushing her breasts against his chest and with a soft cry of surrender, he dug his teeth into the soft pliable flesh of her throat.

Chancella stifled a scream as she felt the pinprick wounds tear to wider lesions that throbbed with an intense, itchy hurt. Valian's arms, initially clamped like two steel vises around her back, relaxed ever so slightly to hold her more tenderly, one hand coming up to cradle the nape of her neck. Chancella leaned back fully into his arms, relishing the shift in his vampire kiss from pain to pleasure. His soft groans, floating faint and intermittently up to her ears, only increased her rapture and she found her arms reaching out and returning his embrace, her fingers playing ever so gently through the dark tresses that, as he drank, regained their sheen and texture.

Forever he held her, with nothing but the warm pressure of his mouth on her throat, his lips and tongue moving in such a way that, even within the confines of his mouth, titillated her. A soft winded moan escaped her lips as she felt wave upon wave of liquid fire being threaded through her neck.

Then as dramatically as he had seized her, it stopped.

Chancella groggily opened her eyes and gaped in wonder at the transfixed form before her. No longer was he the scruffy, sickly figure made frail by the serum but rather, the Valian she had first laid eyes on in the restaurant...handsome, mesmerizing, *alive*.

The blood loss made her dizzy and she began to faint even as Jack's cry of enraged frustration grew dangerously close.

"What do we do?" Chancella mumbled, trying desperately to keep her head from slumping forward onto his shoulder. Blinking to clear her head, she drew in a shaky breath and stared warily at the doorway from where they had just come. "Can you fight him?"

Valian smirked and despite her wooziness she could see that his charm was back—front and center.

"Yes. But I'm not going to."

"Huh?"

She began to tremble as Valian led her over to the edge of the roof. Looking down, she screamed and backed away, her vertigo reeling her head and turning the butterflies in her stomachs to eagles. The eleven-story building was not one for the faint of heart. Turning abruptly to Valian, she recognized the familiar deadpan, emotionless expression that usually adorned the handsome face.

"Hold onto me," he said resolutely.

"Wha...what?" she stuttered.

He stared at her wordlessly as he took a step towards her, their faces mere inches apart.

"Do it," he commanded flatly.

Self-consciously, she lifted her arms and gingerly placed them on either side of his neck, her eyes glued to the ground.

"Tighter."

No sooner had she clasped her hands behind his head, lightly pressing her face against the side of his that was now warm with her blood, than they lifted up in one glorious, speedy motion, knocking the wind of Chancella.

Looking down, she saw Jack burst out onto the rooftop, the wind whipping his pale hair about his wicked, barbaric face, which was now filled with an odd satisfaction. Shouting up at them, his haunting words were carried on the wind, chilling Chancella even more than the night air that sped past them.

"Run where you will, Valian, but the damage is already done. Your pain will live on forever and so, my friend, shall you."

Turning away, she buried her head in Valian's shoulder and tried to tighten her grip but just then, Chancella let out a high-pitched scream as she felt her hands, wet with perspiration, starting to loosen their deathlike grip on her dark pilot.

"I...I can't hold on...I'm going to fall. Aaaaaaaah!"

Before she could stop it, her hands had ripped apart, leaving her to fall down the length of Valian's body, her arms flailing wildly while her fingers scrabbled recklessly for something to grab onto. In one furious flash she slid down him, bumping and bruising against his hard body, first over the swell of his chest, then along the lean, hard muscles of his abdomen and down over his crotch. Her face was just opposite his powerful thighs when his hand strongly closed around one of her thrashing wrists. Like a dog that had reached the end of its rope and was jerked back, pulling her up to eye level.

In a second, Valian adjusted his body and flung her around so that he held her in front of him, the force and suddenness of the move urging another series of squeals from Chancella.

But then there was nothing but the silent world zooming past them as they coursed among the very stars. Chancella began to look around, shivering intently from the wind as she leaned into Valian's strong form still warm from her liquid gift to him.

They ran headlong into all kinds of clouds, wispy tentacles of fog and haze to thick, blinding billows of cotton, through the dark, azure blue of the evening sky to the swirling mists of the atmosphere and the glittering, blinding spectacle of the stars. Far beneath them was a city, a country and a world but here, high above it all and safe in the solid sanctuary of his arms, there was only their two souls.

So this is heaven, she thought to herself, reveling in the rapturous state their angelic flight induced. Closing her eyes, she enjoyed the disembodied sensation, her spirit drifting out free and unencumbered by the heavy trappings of her material body.

This is so unbelievably beautiful.

The whispered response that echoed within her immediately opened her eyes.

So are you.

Looking at Valian, she could see that newfound warmth flicker within his astonishing eyes and without a moment's hesitation she leaned forward to plant a single, warm, moist kiss on his full pale lips. She was delighted at the realization that this time he was not pulling away but rather, kissing her back.

Down through the purple and yellow and red spiraling vapors, on past the heavens' lights through the royal velvet night sky to where, not long after, non-descript shapes began to form far beneath them. Chancella watched in amazement as the grids and divisions of land began to take shape before her very human eyes - tiny houses and cars and buildings and soon even miniscule scurrying animals appeared, which she soon recognized as people materializing below.

Clinging to Valian, she felt their speed slow as the wind no longer whipped her hair back from her face but rather sent it in soft drifting waves about her eyes and mouth. She saw the hard cement rooftop rushing up to meet them and she unconsciously squeezed her eyes shut at the imminent collision.

Then there she was, dizzy and disoriented, the way one often becomes when a fast, prolonged movement ends abruptly.

Opening her eyes, she realized that they had touched down and from whence they came, so had they returned, for now they stood on the rooftop of another multi-story building.

"Thank you," was all she could muster, a swell of emotion buckling her knees.

Valian frowned, not understanding.

"For what?"

Chancella could only motion slightly.

"For the ride."

He stared at her as if trying to digest the full impact of her words. Then he smiled.

"Where are we? Is this your home?" she asked breathlessly, glancing around the unfamiliar area.

"I have no home."

* * * * *

"Lights out!" the guard barked a split second before the holding cells went black.

"C'mon. Let me outta here," Nick whined as he tried to wedge his face between the bars of the prison cell to peer down the length of the darkened corridor, his fingers tightly clasping the icy metal poles.

Down the way, too far for him to see, a voice mimicked his, the affected girlish, petty tone not quite able to hide the drunken state of the speaker.

"C'mon. Let me outta here," the sarcastic, disembodied echo drifted up the length of the dim hall to his ears, the slurred words that had began as a boom fell away to a hushed whisper.

"Shut up!" Nick exploded, banging futilely at the bars in frustration. "This is a mistake! I didn't do anything! I'm not drunk and I'm not insane! There is a vampire out there and he's going to kill me."

The only answer he got was a low, soft laugh that came from the vicinity of the drunk tank.

"I told you to shut up, you goddamn lush!" he screamed in the direction of the sound.

Nothing.

Probably passed out. What a loser. Life was unfair. Here he was, one of the most brilliant minds in the world today and he was surrounded by druggies, drunkards and murderers.

Perfect.

Heaving a sigh, he pulled up his shirtsleeve and looked at his left wrist where his watch normally was. Damn it. He forgot. Force of habit. They had taken all his personal effects when he was brought in. So what time was it? He must've been here for nearly twelve hours already. So it would be, what? Three a.m.? Four? Clearly, he was going to have to spend the night but tomorrow, he would get his one phone call.

They had to give it to him, right? It was a law, wasn't it? Of course it was. They couldn't hold him against his will without giving him his one goddamn phone call—this was America and by God, after that, the shit was going to hit the fan.

But until then, he was stuck like a rat in a trap. Slinking back to the flea-infested sheetless twin bed that had been pushed against one wall, he sat down and rested his head in his hands, working hard to resist the urge to cry.

The silence was now deafening, the earlier commotion of the prisoners' shouts, catcalls and pleas having long since died down.

A hard, heavy exhaustion suddenly came over him and despite the disgusting appearance of the mattress, Nick stretched out, his eyes fluttering closed.

When he next heard the quiet chuckle, it kicked his heart rate into overdrive for he had the distinct impression that it had come not from down the hall but from within his very own cell.

Paralyzed with fear, Nick held his breath, the sound of his own heartbeat banging so loudly that he was certain it could be heard throughout the entire prison. He turned his head slowly and tried in vain to see into the blackness of the cell but without any windows or lights from the corridor, he was in total darkness.

Unfamiliar squeaks and creaks caused him to jump repeatedly, the sound of a water pipe here, the bang of the furnace there.

Frantically he reasoned with himself, talking to himself, reassuring himself. He was just tired and scared. Best to close his eyes and seek out sleep. Tomorrow would be a new day and things would be better tomorrow.

He no sooner decided on this plan of attack, then he felt a cold hard hand clasp over his mouth while another ripped him from the sanctuary of the bed and up to a standing position where he was dangled by the scruff of his neck.

With all his might, Nick struggled against the imprisonment of the steel-like grip that held him, the unseen force holding him from behind.

A cold sweaty chill ran down his spine at the feel of the cool breath against his ear and as the intruder spoke, Nick felt his heart rate go through the roof at the recognition of the rich immortal voice.

"Hello, Nick," was all Jack said.

* * * * *

"Isn't this the first place he'll look?" Chancella panted, their wild, magical flight through the stars having left her breathless, as they touched down on the roof of Valian's penthouse loft.

"No one knows of its existence."

"Jack does."

"He won't come back, Chancella," he stated definitively.

"But —"

"Trust me," he said softly, looking with concern into her eyes. "Jack's out of the picture."

"How can you be so sure?"

"Because he got what he wanted."

"What was that?"

"To see my dream for mortality crushed and all the sweeter, by his own hand."

"I don't understand."

"The formula, Chancella. When used at specific intervals, it reanimates the dead cell. But in the case of an overdose, it —"

Horrified, she finished his sentence.

"It creates the reverse effect — a dead cell with no hope of regeneration."

He nodded quietly and she moved closer to him.

"Valian, I'm so sorry. I know how much you wanted it."

There was a long silence and then Chancella started in again, tentative and for the first time afraid of the answer to the question she was about to pose.

"Back there, what Jack said, was it true? Were you once a priest?"

"Sort of."

"How can you 'sort of' be a priest?"

"I hadn't yet been ordained. I was in the process, studying at the seminary along with Jacariaith."

"So that's what he meant when he said you were brothers once."

"Yes. In his time, there was no one holier than Jacariaith. When he spoke it seemed as if the very light of heaven shone in his eyes, in his words, in his actions. Indeed, it was his enthusiasm and the lure of his conviction that attracted me to the priesthood. I wanted to feel that certain about something. I wanted to feel that assured."

Chancella nodded as the pieces fell into place.

"And so you were the best of friends, until you left."

"Even after. Somewhere he found the strength to forgive me for the life I chose."

"But he couldn't forgive you and Arianna?"

"God, no! That is Jacariaith's twisted take on the whole affair."

"Affair?" Chancella said, trying to hide what felt very much like jealousy.

"I admit I loved Arianna—yes, but not in that way. It wasn't like that, believe me."

"So how was it?"

"Months after I left, Arianna sought me out with a problem—one she felt she couldn't go to Jack with."

"Back up a minute—it's obvious that Jack was in love with her but what exactly was the nature of their relationship?"

"It started out innocently enough—Arianna staying after mass to help, volunteering her time with Jack at the orphanage, that sort of thing. He talked about her incessantly, saying what a blessing she was, an angel, an absolute gift from God but at that point it was all very platonic. He loved her, yes, much the way as one would love a sibling, but—"

"But?"

"Somewhere along the way, it changed. I don't know exactly when but the way he spoke about her hinted that their connection had taken a turn and had become more romantic in flavor. I saw desire in his eyes as he related seeing her in the afternoons at the town square each day and I could sense the fire in his heart when she passed by him at communion, in the rectory, on the street.

"At first I thought I was imagining it but then one night, shortly before I left, he came into my room at the seminary and, weeping with a desperation I had never seen in him, he confessed that he and Arianna had, indeed, become lovers. His flagrant agony was heartbreaking as he related how torn he was between the church and the love of his life and he struggled for some time with what to do.

"In the end, I believe he had made a decision—I think he had decided to leave the church for her. That's when she disappeared."

"And came to you."

"Yes."

"So this problem, what was it? What was so terrible that she couldn't share it with the man she intended to marry?"

"She was dying."

"Oh," was all Chancella could muster, stunned at the cruel irony of the situation.

"I've never known how she knew of my new life or even how she found me but she did and mercilessly begged me to turn her into the very thing I had become. I tried to dissuade her, talk her out of it, but in the end I complied with her wish. To this day, I have regretted it."

"Why?"

"Because instead of alleviating her pain, I think I have only contributed to it. Both hers and Jacariaith's. It is why he has hunted me all this time. To settle the score for stealing the soul of his one true love."

"But she came to you for help."

"I could've said no."

"To a dying woman? I don't see how. And what of Jack? Isn't all this 'thou soul be damned' nonsense just a little hypocritical? I mean, he is, after all, a vampire too!"

"It is, yes, but I have no animosity towards him. He did what he thought he had to."

"We all do," she said tenderly, the remarkable details of his journey from confused mortal to despondent immortal replaying in her mind. "I'm so sorry you have been filled with such doubt, such torment in your life."

"I'm not."

She looked at him in question.

"I have spent a long time searching for an end to the pain and I thought I finally found the answer in the short years of human life but somewhere along the way, I discovered there was something I wanted more than dying."

"What's that?" she whispered.

He stared at her long and hard and for the first time, she saw a warm glimmer shining in his so often cold eyes.

"Living. Chancella, you make me want to *live*."

Their close proximity suddenly became very apparent to Chancella and she fought to keep her heart rate from reacting to the hard body that now pressed gently against her. Hesitantly, her gaze languidly dropped from the moss green eyes, now filled with a wanton desire that filled her with a strange new feeling, down to the full lips that were teasingly parted as if in invitation for Chancella to devour them with her own. The tantalizing thought quickened her pulse even further and unconsciously she licked her lips.

The movement caused Valian's gaze to likewise drop to her mouth, a hard burning hunger mixed with something akin to fear filling the glassy depths. An eternity stretched between them as they stared at each other, hungry for the other's touch and yet, both afraid to make the first move. Then, unable to withhold any more, Valian grabbed her roughly by the shoulders and pulled her to him, his mouth covering hers in an unbridled outpouring of passion, his lips moving against hers, urging them open so as to allow the shuddering entry of his tongue into her mouth.

At its feel, a soft sigh escaped Chancella, her arms reaching up to encircle his broad shoulders and draw him even closer to her.

Valian clasped her tightly to him, his hands running up and down the length of her back, stopping only to loosen her hair from the tight restraints of her ever present bun and running his fingers through her long auburn hair that now hung down past her shoulders. Cradling her head in one hand, he begrudgingly pulled his burning lips away from her mouth to travel down the silky throat, where he suckled the tender area behind her earlobe, a husky half-human, half-animal cry breaking free from him as the scent of her blood filled his nostrils.

"You smell good," he said softly, shaken by the intense emotion she produced in him. Smothering his face in her hair and neck, his hands caressed and kneaded every part of her as the human scents of her body, so long forgotten, aroused him intently.

"I love you," she said barely audibly, her whispered confession urging another tremor from his shaking form.

"I love you too," he replied breathlessly, moving along the curve of Chancella's neck. She swooned at the sensation of his tongue in her ear and clasped desperately to him, painfully aware that his strength was the only thing keeping her up. Held tightly against him, she could feel a swell of desire flare up in her loins and she dropped a trembling hand down along his hard stomach to press firmly against the front of his pants, but his fingers gently closed around her wrist before she reached her desired destination.

"Don't," he said tenderly, his eyes sweet shades of soft turquoise as he nearly shrugged in explanation. "I can't."

The flicker of disappointment in Chancella disappeared as quickly as it came and she wrapped her arms even tighter around him, smiling a sly, seductive smile as she spoke.

"We'll work around it."

The look of surprise that flashed on his face changed to one of uncertainty and a heartbreaking shyness.

"It's been a while since I've done anything like this—"

Chancella put a slender index finger to his lips to silence.

"For me too."

A slow, sexy grin spread apart Valian's tantalizing lips to reveal the hard, jutting edges of his eyeteeth.

"I think it's been just a little longer for me."

Chancella leaned into him then, her lips only inches from his as she whispered.

"Let's stop talking."

Something not unlike a snarl erupted from her vampire lover as she dragged her finger down so as to part his lips, and throwing her arms around his shoulders, clambered even further into his embrace, her lips devouring his.

She could feel his nails digging into her back in response, her sudden gasp muffled by his mouth as he bit her tongue that in an impassioned frenzy, made slow, seductive circles in the deep recesses of his mouth. She moaned softly as she felt him sucking hungrily at the blood that leaked from her tongue. With shaking fingers she hastily unbuttoned the black silk shirt, opening it to reveal his flat, smooth stomach and easing it over his broad shoulders, let it glide down off his marble-like skin and fall to the floor. Holding him on either side, she kissed her way down, starting at the base of his throat where she spent extra time nuzzling and licking his earlobe while he clasped her bottom with a strong hand and pulled her strongly into him.

"I want to make you feel good," he said lowly as she moved down the length of his smooth, cool body, his hands clasped gently on either side of her head, making long slow strokes down the length of her hair.

With a hard, fast motion, he pulled her up to eye level and, bending down, swung her into his arms, his head dropping down to kiss her breasts through the light fabric of her shirt as he walked over to the bed.

Gently placing her down, he lay on top of her, his thighs moving in such a way as to part her legs where he placed a strong knee between them. The weight of his body and the feel of his muscular thigh pressing against her caused her breath to come in short, hard gasps. Her hips involuntarily surged forward against his, seeking to merge with him as he unbuttoned her shirt and began kissing her breasts overtop of the silky fabric of her bra.

Chancella allowed her hands to stray from the silky sleek sensation of his dark hair down along the muscular back and over the swell of his firm buttocks. Bringing both hands around to the front, she began to unzip his pants only to slip a hand under the band of his shorts to gently push both down and off.

Valian's gentleness gave way to need and he urgently pulled her skirt from her hips, quickly grabbing either side of her silken panties and with one single movement yanked them down to her knees where he delicately eased them past her ankles and off. With her legs fully extended, he began kissing her feet and sucking her toes before slowly moving forward, soft, pliable kisses and licks preceding him until her knees buckled over his shoulders on either side of his head.

The firm, moist pressure of his mouth on her inner thighs caused her to twist in a painlike ecstasy, her hips pushing forward as she desperately needed the feel of his lips in her most private place, a hushed, sweet whimpering communicating the extent of her need to him.

Hearing her unspoken plea, he pulled up from her thighs only to bend his head down to that secret garden between her legs, his tongue teasingly licking at her moist cavern of pleasure.

Chancella groaned loudly and arched her back, her hands, now firmly intertwined with the silken strands on his head, urging him deeper. At the feel of his tongue, she swirled into a sweet delirium where she could only hear the pounding of her heart and the feel of the honeyed rhythmic suckling that sent wave upon wave of rapture through her. Her thighs began to tremble uncontrollably as she sped, faster and harder, towards a mind-blowing climax, tears welling, overflowing and spilling down her cheeks as she exploded in an earth-shattering release.

Eyes closed and panting, Chancella lay exhausted from the pleasure Valian had urged from her body. Vaguely she became aware of the pressure of his lips on her abdomen and he kissed his way up to her face, the sweetest, gentlest kiss saved for her lips and eyelids. Without thinking her arms encircled his bare waist, her exhausted passion miraculously flaring up once again at the weight of his hard body atop her.

Forcing him onto his back, she moved over every inch of his alabaster flesh, even that part of him which lay limp and useless between his legs. Although Chancella detected the sweet sad sigh that escaped his lips, she could not have known the pleasure she gave him by worshipping his naked body with her caresses and kisses.

"Say my name," he asked melodiously as he watched her through half-closed eyes.

"Valian, Valian," Chancella whispered, unaware of the bliss she was producing. It had been several lifetimes since a mortal woman had even known his given name, never mind addressed him with it. To have both occur simultaneously was strangely humbling.

Rolling her over, he kissed her lips, his hand falling between her legs to touch her, first a tentative, feathery stroke that graduated to a firm, rhythmic pressure. With slow steady surges he pushed his fingers inside her, over and over again, each entry deeper and firmer than the one before. Hoisting her hips up, she wrapped her legs around his waist, groaning at the feel of his fingers inside her, urging her farther. Biting down hard on his shoulder, Chancella felt another climax overtake her and the storm of her passion flared and faded once again.

In the rapturous aftermath, she become vaguely aware of the slight pain and rhythmic nuzzling on that sensitive area where her neck met her shoulder. No sooner did she realize that Val was drinking from her than he lifted his head and, grasping her hand firmly within his, made a small slice on the opposite side of his neck with her own fingernail. A fresh stream of blood immediately bubbled and flowed down over his shoulder. With his free hand, he lifted Chancella's head, directly placing her lips in line with the gaping wound.

She knew what he wanted her to do and yet she felt the learned human response of repulsion well up inside of her.

"Do it," he murmured softly, his voice filled with a husky need she had never heard. His head dipped down and she once again felt the cadenced pull of his lips on her neck.

Shaking, she complied. Tentatively she licked at the cut that was now spurting blood, afraid of hurting him. The hot earthy flavor jolted her senses and she trembled as she hesitantly lapped at the gushing wound until she felt the warm pressure on her own neck lessen once again.

"Suck it," his voice hissed quietly in the dark and she obeyed, closing her eyes and leaning into him, she opened her mouth further to completely surround the gash, where she began sucking gingerly.

She felt the firm pressure of his hand on the back of her neck urging her closer.

"Harder," he whispered. Chancella complied, locking her lips tighter around the hot fount of his blood and breaking into a rhythmic sucking on his neck. The wave of another climax reared up at the realization that the back and forth movement of his fingers inside her were in perfect synchronicity with their vampiric union.

Whimpering she began involuntarily sucking harder as she dug her nails into his back, suddenly needing to drink in every drop of him. Each pull of their timed suckling sent an electrical jolt of fire through her, each move of her lips filling her mouth with the strangely intoxicating warm liquid, her own moans mingling with those of Valian's.

The simultaneous action of replacing the blood he was taking from her caused Chancella to start trembling uncontrollably in a sort of sensory overload. But Valian's arms held her steady, not prepared to stop just yet, sucking her hungrily as she did him, the loop of liquid love beyond anything either had ever experienced.

Locked and undulating in their mortal/immortal expression of love, they simultaneously fed on each other, the fire inside intensifying and spreading deeper into each nerve ending and fiber. Chancella's muffled cries of ecstasy mingled with Valian's passionate moans as they raced towards the unknown, faster and faster, through blinding light, fire and starbursts until Chancella exploded and she began weeping at the sensation of moving down through the layers to deeper and more intimate unions—to an uncharted area.

Here now, it was as if someone had torn the flesh and bones and muscles from her body and she was just the energy that lived inside her. Nothing physical. No heavy limbs or organs or flesh. Just her. Just Chancella without all the trappings—a beautiful, beaming, all-encompassing light that was bountiful in its warmth and goodness. And into this realm came another light, just as beautiful and warm, merging with hers in a pulsating radiation of light and fiery astronomical like bursts of fire.

Around and around the two beams swirl, touching then parting, merging then separating, toying with each other until they fell together in perfect union, one atop the other, inside the other, everywhere.

They were *one*.

Then gradually she began to become aware once again of the other layers. Up through the layers she could feel the circle of their blood love and then even further up to the next layer, until they lay, spent and silent, in each other's arms. Silently, she stroked his hair, easing the damp strands back from his forehead.

Valian pulled up from her embrace and with a gentle hand raised her downcast face. God, she was beautiful, he thought as he looked at the tear-streaked skin and her petite, pretty mouth that was smeared with blood. His blood.

"Don't cry," he said softly, mildly alarmed by the flood of hot tears that ran down her trembling face.

Chancella could only shake her head and it took her a few moments to regain her composure. When she did, her voice shook as she spoke.

"I've…I've never felt anything even remotely close to that before."

Valian smiled, an unspeakably sexy look of "I meant to do that" on his face.

"Neither have I."

The slightest hint of a frown crossed his brow then and for a split second Chancella had a horrible inkling of Valian's spiritual exodus, a kind of emotional withdrawal from the cozy state that they were in.

But then he smiled, and reassured, Chancella rubbed his chest soothingly and rose up to plant a lingering kiss on one of his still erect nipples before lying back down. Snug and secure in the surprising warmth of his arms, she fell asleep, her body and mind lulled into the sweetest of reposes.

The next morning Chancella awoke to the familiar sounds of the city. Far below she could hear the squeal of tires, horns blowing and the whoosh! of the buses as they stopped. No sooner had her eyes fluttered open and she turned her head then an inexplicable gash of despair stabbed into her, seeping into the afterglow of the night before and absorbing and replacing her momentary brush with happiness and contentment.

There was no sign, no message, no warning and yet, without reason or proof, she knew something and knew it with an agonizingly absolute certainty.

Relieved that she could remember him and every moment that they had shared together, Chancella, evenso, knew that Valian was gone.

For good.

Chapter Eleven

ഇ

The rain fell in one non-stop sheet of icy liquid, as if heaven itself had frozen solid and with one unimaginable gush was instantaneously thawed. Chancella climbed from her car and bracing herself, hurried down the forsaken, desolate street toward the apartment complex, using her arms as a shield from the stinging assault of freezing drops that pelted her face to mingle with the hot flood of tears that were already there.

Bursting into the dry interior of the dismal lobby, she fell against the door panting, completely saturated by the short jaunt from her curbside parking spot to the brownstone's entrance.

Wiping at the beads of moisture that trickled from her hair into her eyes, she walked across to the tenant registry and through her water-logged vision, began reading down the list of names.

For whom, she didn't know.

Without his last name, she wasn't sure she could find him. He had mentioned the name of the building he lived in, but that was all she had. Moving her index finger down the vertical directory of surnames, she moaned in frustration when she reached the end, none of them preceded by the initial R. As if she didn't trust her own eyes, she looked through the list a second time, halting at one of two speaker buttons that didn't have a name beside them.

Firmly pressing the first white square, Chancella leaned forward, preparing to answer into the circular intercom. A loud pop and crackling jerked her upright and she stood warily looking at the grated area. Then, a strong voice boomed out over the cheap intercom system.

"Kai?"

"Oh…yes, I'm sorry to bother you but do you happen to know a—"

An outburst of seemingly irate Vietnamese streamed steadily from the intercom, rising dramatically in volume, finally culminating with an angry disconnecting click.

With a far greater hesitation than before, Chancella pushed the other nameless button, unconsciously taking a step backward as she tensely waited for a response from the tenant.

Nothing.

Exhaling slowly, she pressed again, mentally formulating a plan B as she waited.

"Yeah?" a faint male voice answered.

Chancella's heart skipped a beat as she leaned forward.

"Rio?"

A spell of silence followed and she grew uncomfortable.

"Rio, is that you?"

"Who's this?"

Chancella breathed a heavy sigh of relief, her eyes fluttering shut for a brief moment before she began speaking again.

"Rio, it's Chancella."

More silence.

"Dr. Tremaine," she clarified.

"Yeah?" he said.

"Listen," Chancella commenced, faltering as a whole bunch of emotions, not the least of which was pride, pulled her in opposite directions. Squeezing her eyes shut, she took another deep breath and charged ahead.

"Is Simarone with you?"

She looked down and shuffled her soaking loafers anxiously as she waited for his reply. Every word, every second felt like an absolute perpetuity and silently she cursed her notorious impatience.

"Yeah," Rio finally said.

"Can I come up? Please? I need to talk to him."

This time, the only response she heard was in the form of a loud buzzing, indicating her approved admittance. Taking note of Rio's suite number, Chancella grabbed for the door before the sound stopped and made her way through the labyrinth of poorly lit, loud carpeted hallways that led to his door. Knocking softly, she ran a shaking hand through her drenched hair, which was, uncharacteristically, hanging loosely around her shoulders — a sweet and sad reminder of the night before.

It opened and Rio, shirtless and barefooted, met her, motioning slightly for her to enter.

They went around the corner of the short foyer and into an undersized room that served as a bedroom, living room and kitchen, all rolled into one. Simarone was standing, almost as if he had been expecting her.

As much as she wanted to be polite and exude patience, she simply couldn't contain herself.

"Where is he?" she demanded quietly, working hard to keep her bottom lip from trembling.

"I don't know," Simarone said sadly.

"Don't give me that! You're his blood! You can hear each other's thoughts!"

"Only if desired. He is purposely blocking me."

"Please, Simarone."

"He's telling the truth," Rio stepped up. "I've experienced it firsthand. The blocking thing."

The two young men exchanged knowing glances.

"I'm sorry, Chancella, I really am but honestly, if Valian doesn't want to be found…there's no one who can find him."

* * * * *

Jack was stretched out with inhuman balance on the cold metal tentacles of the construction apparatus that was attached to the thirty-story office building. With a pronounced sigh he locked his hands under his head, stared up into the dark heavens and pondered his next move.

Now that Valian had been reduced to a biology case study, Jack was halfway to finishing what he had started. This truth should have filled him with an unimaginable joy and while the thought of Valian's immortal flesh being cut and sliced gave Jack a momentary thrill, he felt strangely disappointed and empty. Even scaring the hell out of that little shit Nick hadn't given him the kick it should have. Maybe when the real goal was achieved he would feel content. Maybe when he saw *her* again his heart would stop its restless ache.

Valian's questions about Jack's long-lost love played over and over again in his head and the haunting words filled him with a sick sense of truth that he could not run from. Then he began to ask the questions to himself.

Gone to Valian? Why would Arianna have done something like that? What or who was she running from? Why had she remained in hiding all these years?

And then there was the big one, that he scarcely could bear the materialization of the thought in his head and yet there it was, over and over and over again, resounding like some tormented mantra in his mind's eye.

Had she never loved him?

"I did. I always did. In fact, I still do."

The sound, soft as an angel's wing and twice as illusionary, touched his ears and for a moment, he thought he had dreamt the whisper. But then Jack snapped to and realized with the sudden, hard pounding of his heart that he was not dreaming but had heard the long-remembered voice speaking to him.

Frozen with the fear of one that has waited so long for something and yet is strangely afraid to get it when that moment comes, Jack turned as if in slow motion toward the source of the sound.

There she stood, more beautiful than he could've ever remembered, and the tears of a thousand different emotions filled his eyes as he looked upon the beloved form of Arianna.

Through his blurred vision he could still make out the shoulder length black hair, now tied back in a loose-knotted bun, and the calm, steady gaze of her gray eyes. The smooth flesh, once tanned and golden, now had faded to a luscious shade of ivory but still, her eyes were outlined in a deep kohl blue and her wide, full mouth in a brilliant shade of fuchsia were startling contrasts to the pallor of her flesh. His jaw clenched repeatedly as he fought back wave upon wave of conflicting emotions and a barrage of thoughts coursed through his head. Should he run to her and take her in his arms? Perhaps coolly question her as to her reappearance. Better yet, let her speak and see what she had to say.

No sooner had he reasoned himself into the latter, than Arianna spoke.

"I know you have a lot of questions, Jack. Some I have answers for. Others not. Just let me say that the choices I have made in my life may not have been the right ones, but they were mine."

For the first time since Arianna's heavenly materialization, Jack felt the bitter taste of anger in his mouth.

"What's that supposed to mean?"

Arianna sighed.

"We need to talk, Jack. There's so much I want to tell you. I don't know if I can make you understand, but I'd like to try. I'm finally ready to try. Will you meet me later?"

"Where?"

"Some place we can be alone together."

The suggestiveness of the words filled him with a fresh surge of longing and the recollection of their forbidden mortal love and physical expression of it flitted across his mind's eye and he looked away, wincing. He shook his head slowly but was unable to speak. Arianna's voice further cut him.

"Please, Jack. I know you are in pain but I am too. Let me try to explain what happened."

"Why? Why now?"

"Because I can. Because I'm ready."

"And what of me? I have been ready for years! Searching for centuries. Have you not thought of me?" He bellowed as he gruffly turned away, wiping irately at the silver streaks of tears that coursed down the pale skin of his cheeks.

"I've done nothing but," she replied softly, taking a tentative step towards him. "In actuality, I did what I did with you in mind."

"What?" he turned, the anguish now clearly etched on the disbelieving face.

"Please, Jack," she cooed gently, tears now brimming in the ocean blue of her eyes. "I match your agony but let me explain my actions to you. I am certain when I have finished, you will understand the method in my madness."

"And if I refuse?" he snapped petulantly.

"Don't let pride leave you unsatisfied. I can answer all your questions and calm your battered heart if you will only listen."

The words hung in the air and he stared at her for a long moment. An emotional tug-of-war raged within him. His hurt, which had mutated into an angry resentment and bitterness, would not be quelled and a fiery indignation threatened to ruin this so-longed-for opportunity.

But he desperately wanted, needed, to hear her story and learn what had taken her from his loving embrace all those years ago. He stared at her, wincing at the sight of the locket he had given her.

Gritting his teeth to silence the powerful internal struggle of his pain and pride, he spoke out of a forced smile.

"Very well."

She smiled then for the first time, the long-lost sight bringing a fresh pang of desire-tinged pain to him.

"I am so very glad, Jack. Wait here for me."

"What? No! You have come to me finally only to take your leave so suddenly! I won't allow it!"

"Darling—hush. We have a lifetime to catch up. But first there is something I must do and it cannot wait but I promise I will return before the dawn. 'Til then my sweet—"

With that, she lifted up into the heavens, her quickly retreating form but a blurry streak across the evening sky.

* * * * *

The navy blue of the Mediterranean Sea looked almost black despite the shimmer of moonlight that played across its ruffled surface, a fitting hue indeed, for no mood could be blacker than Valian's as he walked aimlessly along the water's edge.

So engrossed in his thoughts was he that he didn't hear or smell his fledging child's approach as he strolled, his eyes tightly closed and a soft stream of hushed words falling from his lips. At the delicate, questioning touch on his shoulder, he literally jumped to face his kin, unable to understand how his whereabouts had been discovered.

"Who are you talking to?"

"Myself."

"Oh? It kind of looked like you were praying."

"You know me better than that."

"That's right, I do."

"So how'd you find me?" he asked in a kind of amazement. He had made sure his block was solid so no one could locate him.

"Lucky guess."

"Sometimes I think you know me better than anyone."

Valian only nodded in silence before looking out at the water, a soft laugh not masking the pain within his eyes.

"I told someone recently that water filled me with a kind of peace. Doesn't seem to be working tonight."

"That's because water has been replaced by another and now you can only find peace in the company of that other form."

Arianna watched her Dark Master closely for a time before she started in softly.

"Valian, what do you think you're doing?" she asked, smiling warmly.

"Isn't it obvious? I'm going for a walk."

"No you're not. You're not walking, you're running and if you don't mind me saying, it's the wrong thing to do."

When Valian didn't respond, Arianna continued on.

"Believe me, I know what I'm talking about. Running from love, for any reason, no matter how good your intentions are, is just plain stupid. You will *never* cease wondering 'what if' and for our kind…never is a long time."

"But she's a mortal. You know what that means."

"Yes I do. It means that this woman loves you enough to take a chance, to step outside of her comfort zone and put herself on the line. Are you?"

"I don't know…I thought I was."

"But you're not sure?"

"You know as well as I do that it's against the rules. Love with a mortal is forbidden."

"I made that very argument to you two centuries ago and do you remember what you told me? You said 'everything's forbidden somewhere to someone.' That's exactly what you said. Ever since I met you, you've always pushed the envelope…deciding and choosing who you want to be and the kind of life you want to lead. Why not decide and choose the person you want to love?"

"I didn't choose her. She was just…there. It just happened."

"Uh-huh. Well, maybe someone else chose her for you."

"Like who?"

"Like the person you were talking to when I first arrived."

"You know I don't believe in that."

"Yes you do, Valian. You just think you don't. Quit trying to direct everything and let go and allow fate to run your life once in a while. You, my darling Maker, are a control freak."

"Is that a fact?"

"It is."

Valian, looking disgusted, only glanced away.

"What do you know about it?"

"Ah, but I know all too well. It was the very same for me. I couldn't manage certain aspects of my life and because I couldn't guarantee or control Jack's reaction to those things, I fled instead of having some faith and letting it ride."

"That was different."

"How so?"

"You left because you didn't want to cause any pain for Jack."

"Is that not the same reason you have abandoned Chancella?"

Again Valian fell silent and this time, when Arianna spoke he listened to her closely, carefully weighing every word as though he might seriously consider what she had to say.

"And if you ask me, it all comes back to love — the other reason I left Jack. I was terrified of how much I had grown to love him and want him and I couldn't bear the thought of losing him. Ever. So I utilized our differences as a way to desert him before he could ever ditch me."

Arianna studied him as he slowly starting walking down the beach, kicking lightly at the white sand under their feet.

"I think you love this woman so much, you too are afraid."

He smiled then.

"Is that what you think?"

"It is. And moreover, I think deep down you know it."

For a time they continued on in silence, Valian reaching out to loosely clasp one of her long cool hands, throwing her a sliver of an emerald sidelong glance.

"Have you spoken to Jack yet?"

"Only briefly. There is so much I need to tell him and I will, but that's just the thing, Valian. I have *forever* to make it right with Jack. You don't have that luxury with Chancella."

Valian nodded and when Arianna continued, there was a sad urgency within her satiny voice.

"Please don't make the same mistake I did. If you love someone, no matter how complicated it may seem, go to them and work it out. Otherwise, your life won't be worth living."

* * * * *

Chancella reached over and flicked off the light. Setting her reading glasses atop the papers that covered the workspace, she propped her elbows on the edge of the desk and, with a deep, heartfelt sigh, rubbed her tired eyes.

These all-night sessions at the lab were starting to get to her but what was the alternative? Go home and veg out in front of the TV each night? No way. At least here she was doing something worthwhile.

Leaning back, she sat for a time in the darkness, the outline of a compact square object buried underneath the avalanche of papers just barely visible. A stab of pain jolted her.

It had all started with that one godforsaken object.

Brushing the sheets aside, she tentatively touched the embossed title of the book, her fingers tingling as they caressed the raised lettering, translating the words *The Cure* over and over again into her mind as if reading it through her very flesh.

Chancella scoffed.

Life can be ironic.

Once someone came to her, seeking it, but now she was the one who needed a cure.

For the first time in a long while, Chancella allowed herself to think of Valian. As if literally opening a door, a flood of memories reared up and she closed her eyes again, letting the emotions wash over her.

It had been almost seven months since that night.

After his disappearance Chancella had gone through the usual stages of loss as surely as if someone had died. For weeks she holed herself up in her place, living in her pajamas, racked by bouts of anguished sobbing and shaking. When she wasn't sleeping, which was most of the time, she lay sprawled on the couch, her new bed, channel surfing through the ghastly selection of daytime television. She ventured into the bedroom only as a means to the bathroom for she couldn't bear the memories that haunted that room.

Soon after came a vague, foggy depression that permeated every aspect of her life. Her music, her books, even her work couldn't manage to hold her interest for more than a few seconds and she could find no relief or distraction from the recollections that snuck into her every waking moment.

Random, merciless sense-surround images jutted into her mind at the most unexpected times. Drinking coffee, brushing her teeth or at the supermarket she would be stunned at the sight of Valian's slick black hair parting and feathering into dark waves of satin as he ran a lean hand, an artist's hand as she always thought, through the silky tresses. She'd freeze at the low timbre of his voice calling her name, soft and dreamy, or urgent and laden with passion, the simultaneous stab of unbearable inner pain and insatiable sexual desire flaring up in response.

Sometimes she would grow dizzy and her mouth would even salivate at the remembered taste of his mouth, his skin, his blood.

No matter where she went he was there.

Everywhere.

And nowhere.

When she began eating again, it was more in the way of picking, lackluster zeal-less toying with her food. However, her sporadic insomnia became quite permanent, her nights often spent staring out at the darkened sky, reliving their one-time trip to the heavens.

Sometimes, if she closed her eyes, she swore that she could almost feel the disembodied, weightless sensation of flying. She could recall that surging upward movement registering in the pit of her stomach not unlike an air pocket on a plane or the drop in a roller coaster, the wind whistling and crying in your ears as it circles and enfolds you like a lover's arms.

Valian had held her loosely but she could recall how their bodies pressed so close together that under other circumstances, the sensation would be decidedly erotic.

Days passed. Then weeks. And months.

Eventually she had traded in her all-night reminiscence sessions for work at the lab. Before the dawn broke each morning she would crawl back to her condo, close all the blinds and sleep the bright of day away, only to awake at nightfall and do it all again.

Twenty-four, seven.

That was her life now.

She opened her eyes, surprised that they were not brimming with tears at her trip down memory lane, and for that she was grateful. Heaven knows she'd cried enough.

Now, in place of the raw agony, there was only a dull, gnawing ache, buried so deep that it almost didn't register.

Almost.

Chancella went to stand up but stopped suddenly, the hair on the back of her neck bristling. Her heart rate went through the roof and her mouth went dry as she froze, only her eyes moving to one side as she tried to utilize her peripheral vision.

Someone was in the room.

As her rationale leapt to the forefront, determined to ease her concern with a series of logical suggestions, her instinct, sharpened and honed through the years, and her most trusted and true ally, continued to silently scream.

At a remarkably controlled rate, she turned her head, masking her fear at the sight of the figure standing some ten feet away by the locked door.

The overhead fluorescent lights buzzed then fired on, flooding the lab with light. Chancella swallowed hard as she stared unwaveringly at the familiar face, a masquerading hatred filling each word.

"What are you doing here?"

The figure by the door didn't answer. Chancella flushed as she stood up and faced him.

"Well?" she demanded. "What do you want?"

The fondly remembered tone caught her off guard when he finally did speak and she had to bite her lip to keep it from trembling.

"You," he paused. "I want you."

Valian walked over to her then, stopping only inches from where she stood.

"Oh yeah? And what—?" she challenged, the shaking in her voice starting to work its way through her body. "You think you can just waltz in here anytime you want a quick pop?"

The monotone of his voice matched the blankness on his face.

"I don't remember it as quick but—"

Without deciding to do so, Chancella slapped Valian hard across the face, the sound of the sharp blow immediately followed by her own gasp as her hands flew to her face, shutting out the sight before her.

Fighting to regain control, she drew in a shaky breath and opened her eyes, wincing at the sight of Valian before her, his head still turned to the left, the angle her strike had forced it. His eyes were downcast, little wisps of hair blown across his forehead from the force of her blow.

He finished his sentence.

"But that's not what I meant," he said sullenly.

She thought she could see the shimmer of tears in his eyes, the enormous pools hovering dangerously close to the dark fringes of his lower lashes, threatening to spill over with every blink.

She resisted the temptation to reach out and touch him and smooth back the silken tresses that had fallen across his face.

"What do you want?" Chancella demanded again, trying desperately to keep the pain out of her voice.

Valian looked at her then and her previous suspicion was confirmed as a single, solitary tear broke free and coursed down over the porcelain finish of his cheek. Confused, he reached up and with a hand that trembled slightly, he wiped the moisture from his face, staring at it on his hand as if he'd never seen it before. He continued staring at his hand as he spoke.

"I told you," he said uncertainly.

"You want me," she repeated, a suspicious sarcasm edging into the confirmation. "Want me how? Why?"

He looked at her then and she saw for the first time a pulsating pain radiating from within the greenish-grey of his eyes.

"I realized that I...I can't live without you."

His bottom lip trembled with the last word.

"If this is about another hare-brained scheme to become human, you can just find yourself someone else to use you as their immortal guinea pig!"

"It's got nothing to do with that," he answered, the volume in his voice raising.

"Good! Because I want no part of your doctor-assisted suicide, so to speak! If you want to keep running from one life to another, jumping at every solution du jour for your problems and are prepared to risk your life—"

The veneer of his resolve crumbled and he reached for her, his hands clasping her roughly as he gave her a solid shake before pulling her close.

"Will you shut up?" he bellowed, his cool sweet breath blowing the hair back from her face. She stared at him dumbfounded. Softening, he started in.

"Chance, listen, I'm sorry," he drew in a ragged breath, a desperate sincerity blazing in the intent gaze, the crease of his brow and the full lips that alternated between a firm, repressed line and a soft, slack tremble, "but I need you to understand. *Really* understand. None of this was part of the plan. I had it all figured out until I met you and then—"

"Then what?"

His eyes searched hers and she had to smile as she saw warmth and a look of wonder sparkling within the emerald depths. He laughed softly and made a motion similar to a shrug as he shook his head in awe. Glancing away, he tried to comprehend it all himself.

"I...I fell in love with you."

His eyes, filled with an intense honesty, found hers again.

"I didn't want to," he continued. "I tried not to but...the more I pulled away, the closer you pulled me in."

Chancella felt the pain and anger of the past seven months begin to melt and she spoke softly as her eyes searched his.

"I fell in love with you too, Valian. Is that a surprise?" Chancella asked, her hands now resting gently on his forearms, her fingers kneading the cool flesh.

He smiled, the beguiling dimples creasing the flawless marble flesh.

"No," he replied softly.

"Then why? Why did you leave?"

His hands moved up to her face then and he tenderly stroked her cheek with the back of his fingers.

"Because I didn't want to hurt you."

"What?" Chancella couldn't keep the astonishment out of her voice. "Have you any idea how much you hurt me by taking off like you did?"

Valian put a hand up as if to silence her but Chancella wouldn't be appeased.

"Well, do you? Do you know what I've gone through?"

"I thought it was the best thing. Life with me would be so complicated," he began softly. "There's so much you don't know about me, about my kind. It could be dangerous. I wanted to protect you from all that."

"So you made the decision for me, is that it?"

"Yes. I knew if we discussed it, you would talk me into staying and I really believed that leaving was the right thing to do."

"Right for who? Not for me. Not for you."

Valian nodded wordlessly.

"And now? Why have you come back?"

He looked down, dejectedly, for a long moment. When he raised his head, there was a clear stoic truth burning within his eyes.

"Because I couldn't stay away. I missed you too much. You gave me something, Chancella. Something I haven't had for a long time."

"So you said," she smiled gently as she let an index finger trail seductively down the length of his forearm. Valian laughed.

"Well, yes, that too, but you gave me something else."

Chancella leaned into him and wrapped her arms around his back, drawing him close.

"What?" she whispered.

Valian returned the embrace as he peered down into her eyes. "The will to live."

Leisurely he dipped his head down and it felt like an eternity before his lips touched hers but when they did, Chancella could tell by his kiss that Valian was back for good.

When he finally pulled away, leaving them both breathless and weak-kneed, there was a glittering amusement in his eyes that spread to his wide grin.

"What is it?" Chancella smiled, a laughing puzzlement on her face. Valian cocked one eyebrow.

"Solution du jour?" he mused. "You think becoming a vampire is a solution du jour?"

"I don't know," she shrugged. "I just—"

But before she could explain, his mouth had found hers again, cutting short her response as he kissed her deeply and before long, both had forgotten the question.

Epilogue

ဢ

Chancella breathed a deep sigh of contentment and leaned back against the plush velvet chair, one of four situated directly opposite the large picture windows of the luxurious coach room.

Letting her head fall lazily to one side, she peered out at the luscious green of the Andorran countryside as it sped by. The softly rolling hills randomly gave way to the dense, imposing mass of the Dagmar Forest where the gnarled cragged roots of the centuries-old spruce trees dug down into the rich, damp soil.

Glancing over, she studied her traveling companion, inwardly marveling at how his remarkable skin was luminous beyond belief, almost glowing in the confines of their private room on this late-night journey.

His supernatural eyes, so often fixed on her face with an increasingly frequent expression of desire, were now staring blankly out the window, and yet Chancella could detect the occasional flicker of something. Ever changing, a light would blaze within the emerald depths, quickly returning to their affected indifference.

There it was again, a flash of, what was that? Anger? Excitement? Regret?

Smiling, Chancella began to look away, mentally giving up on trying to figure out her mystic lover. After months together, she was just delighted to be in his company and bowed to the fact that she would never know his every thought, of which she was certain he had multitudes on the eve of this long overdue homecoming.

Valian's gaze shifted and their eyes met, the insinuation of a smile finding his full lips. His mind was inside hers and in the strangest sort of way, she could feel his presence there, a gentle transcendental probing, delicately searching the deep recesses of her mind's eye to retract the images and feelings that form her thoughts.

Blushing, Chancella returned her gaze out the window.

"Stop it," she demurred. "You know I hate it when you do that."

"What?" he feigned innocence, his eyebrows shooting up in a heartwarming imitation of human surprise.

She resisted the urge to wag her finger at him.

"You know exactly what. I hate it when you read my mind."

"Yes," he nodded, a full grin separating the inviting curve of his lips to reveal the sparkling white of his inhuman teeth. "That along with, let me see now, walking too quietly as in, coming up behind and startling the devil out of you—"

"Interesting choice of words," she interrupted.

Valian squinted at her in mock anger before resuming.

"Ah yes, where was I? Oh yes, there's mesmerizing you with my eyes, and what else? Oh yes, flying too fast."

Chancella rolled her eyes before bursting into laughter.

"You're evil."

He grinned in the most seductive of grins imaginable.

"Absolutely."

With an uncontrollable surge, she flew across the space at him and landed in his lap, her arms wrapped loosely around his shoulders as she leaned in and lovingly nuzzled his neck.

"Are you trying to bite me?" he challenged softly.

Chancella pulled back and in a voice laden with seduction replied.

"Do you want me to?"

Valian chuckled then and pulled her roughly to him, his lips finding hers, a hot, torrid kiss leaving them both breathless as they parted.

Chancella's curiosity about Valian's mindset once again returned and she smoothed back the hair on his forehead as her voice dropped to almost a whisper.

"Are you nervous?"

Valian scrutinized her closely, his eyes locking with hers.

"About what?"

"Going home."

He sighed then, his forehead crinkling in the imitation of a frown as he glanced out the window.

"You know what? It's not my home. I never really had a home, not in the true sense of the word. That is, until I met you."

The look of astonishment on Chancella's face quickly softened to love as she listened to his words.

"Now, as long as I'm with you, wherever we are...I am home."

"But—"

Hush.

The word whispered delicately in her head. She smiled as she leaned into him.

"I hate that too, you know," she murmured, adding yet another item to her previous list of vampire pet peeves.

"Yeah, yeah, I know," he replied lowly before silencing her with a long, deep kiss.

As his lips moved down the curve of her neck, Chancella swooned, not only at the feel of his touch but also at the realization that she, too, was home.

About the Author

❧

Susan Phelan began writing poetry and short stories as a child, always intrigued by both the fantastic and the romantic. Several years ago she began work as an entertainment and travel freelance writer. Today, she is the editor of international tourist magazine WHERE, however she continues to indulge her passion for writing fiction. THE CURE, the first book in the trilogy THE BLOOD TAPESTRY is Susan's first novel.

She lives in Edmonton, Alberta, Canada with her collie, Sadie and her cat Tess.

Susan welcomes mail from readers. You can contact her through her website www.susanphelan.com or write to her c/o Ellora's Cave Publishing at 1056 Home Avenue, Akron, OH 44310-3502.

Why an electronic book?

We live in the Information Age—an exciting time in the history of human civilization in which technology rules supreme and continues to progress in leaps and bounds every minute of every hour of every day. For a multitude of reasons, more and more avid literary fans are opting to purchase e-books instead of paperbacks. The question to those not yet initiated to the world of electronic reading is simply: *why?*

1. *Price.* An electronic title at Ellora's Cave Publishing and Cerridwen Press runs anywhere from 40-75% less than the cover price of the <u>exact same title</u> in paperback format. Why? Cold mathematics. It is less expensive to publish an e-book than it is to publish a paperback, so the savings are passed along to the consumer.

2. *Space.* Running out of room to house your paperback books? That is one worry you will never have with electronic novels. For a low one-time cost, you can purchase a handheld computer designed specifically for e-reading purposes. Many e-readers are larger than the average handheld, giving you plenty of screen room. Better yet, hundreds of titles can be stored within your new library—a single microchip. (Please note that Ellora's Cave and Cerridwen Press does not endorse any specific brands. You can check our website   at   www.ellorascave.com   or

www.cerridwenpress.com for customer recommendations we make available to new consumers.)

3. *Mobility.* Because your new library now consists of only a microchip, your entire cache of books can be taken with you wherever you go.

4. *Personal preferences are accounted for.* Are the words you are currently reading too small? Too large? Too...**ANNOYING**? Paperback books cannot be modified according to personal preferences, but e-books can.

5. *Instant gratification.* Is it the middle of the night and all the bookstores are closed? Are you tired of waiting days—sometimes weeks—for online and offline bookstores to ship the novels you bought? Ellora's Cave Publishing sells instantaneous downloads 24 hours a day, 7 days a week, 365 days a year. Our e-book delivery system is 100% automated, meaning your order is filled as soon as you pay for it.

Those are a few of the top reasons why electronic novels are displacing paperbacks for many an avid reader. As always, Ellora's Cave and Cerridwen Press welcomes your questions and comments. We invite you to email us at service@ellorascave.com, service@cerridwenpress.com or write to us directly at: 1056 Home Ave. Akron OH 44310-3502.

THE
☥ ELLORA'S CAVE ☥
LIBRARY

Stay up to date with Ellora's Cave Titles in
Print with our Quarterly Catalog.

To recieve a catalog,
send an email with your name
and mailing address to:

CATALOG@ELLORASCAVE.COM
OR SEND A LETTER OR POSTCARD
WITH YOUR MAILING ADDRESS TO:

CATALOG REQUEST
c/o ELLORA'S CAVE PUBLISHING, INC.
1056 HOME AVENUE
AKRON, OHIO 44310-3502

Please be advised: Ellora's Cave is a publisher of erotic romance.
Our books as well as our website contain explicit sexual content.

Cerridwen Press

Cerridwen, the Celtic goddess of wisdom, was the muse who brought inspiration to storytellers and those in the creative arts.
Cerridwen Press encompasses the best and most innovative stories in all genres of today's fiction.
Visit our website and discover the newest titles by talented authors who still get inspired — much like the ancient storytellers did...
once upon a time.

www.cerridwenpress.com